Key Largo Blues

The Sequel to *Dakota Blues*

L Y N N E   M .   S P R E E N

ISBN: 153698387X
ISBN 13: 9781536983876

Key Largo Blues

The Sequel to *Dakota Blues*

LYNNE M. SPREEN

For Bill — my husband, my mentor, my friend.

Life shrinks or expands according to one's courage.

—Anais Nin

Chapter One

Staging was everything.

Karen Grace closed her windows against the possibility of noise. Key Largo teemed with Christmas Eve revelers, and the marina was like a parking lot, with fishing charters and pleasure boats coming and going. So Karen took precautions. She couldn't afford to blow her scheme. In one hour, the show would go live.

And the show, if successful, would launch her new business. In the past year, her safe and happy life had imploded. Now footloose and broke, she needed to rebuild everything, starting with finances.

She stood back, considering the optics. During the video call, her new client had to think Karen was calling from a high-end office building, not an old camping trailer.

First, she unfurled a backdrop poster depicting a floor-to-ceiling bookcase and attached it to the wall behind the dinette. Next, the kitchen table got a makeover with the addition of a leather-edged desk blotter, a coffee cup full of pens and pencils, and a monogrammed in-box. Placing her laptop on a stack of books, Karen raised it so the webcam would catch her from the waist up. She lowered the shades to enhance the lighting, adjusted her headset, and tested the audio. Everything checked out.

She showered, put on makeup, gave her blond hair a twist, and anchored it atop her head with ebony chopsticks. She pulled on a pair of Bermuda shorts, a white tank top, and a St. John's blazer, purchased years ago when she and Steve were rolling in cash.

As one last precaution to protect the illusion, Karen dug around in her office supplies, found a thick black marker, and wrote *Do Not Disturb* on a piece of cardboard. Then she stuck it outside and locked the door.

With the flick of a switch, she activated the camera and microphone. Her client needed forty additional nurses to staff a new hospital. Thanks to the recruiting website Karen had designed, a bumper crop of candidates clamored to be hired.

The screen beeped, and her client appeared. Ursula Wahl looked exhausted, her face gray, eyes puffy. By contrast, in the past month Karen had acquired a healthy tan.

"Three more nurses resigned," said Ursula. "I hope you have good news."

"I have excellent news, and after that, we could talk about your turnover situation, if you like."

"Perhaps." Ursula lifted her glasses and rubbed her eyes. "Tell me about our candidates."

"Did you have a chance to review the information I sent you?"

"Not in detail." Ursula shuffled some papers. "It's been a madhouse here."

Karen summarized the three dozen candidates in a few minutes.

"Some of them appear to have erratic work histories," said Ursula.

"Part of that was the recession." Good people had been savaged by the economic downturn, and Karen was eager to see them return to work—not to mention she'd receive a nice fee per hire for her efforts.

"You're too kind." Ursula frowned, the dark circles under her eyes becoming more pronounced. "But I won't settle for mediocre choices."

"You'll be pleased. I promise." Karen knew what she was talking about. This time last year, she had been a corporate executive in charge of human resources for a national firm. She had the expertise to dazzle Ursula, earning a fat paycheck and a great reference. She felt the excitement, a sense of energy rising inside her chest. Her business was ready to take flight. Her future was in her hands. Finally.

A sharp pounding rattled the door of the trailer. Apologizing, Karen paused the call and yanked open the door. At the bottom of the step stood Gina, sporting more jewelry per square inch than Liberace. Her white hair contrasted with a deep tan. "Oh good, you're up. Here's that cocktail dress you were going to alter for me. Remember I told you about it yesterday at the beach?"

"I'm in the middle of a call." Karen pointed at the *Do Not Disturb* sign, which she had put up specifically to ward off unplanned visits from the CRS ladies.

"This will only take a sec." Gina unfurled a bundle of fabric and held it against her chest. "See? It's too tight across the boobs. Not that I'm bragging. Well, really, I am. But I know you can fix it."

"Gina, this isn't a good time."

"Look how beautiful it is. Here, I'll just leave it with you, and you can get to it anytime. Well, any time before Saturday, which is when I need it."

"No, I'm sorry, I can't. You'll have to ask someone else. Now I have to get back to my call." Karen closed the door, hoping Gina wouldn't knock again. She didn't want to be rude, but if she'd learned anything last summer in Cheyenne, it was that sometimes you had to put yourself first.

When she returned to her laptop, Ursula was frowning. "I only have five more minutes."

"Here's a suggestion. Why don't I rank the candidates in order of their qualifications and identify my top choices? I know what you're looking for, and that will save you time."

"Good idea. Thank you." They said good-bye, and the screen went blank.

Karen breathed a sigh of relief. She'd suggested that in the first place, but Ursula had wanted to micromanage the recruitment. Perhaps this was a sign that she would trust Grace and Associates to handle her business.

Twenty minutes later, she sent the email, stored her props, and opened the windows. A boat motor started up, and a tropical breeze floated in the window, calling her out to play. Feeling she'd earned a break, and eager to feel the sun on her face and the wind in her hair, she slapped on sun block, threw some snacks into her back pack, and hurried out the door. She unfastened the chain around the frame of her Buddy scooter, a cheap version of the sleek Italian brand. Karen had bought it to travel around the campground without having to use her truck. The little bike purred along the shoulder of the Overseas Highway, zipping past the line of cars always present during the tourist season. Turning in at Pennekamp Coral Reef State Park, Karen waved her pass at the attendant and headed for the rental boats.

"Haven't seen you for a couple days," said the clerk.

"I've been busy working. Do you have any kayaks left?"

"A bunch. You need a map?"

"No, I'm good." When she had first rented a kayak, Karen would prop the map on her knees while paddling through the mangrove swamp, afraid of getting lost. Her movements had been clumsy, the front of the craft jerking back and forth with her strokes, until she learned that less movement from the paddle propelled her in a straighter line.

Karen tossed the backpack into the kayak, slid it into shallow water, and climbed in, awkwardly pushing off against the sand. The sounds of the marina faded as the kayak slipped around the point and into the mangroves. Her shoulders relaxed, and Karen let out a big sigh. She loved camping with the CRS ladies, but sometimes a person just had to get away.

The gentle late-morning breeze cooled her as she paddled, and she relished the freedom of being able to explore the forest on her own. No one else was within sight or hearing. The only sound was the whistle and chirp of birds calling to each other from within the swamp. The water was crystal clear, the sea-grass bottom visible fifteen feet below. She raised the paddle out of the water and drifted, remembering a time when, as newlyweds, she and Steve had ridden in a hot-air balloon, marveling at the silence as they sailed over farmland and country roads. Except for the occasional heater jet, the balloon had floated in absolute quiet. The passengers had fallen silent, too, as if in reverence.

She felt the same way now, all alone out on the water, rocking gently in the windblown waves, breezes rippling across the surface of the bay. She angled toward the mangroves, alerting a blue heron, which glared at her in indignation before lifting off on a seven-foot wingspan. Nearby, a turtle splashed into the water from its resting place on a tree root. Karen tied up to a root, in the shade of the overhead canopy. Between her own self-imposed workload and the competing clamor of the CRS ladies, a solo kayak trip was the perfect respite. She cracked the seal on her water bottle and unwrapped a granola bar, finally able to relax.

***

Later that day, she went looking for a present for Eleanor, the oldest and most reclusive of the CRS ladies. Eleanor had been under the weather lately and wasn't expected to show for the Christmas Day beach party. Karen remembered seeing a gift shop a few miles south. With the windows rolled down, she turned onto the highway, with Jimmy Buffett on CD, since the old pickup truck had been built before Bluetooth.

In the month she'd been in the Keys, she hadn't played tourist much. Now she dawdled along the crowded highway, eyeballing the cute pastel cottages nestled in a jungle-like backdrop. Overhead, cottony-white clouds scudded across the tropical blue sky. Key Largo, familiar yet exotic, was on the same latitude as the Bahamas. At times, the clouds would darken the sky, and an occasional raindrop would land on her windshield, but then the sun would come out again and dazzle the eyes.

A mile south of the campground, the island broadened, allowing for a smattering of residential neighborhoods. On impulse, Karen turned down a side street. The trees, bushes, and flowers were so different from what she was used to. Almost every yard had a planting of fishtail palms, and many properties were right on the water. If she drove slowly enough, she could peer through the sapodilla and gumbo-limbo trees to the water's edge, where old pilings spoke of sunken docks and the power of past storms. From time to time, a resident would look up and see her, and Karen would give a neighborly wave, which was always returned.

At the end of a rustic lane, the pavement turned into a dirt path leading to the water less than fifty yards away. Karen rolled to a stop, and the coastal breeze carried the tang of brine through the open cab. The beach in front of her was deserted. She caught movement on the periphery of her vision, and saw a lone windsurfer gliding high over the water before dipping down and lifting off again. Mesmerized, she studied his movements, the way he'd catch the breeze and float so naturally. She imagined herself under the sail, and the sense of freedom and longing made her dizzy. The air felt soft, almost weightless, as it brushed her skin. It smelled of jasmine and citrus. She sighed, amazed that people could live in such an Elysian setting.

Maybe if she worked hard, she could make enough money to retire completely in a couple of years. She pictured herself lying around in a hammock all day, reading tabloid magazines and sipping rum punch.

A watery splat of bird poop hit the windshield. So much for her dreams.

She started the truck, rolled up the windows, and hit the wiper/wash button. The bird was right. After two weeks, her natural restlessness would kick in and she'd be looking for something to do. All her life, she'd struggled to find the balance between work and leisure. Work usually won. She'd been told it was a failing, but she enjoyed her career. Until her marriage ended, and reality hit her in the face.

On the way back, she pulled in at the gift shop, a ramshackle white clapboard with pastel trim that hadn't been touched up in fifty years. Wind chimes and dream catchers twirled on the front porch, and a bell jingled when Karen opened the door. She wandered the aisles of trinkets and doodads, discovering a small jeweled box lined in velvet. Karen had met Eleanor at the clubhouse a few weeks ago, enjoying Sunday brunch. The older woman wore a sapphire cape and a dozen gold and silver bracelets. Cut-glass rings in every color adorned her fingers. The jeweled box would be perfect.

On her way to the cash register, a bit of pink caught Karen's eye. Delighted, she extracted the faded pink flamingo from a sagging cardboard box. Last summer, in a desolate campground in south Wyoming, one of her two birds had been shattered by gunfire. Ever since, the survivor had looked rather lonely, stuck in the ground beside the RV.

Back at camp, Karen found a black felt-tip pen and gave the flamingo two new eyes. Then she went outside and hammered it into the ground next to the original bird. She stood back and admired her work, thinking that maybe things were getting back to normal. If Frieda were around to see it, she would be glad, too.

Chapter Two

*I*n the late afternoon, Karen knocked on the door of Eleanor's trailer. She heard shuffling inside, and then the door opened with a creak.

"Yes?" Eleanor wore a purple beret over gray hair cut as short as a man's, a sparkly sweater, and chartreuse stretch pants.

"I don't know if you remember me. I'm Karen Grace. I'm with the CRS ladies."

Eleanor studied her for a moment, her pale gray glance steady. "Of course I remember you. Come in." Inside, a pot bubbled on the stove, infusing the room with the smell of tomato and basil. "I was about to have dinner, if you would like to join me."

"Thank you, but I have something already planned."

Eleanor stirred the sauce while Karen looked around. The inside of the RV was like a museum, full of neatly displayed artifacts from around the world. A full-sized globe stood on the kitchen table, and a map of the world hung on one wall. The map had dozens of colored pins stuck into it. A Haydn symphony wafted from the radio.

"Make yourself at home." She dug around in the refrigerator, pulled out a bottle of water, and handed it to Karen. "I'd offer you wine, but I don't drink it anymore." Eleanor was bent from osteoporosis, so she had to turn her whole body to make eye contact.

"Thank you." Karen took the bottle and sat on the sofa. "I brought you something. An early Christmas present."

Eleanor took the wrapped package, turning it over and examining it. "Why would you do that? We don't even know each other."

Karen remembered Eleanor, though, from the campground in Moab. At the time, the older woman had been digging a trench around her RV, with no help except the company of an Aussie shepherd. Today there was no sign of a pet.

"Did Fern put you up to this?" asked Eleanor.

"She mentioned you're under the weather."

Eleanor waved her hand. "I'm fine." She winced, lowering herself into the chair across from Karen. As she unwrapped the package, her fingers shook, but when she had the paper off, she held the box up to the light of the setting sun. "Exquisite," she said. The colored glass stones threw a prism across the room. "This'll go great with my Egypt collection, and I can use it to hold my rings at night." She set it down. "I didn't get you anything."

"No, I didn't expect—anyway, it was just spontaneous."

"Um hmm." Eleanor fingered her necklace. "They sent you over here to check on me, didn't they?"

"Well, yes, but also, I wanted to say hello."

"You may report back that I am fine." Eleanor's eyes crinkled with mirth.

"I will." Karen smiled back. "They tell me you started the group. The CRS ladies."

"Ha." Eleanor laughed up at the ceiling, revealing perfect little teeth. "More like I couldn't shake them. And I hate that name. 'Can't Remember Shit.' Fern thought that one up."

"You didn't create the group?"

"Do I act like I want company? Sorry, I didn't mean you. But the truth is I like my privacy, unlike that mobile sorority. There is little in life more enjoyable than being able to read a complete paragraph without interruption." Eleanor looked around the room. Her eyes stopped on the map. "I was north of El Paso one year, at a place I call Elephant Butt. It's actually 'Butte.' We stayed there quite frequently when I was younger. One morning, I was outside my trailer, doing tai chi, and this woman, Doc, approached me. Have you met Doc?"

"I have. She's the scientist."

"Heck of a gal. Probably the smartest of all of them. Anyway, she asked if she could join me, and pretty soon there were a half dozen of them exercising with us every morning. And then I couldn't get rid of them. They started following me from state to state."

"They hold you in high esteem. And now they're worried that you're sick."

"Everybody has something." Eleanor worked her rings around so they were aligned with the stones facing upward. "I either stay here or go into some nursing home, and I'm not in favor of that."

"Is there anything you need?"

"Can you get me another lifetime?" Eleanor held up the box, admiring it again. "Failing that, I would like a little less interference from that gang out there...I sound cranky, don't I?"

"You've probably earned it."

"What about you? Where are you in life?"

Karen reached into a pocket and pulled out her business card.

"Grace and Associates," Eleanor read. "That would be you and your cats?"

"No, it's just me," Karen said. "I'm working solo. Running away from the corporate world. Hanging out my own shingle."

"Are you married?"

"Not anymore."

"Family? Boyfriend?"

"They're in North Dakota, lobbying me to come home."

"But instead, you live in a camping trailer. Starting a business. How self-sufficient." Eleanor handed the card back. "I envy you."

"It's a fight every day. I feel guilty and then resentful and then guilty again. And I miss them."

"Stick to your guns."

"I will."

Eleanor pushed herself to her feet. "Thank you for coming, and for the lovely gift."

Karen stepped outside, and the door closed behind her. The sun was dropping into the Gulf of Mexico, and the temperature was dropping as well. Christmas lights, strung from trailers and trees, blinked on and off, giving the campground a kitschy, homey appearance. She walked past the various displays—a waving Santa, reindeer whose heads went up and down, a palm tree dressed with lights—and remembered when her mom and dad would drive her around their Dickinson neighborhood to look at lights. It was always just the three of them, in the old Chevy station wagon with bench seats and manual window cranks. They'd cruise the snow-dusted streets, her mother pointing out each twinkling display with delight, her father's hand resting lightly on the steering wheel, a satisfied smile on his face.

A wave of sadness threatened to swamp her. Her dad had been dead many years now, but with her mother, it was too soon, and it still had the power to bend her in two with grief. She felt like an orphan. At fifty, was she too old to call herself that?

Back at the RV, Karen opened a can of chicken soup into a saucepan and turned it on low. She poured a glass of Pinot and found a Christmas music station on her phone. Although nights were harder, she knew that tomorrow morning she'd awaken with a new attitude. She would open her presents, make some phone calls, and enjoy Christmas at the beach with the CRS ladies. She didn't know exactly where this new phase of life would take her, and it wasn't without difficulty and trepidation, but she felt as if she were on the threshold of an exciting new world. If only she could make it happen.

She propped the book in front of her nose. It was a collection of essays on midlife reinvention.

Chapter Three

*C*hristmas morning announced itself with a pair of grackles fighting in the trees overhead. Karen lay in bed and listened to the distant sound of church bells. Last Christmas she was alone, too, because Steve had moved out and left her to wander around in their Newport Beach mansion alone. The memory was too bleak. She got up and put on her robe.

In the kitchen, she turned on the coffee maker, lit a pine-scented candle, and plugged her iPod into the speaker. "Little Drummer Boy" played as she sat on the couch and admired her decorations, a tabletop tree with permanent lights, and a small wreath hung over kitchen table. That was it. There wasn't much room in the trailer for more. But for the time being, it was home, and it was hers.

After finishing the first cup of coffee, she went to open one of her two presents. It was from Aunt Marie, a shoe box wrapped in white tissue paper and tied with a green bow. Inside, wrapped in more tissue paper, were a can of poppy-seed filling and a recipe written on an index card. The card was yellowed and stained, and Karen's breath caught in her throat as she recognized her mother's delicate cursive. On the back, Lena had written, *Be sure you pinch the ends closed tight.* How many years ago she'd written it, Karen could only imagine. Thirty? More? She closed her eyes. The pain was literal, a thudding ache in her solar plexus. Holidays had to be the worst after losing someone. How long before it receded?

Snap out of it. They're fine.

Karen's eyes opened, and she smiled. Frieda's voice never left her—a gift, in its own way. Of course, it was only her subconscious playing games, but at times it seemed so real. Chalking it up to the depth of her feelings for the old woman, she moved on to the second present.

It was from Curt, and she hesitated before ripping open the green foil paper. The last time she'd seen him, he'd tried to talk her into staying in Dickinson with him. They'd snuggled in front of the fire in his two-story farmhouse, rediscovering a love that began in high school and never really faded, in spite of a lifetime apart.

She opened his card. The note, written in dark lettering, said, *Let me build a fire.* Nothing else. So he was thinking about it, too.

In the morning, he hadn't wanted her to leave. They stood in the kitchen, listening to rain pelt the kitchen window. She explained her promise to the CRS ladies.

"They'll understand," Curt said, but in the end she'd left, and he was the one who didn't understand.

Karen ripped the wrapping paper from the box. Inside she found a framed photo of the two of them in front of March Hall, Curt tall, dark, and gorgeous in his tuxedo, his arm around her in that slinky blue cocktail dress. She was laughing at the camera. He was looking at her.

She pulled on a sweater and went outside. A woman stepped out of the motor coach next door. She wore an antler headband and a bright red sweater. Her husband followed behind, juggling a stack of presents, heading for a party. When Karen wished them Merry Christmas, the woman smiled, but the man kept walking. He acted like he was mad every time she saw him. How you could be mad in Key Largo, Karen didn't get. She kept walking.

A quarter mile from the RV, she turned off the campground lane and followed an oyster-shell pathway to the gazebo on the point. It was white with a peaked roof. Underneath stood a picnic table, painted aqua. From that vantage point, one could watch boats entering and leaving the marina next door, but for now the place was quiet. Nothing but the sail rigging, clanging against the masts in the occasional breeze, broke the silence. Karen sat atop the table and pulled her phone out of her sweat shirt pocket. It was early in North Dakota, but Curt would be up feeding the horses by now.

He answered on the first ring. "Merry Christmas, darlin'. Did you get my package?"

"It's beautiful. Thank you."

"I made two. I'm looking at mine right now…I wish you were here."

"Did you get mine?" Karen had sent him a fruit basket. "I know it's kind of corny, but it's hard to find oranges there, so I thought you'd enjoy them."

"They arrived a few days ago. Thank you."

"Is Erin there with you?" She kept her tone light.

"She's home for winter break. Santa brought her a personalized leather backpack for when she goes back to UC Davis."

Karen had met Erin last summer, home from college to visit her father. She'd reacted warmly to Karen, glad to see her father happy. "What about you? Did Santa bring you everything on your list?"

"That depends," he said. "Are you in town?"

"Not exactly."

He didn't answer, and she struggled to say something that would comfort him, knowing she couldn't give him what he wanted. "I won't be rambling around forever."

"So you say."

She left it alone. She actually didn't know how long she'd be away from North Dakota, and him. The future was too unsettled to be able to say. "Curt, please be patient."

"Sorry. Don't listen to me." He gave a rueful chuckle, as if embarrassed. "I guess I'm feeling it more, with the holidays and Erin leaving in a few days. Hang on." Curt's voice became muffled. "Two for me. No bacon." He returned to the phone. "She's making breakfast. We just got back from church."

"'We'?" She smiled into the phone. "You're reforming?"

"Not at all."

"Good." She felt the pull, drawn to his farmhouse and the bittersweet nostalgia of a Dickinson Christmas.

"Erin's going back to Davis sooner than I expected," he said. "They're doing veterinary trials over the holidays, and she's helping out."

"She's on her way to a great career."

"This old farmhouse is going to be mighty quiet."

"Well, but you have your work, and friends. Have you been golfing?"

"Uh, Karen? It's December."

She grimaced. All around the campground, tropical flowers perfumed the air. She had forgotten it was winter in the Dakotas.

"Hey, listen. Don't worry about me. I've just got a little empty-nest syndrome, but classes start in a few weeks. Unless you wanted to meet somewhere warm before that, like, I don't know, Florida?"

Karen slid off the bench and padded across the sand to the water. In spite of the balmy weather, it chilled her toes.

"Are you still there?"

"Babe, I would love to see you," she said, "but I'm buried in one contract, and I have a couple more lined up. It's not a great time for me...I wouldn't be good company."

"I understand. Don't get mad if I go somewhere exotic and tropical without you."

She grinned into the phone. "How's Aunt Marie? Have you seen her?"

"Going great guns," he said, "but your house needs a new roof. If you'd like, I can help her find a good contractor."

"That shouldn't be your responsibility. Can it wait until I get back?"

"Depends on when that'll be." When she didn't answer, he said, "I have to go. Erin says my pancakes are getting cold."

"Well, Merry Christmas, then."

"Take care."

"You, too." She wanted to say *I miss you already* or something else that would soften their ending, but he'd already hung up.

Chapter Four

"*H*ow do you like it, Dad?" Erin sat across from Curt.

He looked up from mindlessly picking at the stack of pancakes. "They're good, honey. Fantastic."

"Did you notice how pretty the table is?"

She had laid out holiday place mats and cloth napkins, along with their nice china and cutlery. "Beautiful. It's real special."

"And did you like the way I mixed strawberries into the batter?"

"Delicious." He poured more maple syrup over the pancakes and tried to act like he was enjoying his meal, but he felt stung by the tone of his conversation with Karen. He thought about the unsigned contract on his desk.

"Dad."

"Hmm?"

"What is going on with you?"

"I'm fine." He stared out the window. The lawn was shriveled and brown, the trees naked and still. The rosebushes lining the split-rail fence were cut back to almost nothing. A bit of snow clung to the edges of the driveway, but it had been a dry month, clear and cold with serene blue skies and no clouds.

"What did Karen say?"

"Merry Christmas. The usual."

When Erin smiled, her smooth skin revealed a dimple in her left cheek. He had a matching one, but on the right. Both had the same thick head of hair, although his had acquired a dusting of silver around his temples.

But Erin was not smiling now. "Why don't you and she—"

"Seriously, these are delicious. What a fabulous Christmas breakfast."

Erin got the hint and turned back to the stove. A song emanated from her iPod. It sounded like hip-hop. His students listened to that stuff, loud, when they were out on digs, and he tolerated it. Tried to like it, even, but without success. He still thought Fleetwood Mac and Led Zeppelin ruled.

"Are you going to see each other pretty soon?"

"Not sure." Curt made a big deal of cutting and organizing the sections of pancake on his plate. Like everyone else, he'd been disappointed when Karen had left North Dakota on this big foray to find herself. They had all expected her to stay in Dickinson for good. No such luck.

He wondered if she'd ever come back, and then wondered again at his sense of loss. It wasn't logical. He was never lonely—well, he was never alone, anyway. While Erin was smaller, he'd dated discreetly, if at all, not wanting to upset their routine. Then, when she went off to college, it was like the shackles were off. Friends had been eager to fix him up, and with his job at the university, there were always plenty of opportunities. He took full advantage of his new freedom.

Then Karen had walked back into his life, and he understood what had been missing. Right away, he made certain assumptions, but she'd kept him at arm's length. It was too soon, too much going on in her life. He had been happy to wait while she decided what to do next, but he'd hoped she'd settle in North Dakota. Now she was off running around Florida, talking about starting some new business.

When Erin wasn't looking, Curt took his unfinished breakfast to the sink and rinsed it down the drain. When he'd received the offer to do a year in Spain, he was thrilled. He'd pictured dining in cozy neighborhood cafés, checking out old castles and ruins, swimming in the Med, and lingering over dinner until midnight. He never figured on doing it alone.

Curt felt Erin watching him, so he dried his hands and kissed her on the cheek. "Thanks for breakfast, sweetie. I'm gonna go feed the animals." In the mudroom, he pulled on a pair of boots and a mackinaw, slapped on his cowboy hat, and grabbed his aviators. He crossed the yard to the barn and hauled open the big door. Duke, the buckskin gelding, eyed him from a stall. Curt climbed up into the hayloft, grabbed a pitchfork, and started throwing forkfuls of alfalfa down into the feed bins. A clump of hay landed on Duke, who stomped a hoof and shook his mane.

"Merry Christmas, you old bag of bones," Curt said. He finished that chore, hung up the pitchfork and climbed down. Missy, smelling breakfast, trotted in from the corral. Her colt, almost as tall, tried to muscle his way around her, but she bared her teeth.

Curt filled the oat buckets, soothed by the sound of their contented munching. When he went to Spain, he was going to have to figure out what to do about them. Maybe he could board them with Patrick for the year.

Erin appeared at the barn door, her black hair woven into two long braids. She wore the Stetson and boots he'd given her for Christmas. "Want to go riding?"

"The horses are pretty sour," Curt said. "Especially him." He gestured toward the gelding.

"You're tougher than he is." Erin slipped into Missy's stall. "Hey there, girl. How's my baby?" The mare nickered in welcome.

Curt watched. Erin was twenty-two and almost gone. He figured once she finished her DVM in Davis, she'd end up in California. He wouldn't have that many more opportunities to ride with her. Suddenly the future felt like it was closing in.

"Okay, sure. Let's ride." Curt snapped a lead on Duke, tied him to a rail outside the barn, and laid the pad and saddle onto his back. Other than flinching at the withers, Duke accepted the load. Curt pulled the belly strap tight. "I think the highline trail would be safer this time of year."

Erin slipped the bridle over Missy's ears and threaded her forelock through. "I don't care where we go. I just want to ride."

When Curt stuck the toe of his boot into the stirrup, Duke skittered sideways. "Whoa," he shouted, and the horse stopped, shaking his head and mouthing the bit.

Erin swung up into the saddle. Missy trotted toward the gate, eager for some exercise. Out on the lane, they cantered away.

With a nudge from Curt's heels, Duke sprang forward in a fast trot, chasing after his stablemate. Curt slipped easily into a post, and the ride smoothed out. He watched with admiration as his daughter rode Missy in a slow canter up ahead. When she was small, she'd been thrown, not enough to be hurt but enough to scare the hell out of him. It was never far from his mind.

Now she was lithe and strong, an accomplished horsewoman and on her way to becoming a professional veterinarian. The trajectory of her development both delighted and sobered him, for it served to mark the passage of time.

One hundred yards ahead, Missy trotted past an overgrown windbreak, and a flock of pheasant burst into the air with a great thunder of wings. Erin cried out, and the horse shied and bolted. While Curt watched, helpless, Missy took off with Erin bent low over her mount's neck like a jockey. Curt gave Duke his head, and they tore after the mare, hoofbeats pounding against the frozen ground. At the top of a rise, Missy slowed as Erin regained control, first to a canter and then a fast trot. By the time Curt drew alongside, his daughter was comforting her horse with soft words and touch.

"Jesus," Curt said, his heart pounding. He could feel Duke's sides expanding and contracting as the horse blew. Missy stretched her neck and shook her mane.

"Sorry, Dad. The birds scared her. We're okay." Erin patted her horse's neck.

"Let's walk it off." They nudged their mounts forward, and soon the steady clop-clopping of the hooves began to relax him.

Erin gestured at the endless blue sky; the distant farmhouses, each with a windmill; and the plowed fields lying fallow in the wintry cold. "I miss all this at Davis."

"It's not forever." Although sometimes, sitting in that silent farmhouse alone, he thought it might be. Erin would be awarded her undergraduate degree in the spring, but it would take her another few years to earn her DVM. For all intents and purposes, she was already grown up and moving on. He had to think of his future too, but at least he didn't have to worry about Erin.

In companionable silence, they rode down a slope to a dirt road that ran alongside a semifrozen pond. Out in the country, there was no sound except that of the horses and the occasional trill of a meadowlark.

"Dad, can I ask you something?"

He pulled his hat lower over his eyes. Erin had displayed a tendency of late to try to run him the direction she thought he should go. He figured that came with womanhood, but under the present circumstances, he knew who she wanted to talk about and wished she'd give it a rest. "I think you're going to, regardless."

"It doesn't make sense that you're alone, and now you have a shot at this amazing woman..."

"I'm glad you like her."

"I do, and I think she'd be awesome for you. So what are you going to do about Karen?"

He looked at her from behind reflective sunglasses. "What we're doing. We're friends."

"But when are you going to be more than friends?"

He glanced up at the sky, where a dozen vultures soared in a lazy circle. What difference did it make what he wanted? Karen's mind was made up. The sooner he accepted that, the sooner he could get on with his life.

"When you were with her, you seemed really happy," Erin said.

"You mean I wasn't my usual crabby self?"

"I'm just saying it's not good for you to be by yourself all the time."

"I'm around people all day long."

"Not that kind of people. Girlfriend kind of people." She leaned forward in her saddle, grinning at him. "Soul-mate kind of people."

"Erin, I'm fine. Leave it alone."

"But Dad—"

"Drop it." He leaned forward and clucked at his horse, leaving Erin's words hanging in the frigid air.

Chapter Five

*E*arlier that Christmas Day, Jessie stood near the sink, trying to choke down a bologna sandwich and get back to her books before the baby awoke. Now it was almost two o'clock, and she still had thirty or more pages to the end of the chapter.

What a screwed-up Christmas. She had planned to make a special holiday dinner for Lenny and sit down like a family to a nice meal. But Kegger had pounded on the door yesterday, saying he'd found them work. Jessie was incredulous. They hadn't worked for weeks, and then all of a sudden, here comes a job on Christmas Eve, tearing down a couple of decrepit outbuildings on a nearby farm. Money didn't grow on trees, so Lenny had left that morning, right after they opened their presents.

Jessie leaned down and slurped a drink of water from the faucet. The gift giving had left something to be desired. She had received a bottle of perfume from Lenny, a scent that would work better as roach killer, and a book from her mother and dad, which she tossed in the box to donate to the thrift center. Maybe next year, she and Lenny were more settled, Christmas would be more fun.

Wiping her chin with the back of her hand, she stared out the window at their sad excuse for a yard. Nothing grew in a thirty-foot radius from the tree where the dog was chained, and pretty much everywhere else was bare and ugly, too. One of these days, she'd fix it up, as soon as she could talk Lenny into hooking up a drip line.

He'd promised they would have their holiday dinner on New Year's Eve instead, so today, with him gone, she had the luxury of messing up the whole table with her school books. By the time he came home, she'd have them stashed out of sight. He got irritated at all the attention she paid to her classes, even though, as a concession to not having a babysitter for Sunshine, Jessie could only attend online. But that was okay. She was still learning.

And her classes were helping her make sense of her new life. According to her psychology book, Lenny was probably acting like a jerk to hide a lack of confidence. This was understandable since he was only twenty-three. Plus, her being the girl, he probably felt intimidated. Although Jessie felt sorry for him, she was happy to learn this about people. It made her feel safer somehow, understanding things. Even though she was younger than Lenny, she was pretty mature. Men grew up later. Lenny would be okay in a couple of years. Until then, she'd have to look out for all of them.

Sunshine began to whimper. You sure didn't need a baby monitor in a single-wide. Every cough and fart could be heard clear out to the driveway. Jessie washed down the last of her sandwich with a slug of water, bitter today. The well must be getting low. They hadn't had enough rain in the last couple years, although the weatherman had said things might improve soon. If this drought kept on, the wells would go dry. She wondered what they'd do then, out here in the country without a regular water supply. Lenny would never let them move closer to Atlanta. Maybe she could start stockpiling. There was room in the shed behind all his junk. Maybe if she got a little bit ahead, she could buy a bottle or two at a time and hide them.

Jessie tied her long white-blond hair in a ponytail and hurried to the bedroom. Sunshine, who had begun wailing in earnest, stopped when her mother, cooing and smiling, reached down and picked her up. Lenny had jammed a crib between the bed and the wall, but pretty soon the baby would be too big for the arrangement. The bedroom could handle a baby bed and a twin, though, so maybe Lenny would agree to sleep on the couch. He usually fell asleep there watching TV anyway, whether from too much beer or worn out from the occasional construction job.

The trailer was quiet, except for the baby fussing and Booger, the dog, barking in the front yard. Jessie sat back down at the kitchen table with Sunshine on her lap and gave the baby her sippy cup. The baby made happy little grunts as she filled her belly, and Jessie stared at her, mesmerized by the porcelain skin, the eyelashes that grew from flawless lids, the miniature nails on perfect fingers. Soon enough, the infant would be a toddler, and Jessie would miss these days, although they were a challenge with Lenny around. But hopefully he would get hired somewhere regular and they could move into a bigger place, maybe a double-wide. Maybe even a house someday, and then she could have another baby.

This morning, she had made his lunch, hurrying as fast as she could. He and Kegger drank coffee and fidgeted in the living room while she worked. The trailer would jiggle and rattle every time one of them got up, sat down, or got up again to look out the window.

At least he had a job today. He would make a few bucks. The further ahead they got, the less likely he'd split a gut when she asked for the money to enroll in the new semester. Finally, she'd finished his sandwiches, stuck them in a plastic grocery bag, and stood at the front door, holding the bag in one hand and Sunshine in the other. Lenny had kissed her, pushing her against the wall and sticking his tongue down her throat in a show of ownership while Kegger laughed. Jessie went to rinse her mouth out. Lenny wasn't a stickler for brushing his teeth.

After they left, Jessie played with the baby for a while. Her daughter was amazing for not even a year old, already pulling herself up and trying to walk. Sandy had sent a wheeled walker as a peace offering, but it had stayed in the box since there was no surface in the trailer where the wheels could roll. They'd sold it on Craigslist and met the buyer in the parking lot of the Circle K store. Lenny had sat in the truck while she did the transaction. He had said it was for her protection and that he wanted to make sure the buyer didn't knock her in the head and run off. Lenny had gotten mad when Jessie put her foot down and said the money was for baby food and diapers.

"The whole twenty bucks?"

"She needs it more than we do." Jessie had talked fast as she got Sunshine out of the car seat. "I'll be right back." With that, she'd hurried into the store before Lenny got the idea to chase after her and take the money.

Now, in the quiet trailer, only the drone of a distant tractor broke the silence. That, and the baby's hearty burp. She played with the baby for a while and then let her amuse herself with a walker that didn't walk anywhere but held bells and buzzers and all manner of infant toys. After putting her down for another nap, Jessie went into the kitchen and filled an empty milk carton with water. She opened the door as quietly as possible so Booger wouldn't start barking. The dog, tied to the thick elm with a rope, watched silently. Jessie tried not to look at him. Booger was a mean old mutt with an overdeveloped sense of territory. He tended to behave better if you didn't make eye contact.

A cloud passed over as she dribbled a thin trickle of water on the azalea bush next to the porch. The lady down the road had given her the flowers last May when Jessie came home from the hospital with Sunshine. Jessie didn't know the woman, except for the fact that she lived over the next hill. Still, it was a nice gesture, and the plant was doing well, even though one time Booger got loose, ran straight to the azalea, and pissed all over it. Jessie got real mad while Lenny laughed so hard he about peed himself. But the azalea seemed to thrive even then. Maybe pretty soon it would rain, and then she wouldn't have to water it so much. Jessie emptied the last drops of water on the plant and went back inside.

Before she resumed studying, she did the dishes, swept the kitchen floor, and straightened the living room. The place was small and tight, bad enough when it was just her and Lenny. Now, with the baby, there was more pressure on all of them, especially Lenny, who was big. She hadn't wanted kids, but there was that party last spring, and now here they were. But you couldn't say it was a mistake when it got her the cutest, smartest, most adorable little kid in the whole wide world.

Outside the trailer, Booger howled. The dog was circling, making a spot for a nap. Jessie slipped on her black retro reading glasses. They looked like rhinestoned butterfly wings, which Jessie loved and Lenny hated. She piled a stack of textbooks on the coffee table, folded one leg under herself, and went back to studying for her psychology exam.

Chapter Six

*T*his is what it would feel like to not have him in your life, she thought. Karen set the phone down. The party would start in an hour, and she needed to get a move on, but Curt's phone call had chilled her.

What did you expect?

She picked up the phone again and studied the screen, thinking she could call him back. Promise to do something, throw him a reason to hope. But would she be leading him on?

She wished he understood. She needed to talk to him...really talk. He would understand. She eyed the phone.

It would have to wait until later. She would call him after the beach party, when he'd had time to settle down and she'd thought of what to say.

She reached into the fridge for her contribution to the potluck lunch: her special macaroni salad, a holdover from California. The Dickinson relatives had loved it, even if avocados were impossible to find. Karen divided the salad into two smaller containers suitable for transporting in the compartment of her Buddy.

As she motored toward the gate, another rider fell in beside her. It was Rita, also on her scooter. They rode two abreast to the park, passing the docks where dive and snorkel boats were loading passengers. Farther down the lane, a playground swarmed with kids who rode the swings and took turns going down the bright-yellow tube slide while parents perched on the picnic tables. The park quieted as they approached the mangrove forest, a self-guided tour area where one could trek the boardwalk under the spreading limbs of the oddly shaped trees. The road ended at a beach, where the CRS ladies had laid claim with shade covers and folding chairs.

They parked next to Fern's black Silverado with the dually tires and the fifth-wheel hitch. Fern had owned a Chevy dealership back in Phoenix. Now retired, she and Belle went first class all the way. Belle, wearing a floppy red hat with miniature ornaments around the band, waved Karen over to a table laid out with casserole dishes, fruit bowls, and appetizer trays. At a second table, Fern tended bar. She handed Karen a red Solo cup filled with wine. "Glad to see you out and about. Nice of your boss to give you a break."

"She's a pretty decent gal if you give her a chance," said Karen. She and Rita headed for the CRS ladies, who had set a circle of chairs in shallow water. The chairs were shaded by brightly colored umbrellas stuck in the sand.

"Hey, look who's here," said Margo. Her gold bracelets glittered against dark-coffee skin. "Come and sit with us."

"I can make room." Candace, a Paula Deen look-alike, raised her heavy body and scooted her chair around.

At the water's edge, Karen and Rita kicked off their sandals and waded in. Largo Sound was clear and warm, and an offshore breeze riffled the water. All around the circle, women laughed and chattered in twos and threes. After saying hello, Karen settled into an empty beach chair, wiggling her toes until they were buried. Rita sank into the chair next to her and sighed. Grinning, the two women tapped cups. One year ago, Karen had been slaving away for a jerk of a boss in a soulless corporation. Now she was free. Well, sort of free. Broke, single, and homeless, unless you counted the RV, but still free to make up her own rules. Which were

1. I work for myself (because after a long career, she'd been fired);
2. I live alone (because after a long marriage, her husband had left her for a hot young thing);
3. I am not a doormat (because if the incident on the highway outside Cheyenne had taught her anything, it was that sometimes you had to put yourself first).

It wasn't easy trying to become a new woman at fifty. She had done everything wrong in the first forty-nine years, and now things were going to be different. As Frieda used to say, you had to decide how you were going to live your life, or someone else would decide for you.

If Karen acted like a mole at times, hiding from society, working out of her fifth wheel, trying to make an independent life, it was only because of her new rules. And when she needed company, the CRS ladies were there, ready to include her in whatever they were doing, even if it was just a walk through the palm-shaded campground or sitting around in someone's trailer, having a cup of coffee or a glass of wine. She could count on them.

Some of them still worked part time. Rita drove an eighteen-wheeler when the routes suited her, and Doc, a semiretired scientist, still did odd jobs for the government. But the rest of them—Fern and Belle, Candace and Margo from Beverly Hills, and Patti from the Bronx—were all permanent pensioners.

"What are you working on, Karen?" Doc leaned forward, her gray hair gathered into a long braid under a khaki field hat.

"I landed a couple of contracts recently. Mostly recruitments. Headhunting. How about you?" Karen leaned down and trailed her fingertips in the water.

"I'm analyzing metadata for the HHS. They want to know about the impact of sustained Internet usage on the brain."

"Oh, it absolutely fries them," said Candace. "I worry about the kids these days. They're like zombies."

"It's not just the kids." Patti held up her phone. On the back, it had a FDNY decal, the same as her ball cap. "I couldn't live without this."

"Me, neither," said Margo. "I'm on Facebook and e-mail. And I read the morning paper. And there's weather, fitness tracker, movies—you can't get away from it."

Rita nodded. "I even have a dashboard mount in my truck for my laptop."

Doc grasped at her hat as a freshening breeze whipped the umbrellas around. "Actually, we're finding it may foster the growth of new brain cells, particularly in older populations."

"Thank God," said Karen. "I'm on the computer constantly. My problem is I have to find job candidates by searching the web, and that's really labor intensive."

Doc looked thoughtful. "Isn't there some way to automate the process?"

"Not that I know of. You go one by one—making calls, reading résumés, doing screening interviews on video calls. Sometimes I get anxious, wondering if I'll be able to deliver."

"Try stepping away every ninety minutes," said Doc. "Rest your eyes and your mind. It'll recharge you as well as a nap."

"Or just take a nap." Fern held the jug out and refilled their cups.

"I'm too busy for naps," Karen said.

"Pretty soon, you'll be old enough to retire," said Candace. "Then you can do whatever you want."

"I'm already doing what I want. I love my work."

"Uh-huh." Margo looked at Candace. The two women burst out laughing. "You are one sad case, honey pie."

Karen took a sip of wine. She'd heard the charge all her life. It didn't bother her anymore.

Gina joined them, rhinestones sparkling from her visor all the way down to the cuffs of her capris. "Hey, Karen, you never got back to me. I need you to alter that ball gown for me."

"You sew?" asked Candace.

"Not so much these days." Karen tipped the cup back, savoring the fruity, cold wine. She enjoyed sewing and had even brought her machine along on this trip for occasional fixes.

"It's a cocktail dress," said Gina, winking. "It's too small in the boobs."

"Again? You didn't." Margo eyed Gina's front.

"Like 'em?" Gina stuck her chest out. "Went the full double D. So, Karen, I'm going to this New Year's party."

"I'm sorry, Gina, I've got too much on my plate right now."

"Can't you find a tailor in town?" asked Patti.

A red speedboat roared past, drowning out Gina's answer and distracting her momentarily. Using the boat as a cover, Karen went to see if she could help with the food.

Belle was just setting down the last dish on a table jammed with casseroles, salads, and platters of turkey. "Would you call everybody? It's ready." The women gathered around the table to say grace before loading up. They held hands and bowed their heads. Karen had been raised a Catholic but at this point, she felt more spiritual than religious. Still, she appreciated the spirit of community and fellowship.

"Lord, we ask you to bless our families and our friends and this great country of ours. Thank you also for this beautiful day in Key Largo and for the privilege of good health so that we may enjoy it."

"And Eleanor," said Candace.

"Amen."

As the women returned to their chairs, Gina called out to Karen. "Sit by me. We can talk about my dress."

When Karen glanced around in dismay, Rita plunked down next to Gina and extended her hand. "Hi, I'm Rita Lopez. I drive a Peterbilt."

"Lovely, dear." Gina looked her up and down. "Is that some kind of RV?"

"No, I'm a long-haul trucker."

"Delighted." Gina began poking at her food.

"Want to hear about my truck? I just overhauled the motor."

"No thank you."

Karen sat on Rita's other side. "Thanks," she whispered.

"You owe me." Rita picked up a turkey leg. "Isn't this great? I'm so excited to eat home cooking."

"You must eat at a lot of restaurants," said Karen.

"Fast food and cafés, mostly," Rita said. "Or I'll make something in the back of the truck. It's not too bad. I've got a fridge and microwave in the sleeper."

Karen had loaded up with both white and dark meat, stuffing, potatoes and gravy, cranberries, and a sampling of casseroles. It was amazing what these women could do with the small kitchens in their RVs. The turkey had been a shared project, with several of the campers volunteering to cook up individual parts of the bird. "How did you fall in with these guys?"

"Rita saw us caravaning," Margo said. "We were about two dozen rigs. When we all hit the road at the same time, it's quite a sight."

"It was a convoy," said Rita. "You pulled in while I was getting gas, and I couldn't stop looking. Then I made it a point to strike up a conversation."

"I believe we were standing in line at the restroom," said Candace. "You looked like you needed a friend."

"When we first met her, Rita was a scared little thing," said Patti. "We couldn't believe she was driving a big old semi all by herself."

"How did you get into that line of work?" asked Karen.

Rita looked at her food. "How about we talk about something else?"

Candace patted Rita on the arm. "I used to work. I volunteered a lot when the children were small," she said. "Now that they're grown up, I don't do as much. One of these days, I want to get back in shape and start helping again."

"I used to run into burning buildings," said Patti. "Not anymore."

"You miss it, though," said Doc.

"Sometimes."

"So, how do you all organize your trips?" asked Karen. "How do you come together?"

"Fern tells us the itinerary, and if we can, we meet up with the group, usually for months at a stretch," said Margo. "At first, my daughters were unhappy that I wasn't available to babysit a hundred percent of the time, but they adjusted."

"That's a problem sometimes," said Patti. "People don't always understand."

"You get to a certain age, you want to do your own thing," said Margo.

"I mean, you give them the first half of your life," said Candace. "The second half is for you."

"I don't understand you people," said Gina. "I usually do whatever I want."

"Throughout history, man has tried to find balance," said Doc. "Too much of any one element can result in negative outcomes."

"Not for me," said Gina. "Let's open presents."

They had agreed on a limit of twenty dollars. Fern, wearing a Santa hat, handed out the unmarked gifts, the randomness of which caused peals of inebriated laughter. Belle got a new tool belt and

Fern a bottle of perfume, so they switched. Candace got a yard-art palm tree and Margo a shovel, which drew a frown. "I'll trade you that for this," said Doc, handing over a breezy, floral sundress. "It's attractive, but I prefer slacks."

"I can't wait to try it on." Margo held up the sundress. "And it's got a wrap with it. How inventive."

"I made it," said Karen. "It seemed right for the Keys."

"You are really creative."

Karen opened her own present, which turned out to be the book *The Four-Hour Workweek*, by Tim Ferriss. She looked up and saw Fern watching. "Is this from you?"

Fern nodded. "Thought it might help."

"What am I supposed to do with this?" said Gina, unwrapping a rhinestone-encrusted dog collar.

Rita elbowed Karen, who bit her lip to keep from laughing.

"I really meant it for Patti's little dog," said Belle.

"I got a year's subscription to this." Patti held up a copy of a Hollywood tabloid. "Would you like to trade?"

"Definitely." As Gina began pawing through the magazine, Karen glanced at her watch, a Rolex left over from the glory years. "It's almost five. I have to run."

"Back to work?" asked Rita.

"Back to work," said Karen. As she packed her scooter, Belle hurried over.

"Are you coming to the party on Friday?" she asked.

"Tomorrow?"

"It's Fern's birthday. We're just having a little get-together. No big deal. I know she'd want to see you there."

"I'll try," said Karen, "but don't be mad at me if I don't show."

"You wouldn't have to stay very long. I'd hate for you to miss it."

Karen's answer died on her tongue. What was the point of arguing?

Back at the RV, she went around opening windows, letting the breeze in. Then she plugged in her tabletop Christmas tree and set the new book, poppy-seed mix, and photo next to it.

While the computer started up, Karen massaged her temples. She had a headache from the wine and the sun, and she felt worn out. Yet she still had work to do. Doc's question nagged at her. Everything else was automated these days. Why not employee recruitment? She could do some of her work in her sleep, so why not create a search engine to handle it automatically?

She heated water for instant coffee, poured it into a thermal cup, and went outside, hoping a brief walk around the campground would clear her head. Karen set off along the perimeter road, admiring the Christmas displays.

At the far end of the campground, where the road began to circle back, stood Eleanor's trailer. The site wasn't close to the beach or in view of anything pretty, but Eleanor liked her privacy. Karen admired the woman for her individuality. Even before she had gotten sick, she'd preferred to be alone, and she didn't let the CRS ladies tell her how to spend her days. Yet they loved her. Karen wondered how a person walked that particular tightrope.

A few minutes later, she hung up the Windbreaker and plugged in her iPod. With Keiko Matsui pounding away on the piano, Karen got out her paperwork and settled in at the dinette.

She opened the folder, making final notes and organizing while her attachments uploaded. Just as she hit send, a breeze gusted in the window and blew her papers to the floor. When Karen leaned down to pick them up, she hit her head on the table, knocking loose a piece of decorative edging, the same one she'd reglued yesterday. Sighing, she set it aside, took another slug of coffee, and returned to the keyboard. It would be a long night.

Chapter Seven

*T*he next morning, Aunt Marie called. Her voice sounded like she was in a tunnel.

"Are you down in the basement?" Karen pictured her aunt, now in her mideighties, climbing down the narrow ladder into the root cellar under the house.

"Yes, but I have you on speaker so my hands are free," said her aunt. "I'm rearranging jars. How was your Christmas?"

"It was great. Thanks for the poppy seed and the recipe. Are you alone down there?"

"*Ach*, don't worry about me. I have the phone. Oops." There was a loud crash. "Just some tin plates. Nothing to worry about. Listen, dear, I called to tell you I'm thinking of moving into the mother-in-law cottage at Lorraine and Jim's."

"That would be great. You'd have your own little place, but there would be people around, too."

"And then you could come back and live in your house."

Karen sucked in her breath. It was a bold new ploy and she had to give her aunt credit.

"Lorraine and Jim are thrilled. I'll probably be out of here in a few weeks."

"I suppose I could rent it," Karen said, "with all the oil workers in town."

Her aunt fell silent, probably calculating her next move.

The house was ancient, but it had weathered tornadoes and blizzards and floods. Her great-grandfather had built it prairie style, with dirt packed into the space between the interior and exterior wood walls. The flooring sagged in places, and the plumbing was temperamental, but during the oil boom, housing was so prized in Dickinson she'd have no trouble renting it out. Besides, she could use the income.

"But the boom's petering out, and besides, renters can be hard on a house," said Aunt Marie. "The neighbor down the street rented hers, and they slept six to a room, lined up on the floor. They ruined the plumbing, and oh, the filth."

"The only reason you should move is if it makes you happy," said Karen. "Not because you're trying to make room for me."

"I would be happy if you were back in Dickinson. And I'm not the only one."

"Who've you been scheming with, Aunt Marie?"

"Not scheming. Just talking. The professor came by a couple days ago to drop off his homemade chokecherry jelly. It's so good I told him he could sell it. That man can do anything. You're missing out."

"We talk on the phone."

"You know what I mean. Men like Curt don't grow on trees."

"I know," Karen said. She loved being with Curt, loved waking up in his big farmhouse, loved going on digs with his geology classes, loved everything about him. But she'd been married for almost thirty years, and her divorce had only become final a few months ago. Right now, she liked the feeling of being on her own—even if it was in a shabby trailer in Florida.

Aunt Marie sighed. "You know I'm not getting any younger. I'd sure like to spend more time with you, and I can't travel anymore."

"I promise I'll come home in the spring, okay?"

"To stay?"

"To visit."

"I'll be looking forward to it."

Karen hung up, gathering her clothes and towels for a trip to the Laundromat. As she hunted for quarters, she thought about Dickinson. After all the years in California, returning to her hometown had been deeply satisfying, even though for the sad occasion of her mother's funeral. She'd enjoyed renewing old friendships and getting to know her family again. Leaving hadn't been easy, but she had told herself it was just for a promised rendezvous with the CRS ladies in Florida.

The problem was, she hadn't said when she'd be back, and when anyone asked, Karen had dodged the answer. In truth, she didn't know when she'd be back, or if. After thirty years in one place, she wasn't ready to decide where she'd settle down. She knew she could work from anywhere if she set up a human resources consulting business, and until that grew, she would delay the decision.

Of course, there was always the little voice in her head asking why she was working so hard trying to get the business up and running when she could simply move home and live in her old house? Employers were screaming for staff. There was such a labor shortage she could probably flip burgers for twenty bucks an hour.

Sure, I'd like to see that.

Karen stopped what she was doing. All her life she'd been accused of being in her head too much, but this time either the voice was real or she was having a stroke.

Where are you?

Where do you think?

Karen looked around the trailer, half expecting a curtain to move. She placed the laundry basket by the door.

So what are you going to do?

I'm going to make up my own mind, Karen thought, *just as you would have.* Frieda, at ninety, had demonstrated curiosity and self-improvement right up until her death. Karen wanted to do the same.

The Laundromat was crawling with snowbirds, and she was lucky to grab a couple of washing machines. After dumping in all her clothes, she found a chair in a quiet corner and opened her spiral notebook. It was time for some serious strategizing. What contacts did she know from her career in the health-care industry, and what services could she offer? As she thought about the various companies and offices in California and the Southwest, the page began to fill with names and ideas. She transferred her laundry into a couple of dryers, selected her first target, and dialed the number.

"What a nice surprise." Peggy's voice was raspy from cigarettes. "I thought you died, kid. What can I do you for?"

Karen laughed out loud. She'd always enjoyed working alongside the older woman. Even now, she could picture Peggy's craggy face, her smile askew, bright red lipstick bleeding into the wrinkles around her mouth. After a few minutes of catching up, she said, "I'm looking for work."

"Century Health is hiring," Peggy said. "That outfit up around Marin County. They pay a lot, but housing's expensive."

"What I meant was I'm freelancing. I do contract work."

"Is that right? Are you turning into one of those people who stay in their pajamas all day?"

"Almost. I'm at a Laundromat right now."

"Sounds very glamorous."

"Doesn't it?" Karen loved that she didn't have to pretend with Peggy. "And I can see the ocean, if I squint. It's right on the other side of the highway."

"Me, too, as you recall. Big deal." Peggy laughed, a hoarse cackle. "So, what do you need?"

"More like what do *you* need? I know you're up to your eyeballs in work. How can I help?"

Peggy ran things now at Global Health, Newport Beach. She had become even more formidable since returning from a failed retirement and demanding her job back. She held the corporate checkbook and the power to decide whom to hire. "You worked here for thirty years. What do you suggest?"

"To start with, your recruitment system is out of date, and your training was never legal." Karen listed all the areas of need she remembered from her days at Global. She was betting not much had changed, except perhaps to worsen. "And, as I recall, if anybody wanted to raise a fuss, you'd be on thin ice with the EEOC—"

"All right, all right. Jesus. You can start with a policy review, and we'll go from there."

"I'll send you a proposal. Now, I heard Ben left to start his own firm. Do you know what he's up to?"

"He bought into some smaller version of us. Him and a few guys started a partnership." Peggy exhaled, and Karen remembered how smoky her office used to be. Peggy didn't really care about environmental laws. "Hey, now there's an idea. He could probably use your help."

"That's what I'm thinking. Do you have any contact information?"

"I think so. Lemme look. Yeah, here it is. Savannah." She read off the number. "Go get him, Tiger."

Ben Washington had been her protégé, the most promising of dozens of young talents she'd brought along. After saying good-bye to Peggy, she found him at Savannah Health Solutions, listed as one of the founders. A quick search of the Internet told her SHS was new and expanding rapidly. She made a tentative list of the services he'd be likely to need and dialed the number.

"Karen. What a surprise." He laughed in the deep, rich baritone she remembered. "What've you been up to? Are you still in South Dakota?"

People always got it wrong, but she left it alone. "Actually, I'm doing consulting." Karen filled him in, not exaggerating but not explaining everything. He didn't need to know she worked out of a trailer. After a decent amount of getting-reacquainted chit chat, she said, "I have business in Savannah next week." She hoped he wouldn't press to expose her lie. "I wondered if you'd want to get lunch. Say, Monday?"

"That'd be fantastic. I'll clear whatever else I was doing. There's this great little place overlooking the river."

Karen hung up, grinning like a fool at her audacity. First the contract with Ursula, then Peggy, now Ben. It was almost as if she could conjure up work just by thinking about it.

The travel logistics would be a hassle. To keep costs down, she planned to take the truck, leaving early Sunday and driving all day. All she needed to do was figure out what to bring and where to stay, someplace cheap but clean. She began folding clothes, wondering how much leeway she had on her credit card.

Back at the trailer, she grappled with the question of what to wear. Savannah would be cooler than Key Largo. Karen pulled a box out from under the bed and unfolded a cute sweater and matching turtleneck. She would also pack the camisole that could be worn under a blouse for more warmth and provide a sexy little glimpse of lace at the bodice. Curt had loved that look. At the thought, she remembered she'd promised to call him, but their last conversation had ended on a down note and she struggled to think of what to say. Why couldn't it be easy? She loved his company and missed him like crazy, but the next few weeks would be nuts. But maybe after that? She could check her calendar. Maybe they could work something out. She folded one more top and put it away.

After lunch, she went back to her workstation in the kitchen. She worked until evening, made dinner, and then worked some more. All the while, her phone sat silent and accusing, but she didn't know how to give Curt what he wanted.

Chapter Eight

*C*hurch bells rang through the truck's open window as Karen left Paradise Shores. Cruising toward the mainland, she savored the balmy air and the quiet of a Sunday morning. It felt good to escape, to be moving toward something positive and exciting.

Karen had always enjoyed driving long distances alone. The automatic movements over droning blacktop freed her imagination, often sparking creative thoughts and solutions to tricky problems. When she had lived in California, business sometimes required her presence at the office in Monterey, and whenever possible, she drove from her home in Newport Beach. She'd leave early and stop in Santa Barbara for breakfast, continuing on to her favorite motel on Cannery Row.

Now, she was happy to have the time to think about Savannah. Ben Washington had been one of her most promising young managers at Global Health, and she was eager to see what he'd done professionally. Also, she hoped to find time to see the city, with its lavish gardens and monuments and its antebellum structures still intact. Maybe Ben could show her around.

So she settled in to think and plan, but the first name to pop into her head was Curt's. She missed him, but she couldn't afford the indulgence. If he were around, she'd want to spend languid days and torrid nights not working. She knew from their time together in North Dakota that when she was with him, she couldn't focus on anything else. If he were to stay with her, even if only for a week or two, her resistance would falter. He lit up her body like she was seventeen again, which was when she'd first had a crush on him, but they'd gone on to create wholly separate lives.

Now they were both free, but Karen was hesitant. In her world-view, relationships had a way of taking you over. Before you met a guy, you'd be chasing your own goals. Then you fell in love, and it was all so exciting you could barely stand to get back to work. But you did, in little bits and shreds of time, while wishing you could be back with The Guy, doing whatever. And he'd be sending you texts about dinner or golf or hiking or taking a vacation. Which was way more fun than working.

As a result, your work would slide, until one day, you'd realize you're seriously behind. So you'd lay it out for him, and he'd agree, and you'd go back to your charts and graphs, but time would pass, and you'd feel conflicted. Here you'd have this perfectly wonderful man, and he was ready to offer you the moon, and all he asked of you was time. Which you wished you could give him.

So you'd set the work aside and tell him yes. Maybe you'd have a drink or two, followed by dinner. Maybe see a movie and spend the night together. Days came; days went. It was heaven, and you were living the life.

Only problem was, it was *his* life. Because you had goals and dreams, and with him around, they were getting pushed aside, and against all odds, that was okay. Only it wasn't.

Karen stared at the highway unfurling in front of her. Would relationships always be this way, a zero-sum game with no compromise? How did other people balance them?

For now, her only response was to ask Curt to be patient until she got her business off the ground. Then she'd be able to relax a little and maybe even invite him to come stay with her in Key Largo. That would be romantic. Her hormones stirred at the thought.

She enjoyed the feeling. It was something she had feared losing as she rounded the corner toward fifty, a dull, married woman with a libido as flat as the North Dakota prairie. Then Curt had come back into her life, and she'd discovered that sex at her age was even more spectacular than in her youth.

In fact, it wasn't just sex. At fifty, she felt like she was starting all over again, as motivated and excited as when she was young but with a much more capable mind. These were early days, adrenaline-soaked ones in which Karen was free to take chances and pursue her dreams. It was the silver lining that remained after the upheaval and loss of the past year.

But there was still the dark undertone of risk. What if she lost him? What if she failed in her quest to build financial independence?

Stop whining. Life is to be lived.

Karen grinned. Call her crazy, but there were benefits to having a great imagination. She felt as if Frieda were in her head, riding along with her. It was a comfort.

You're welcome.

She took an off-ramp, found a fast-food place, and bought a burger at the drive-through. Under the spreading limbs of a giant eucalyptus, she ate lunch and then got back on the road. Traffic was heavier now on the Interstate northbound toward Savannah. Signs beckoned travelers to stop at any number of historic points of interest. A historic seaport, an old plantation, and an entire community on Jekyll Island all called out to her. She would enjoy seeing them if she had more time.

But a person could only do so much. There had to be a way to systematize or automate the search work she was doing. What if she could direct her computer to alert her when certain searches were conducted online? She had already set up alerts when people asked about her business. Some of these turned out to be headhunting gold, the pursuit of which yielded qualified candidates for her clients.

Surely there was some kind of software out there. And if there wasn't, could she develop it? And once developed, could she sell it to a big company and become rich?

She jammed on the brakes, almost rear-ending the guy in front of her. What a great idea.

It was worth thinking about anyway. She filed it away and went back to driving.

Trees bordered the highway, two lanes on each side separated by a wide strip of grass, and the sky was a perfect deep-blue backdrop to drifting, fluffy-white clouds. At times like this, Karen—child of a small town in the Midwest—felt lucky to have lived in several different places in the country. From the Dakotas to California to Florida, she'd loved some part of all of them, although her hometown would always represent her foundation.

Toward evening, she drove into Savannah, crowded with traffic and hopping like the busy riverport city of old. Her hotel, though economical, was clean, new, and geared for business. In the old days, when she had been wealthy, she almost didn't appreciate a decent hotel as much as she did now, when every dollar was so precious. Humbled at the realization, she went downstairs to find a place to eat dinner.

The hotel opened onto a busy side street lined with crumbling brick facades. The brickwork moldered with the black patina of southern damp, and castor-bean trees sprouted from underneath buckling sidewalks. Yet she walked without fear, joining a crowd of tourists and businesspeople, the former laughing and sipping beer from paper cups, the latter scowling into phones or jabbering at Bluetooth earbuds.

Three blocks away, she found a down-home diner furnished with the aluminum-edged laminate tables of her childhood. Overhead, a collection of hand-crank eggbeaters hung from the ceiling. A well-padded waitress took her order of shrimp and grits fancied up with smoky andouille sausage. The restaurant was filled with a mix of family types and worker bees.

Other than Ben, she knew no one in the city. She wondered what he'd be like now. Sometimes the people you mentor break away in a bid for independence that makes continuation of the relationship awkward. She hoped they'd still have their easy camaraderie.

She looked around the diner, taking in the fact that everyone else seemed to be here on holiday, relaxing and enjoying their leisure, but she was gearing up for a business pitch. So this was her life—at fifty, she was working as hard as a kid again.

Her phone rang. It was Curt.

"Perfect timing." She smiled into the phone.

"You sound happy. Where are you?"

"I am, at this very moment, having dinner in Savannah, Georgia."

"My rambling woman. What's in Savannah?"

As Karen explained, she heard the joyful lilt in her voice. Somehow, talking to him about her plans made them seem more possible. "Thanks for your faith in me," she said. "It helps."

"You'll be successful, Karen. You always are."

She felt the warmth, and a wave of longing nearly overwhelmed her, but she had to stay strong. As if sensing it, he closed in. "Why don't I come visit you when you get back to Florida?"

She hesitated, trying to find the right words.

"Is there a problem?" he asked.

"No, that sounds wonderful," she said. "It's just that I don't know how much fun I'll be, working and all. If you came to visit, I'd want to spend all day with you, but I really have to focus."

"I understand."

"I really appreciate that."

They hung up, and Karen went back and forth between regret at not being nicer to him and frustration that she felt guilty. She enjoyed his company so much, and the lovemaking—she shifted in her seat at the memory—well, it was first class. But she wished he would cut her some slack.

She flagged down a waitress and ordered a refill on the wine.

Chapter Nine

*D*ownstairs in the buffet line, Karen followed a round-shouldered giant who scooped a mound of scrambled eggs and sausage onto his plate while talking to the party in his ear. Most of the tables were taken, filled with tourists in bright florals and working people in beige and black. She grabbed a cup of coffee and a bagel and returned to her room, where she spread the newspaper on a small round table and read while eating. Savannah was recovering from the recession, thanks to tourism, but well-paying jobs were still scarce. That would make it easier for her if Ben needed employee recruitment. She scanned the rest of the paper, folded it to the side, and mentally rehearsed her pitch for the variety of services she could offer. Then she drove through downtown traffic to Savannah Health Solutions, a granite ten story overlooking the river. When the elevator opened onto the fourth floor, a receptionist led her down the hall to Ben's office.

He stood at the window, hands in his pockets, gazing out at the riverfront. His posture was relaxed yet elegant, French cuffs perfectly white against dark skin, hair trimmed in a classic fade. At the receptionist's voice, he turned. His face broke into a smile, and he crossed the room in two steps and swept Karen into a hug.

"Where on earth have you been?"

"Working. I'm in Florida right now."

"You look great." He led her to a conference table. "Tell me everything."

She didn't, of course, having rehearsed the update speech last night until she could say it with apparent spontaneity. But she told him enough to get him excited about her new business.

"So you've become your own boss, Karen. Congratulations."

"And you, Ben. What a gorgeous office. You must be doing very well."

"We're rockin' and rollin' here. Nothing but blue sky ahead." He reached for her hand. "I owe you. You got me started."

She returned the squeeze. "You would have made it under any circumstances."

"No, you brought me along when I was in a bad place. Trained me up, got me thinking like a CEO. And now look." He gestured toward the whole of his lavish office. "Who'da thought?"

"Me."

"Yes. You would have." Ben pulled a file out of a drawer and handed it to her. "These are our growth projections. We'll need additional staff, from physicians to desk crew. Second, we need compliance manuals and other internal forms. Third, work fast, because there's always something coming down the pike."

As Karen listened, she marveled at his maturity. He'd ditched the slouch, the two-day growth of beard, and the baggy slacks. This Ben was a grown man, a professional. Maybe she'd never been privileged to have children, but her work in human resources gave her plenty of opportunities to help young people get a start. Looking at

Ben, seeing his confidence and hearing the enthusiasm in his voice, she could not suppress a proud smile.

After showing Karen around and introducing her to his staff, Ben took her upstairs to the Bayou, a white-linen restaurant on the top floor. "Try the ham," he said. "They bake it in a bourbon-molasses sauce that is out of this world."

"I'd love to, but…" Karen looked over the menu and, mindful of her shape, ordered shrimp salad instead. They chatted as they ate, while watching barges, tugs, and pleasure boats ply the Savannah River below. "The view is spectacular."

"It is. They demolished a warehouse and shoehorned this one in."

"Must be pricey."

"We can afford it."

On the far banks lay a sprawling convention hotel surrounded by a lush, manicured golf course. "Did you ever take up the game?" she asked. "I know you wanted to."

"I did. It used to greatly annoy me, watching you and the other execs head out for a round while I was stuck at the office."

"That's why I learned," she said.

"Do you still play?"

"Every chance I get." It was a lie. Karen hadn't golfed since the Bully Pulpit, early last summer with Curt. She remembered her delight at running into him that afternoon. They'd played the Dakota Badlands, renewing their friendship after thirty years apart. Afterwards, he'd asked her to be his date at a black-tie dinner at the university, and they'd ended the evening in his bed.

She realized Ben was talking, and tried to focus. "It's hard to find the time though," he was saying, "between work and family."

"You moved here because your mother-in-law is ill?"

"She was," he said. "Unfortunately, she passed last August. We intended to move back to California, but I found this opportunity, talked it over with Yolanda, and we agreed to stay."

"I'm sorry to hear about her mother. How is Yolie?"

"Great, busy with the kids, but we're doing well."

"Do you ever miss Newport?"

"I miss looking out the window and watching the sun set into the ocean, right from our office," he said. "But there's a lot I don't miss. The crowding. The lack of civility, at times. It's different here. Very southern. What about you?"

"When I moved to California, I was so young. I fell in love with it, and it felt like home. I miss it."

"So, why Florida?"

"It's temporary."

"Until what?"

She shrugged. "Business, family, life. I can't say for sure."

They sat quietly for a moment, remembering. Then she folded her napkin next to her plate. "About your plans."

"Okay, long term, we want to open a string of clinics, first in Georgia, then expanding to other states."

Karen took notes as Ben elaborated. By the time he wrapped up, she had several pages' worth. He flagged down the waiter and ordered coffee. "Now that you know my needs, *Ms. Grace*, tell me how you plan to meet them."

"Show-off."

"Uh-huh. Feels good."

"Well, *Mr. Washington,* as it turns out, I have already conducted this kind of work for several large firms, so there will be no learning curve." Karen hoped he didn't notice the tremor in her voice. She wanted this contract so badly her pulse had accelerated. To get a toehold in Savannah, with all of Ben's contacts, would set her up for life. She described for him her capabilities, and when she finished, he nodded.

"That's what I want to hear," he said. "And what about timelines? How long will it take and when can you start?"

"A couple of days here in Savannah to get everything rolling. Then I'll head back to my home office and continue, updating you periodically until we've met your objectives. I estimate three to four weeks for phase one." She set her pen down. Her hand was shaking, and she took a deep breath. Their association would create a lot of work, but come hell or high water, she would deliver.

He laughed, a deeply resonant sound. "Same old Karen. Organized to the max and ahead of the curve."

"Of course." Her bluff was working. He hadn't noticed how anxious she'd become.

"I asked about your Florida office. Why not move to Savannah? You could be like our HR office down the hall, except you'd be independent. You'd have other clients besides us, and you'd be busier than you could ever imagine."

Karen smiled, but her chair seemed to be tilting, and she had to grip the table to steady herself.

"Karen?" Ben was staring at her, frowning with concern.

"I just need to—I'll be right back." She hurried across the restaurant to the ladies' room. Inside, she sank into an overstuffed chair in the lounge. Across the room, she saw herself in the full-length mirror, dripping with sweat and as green as the salad that was churning in her gut. Her heart pounded, and she couldn't catch her breath.

She leaned back, resting her head against the wall and breathing slowly. She hadn't had a panic attack in years, not since her first promotion to C-level at Global had her reeling from anxiety and fear of failure. She had gotten through that, and she would get through this.

In a few minutes, her pulse slowed, and she rose and crossed the room to the sinks, regaining her strength with every step. Cloth towels sat in a woven basket on the counter, and she soaked one in cold water and held it to her face and throat.

With Ben's offer, she was truly at a crossroads. She could live in a trailer and work part time, or she could build a brick-and-mortar business. When he had suggested the latter, she saw herself being responsible for dozens of people and relying on and trusting them. She couldn't. Not now, and maybe never. Not after the implosion at Newport and the end of her corporate career. She could never again see herself with that kind of responsibility.

Yet Karen was driven to build something that would sustain her into old age. Without help, that was unlikely.

So what was the answer? Killing herself to maintain the facade with her clients, pretending she was more than one woman working out of an RV? Dying under an oversized workload?

She knew what she had to do, if only it were possible.

When she sat back down at the table, Ben was concerned. "What happened? All of a sudden, you looked ill."

"Fine. Good. Just getting over a bug," Karen said. "But there's something I'd like to ask your opinion about."

In a gesture she remembered from Newport, Ben leaned forward, all concentration, ready to help. "Tell me."

"I've been thinking about developing an app. A piece of software that'll help me find viable candidates—while I sleep. It's something I've been kicking around for a while. I think it has huge potential, but I need a second opinion." She pulled out her notebook and began to sketch a diagram. "A few years ago, a major department store figured out a way to pick up on which of its customers were pregnant. They even figured out how to predict the approximate due dates. All from mining the purchase data."

Ben nodded. "I've seen that kind of thing. For my daughter's eleventh birthday, I did a search for sparkly tap shoes. Now I see the damned things everywhere."

"That's a little different. In my case, it's more about sifting through the information people volunteer in public forums. Like social media." She drew a few more boxes connected by arrows. "My idea is to create something similar that would help me find employees. Say there's a public forum where people are talking about the health-care industry. If you had the right algorithms, you could find potential candidates and make them aware of job openings."

"You'd be overwhelmed by data," he said.

"So I'd figure out a way to filter it. But my software could identify a person, and I could follow up with an automated invitation. All I'd have to do is front-load the particulars for each recruitment and then sit back and wait for the résumés to roll in."

"Only one problem," said Ben. "If it works, you'd be out of a job."

"No. The app would deliver the data to a human, who would then use it as necessary. I could use it when I recruit for smaller companies, for example, and I could license the rights to larger corporations to use in-house. Either way, I win."

"Sounds good, but aren't you afraid of annoying people? What about privacy?"

"It would only be able to find data that's volunteered on public sites. Then I would reach out with a courteous and respectful inquiry, as I do now, but it would be so much easier to find prospects. See?"

"Damn, Karen."

She sat back, happy that she'd finally had a chance to tell somebody about it, someone with the expertise to appreciate it. She felt happy to be part of the commercial world, producing at the top of her game again, at least in theory.

"So what's next? What's the next step?"

"That's a little bit of a challenge," said Karen. "I need to find a programmer I can trust, get it built, do beta testing, and then launch it. I could put it together in a few months, if that were all I did all day. But, knock on wood, I'm pretty busy."

"And I just loaded a bunch of new work on you."

"I'm not complaining."

"Yeah, but you can't do it all." He drummed the table with his pen. "There's a business incubator in Savannah. I know about it because I'm friends with some of the guys. They look for start-ups—businesses, usually, but sometimes it's products they can either buy the rights to or sell for a cut. I wonder if they'd be interested."

"You mean they would fund me while I take the time to develop it?"

"They might, if you could talk them into it. Do you have a number? How much you'd need?"

Karen swallowed. "Fifty thousand should get me started."

"Let me see." Ben got up from the table and walked away, his phone at his ear. She watched him meander back and forth, talking. The longer it took, the more she doubted, but when he returned, he was smiling. "You have an appointment Wednesday morning."

Thirty-six hours from now. Karen blanched. At this point, all she had was her squiggles. To impress the panel, she'd need a complete deck of slides, charts, and handouts. "Most of my materials are at my office. I'm not sure I can pitch them on such short notice."

"You just pitched me, and I'm convinced."

"Day after tomorrow," Karen said.

Ben nodded. "New Year's Eve. Matter of fact, we're throwing a party at the St. Regis. Some of the investors will be there. It'd be a great opportunity for you to mingle."

Ben was right. This would be a chance to rub elbows with Savannah's movers and shakers. Besides, it would be fun to go to a party on New Year's Eve in Savannah. She remembered passing a fancy little dress shop on her way to the meeting this morning.

"You took a chance on me. Now let me return the favor." After he paid for their lunches, they went back downstairs. Ben found her a spare desk in a vacant office, and she began preliminary work on his first project. At seven, she said goodnight to the few remaining workers and drove back to the hotel, grabbing a hamburger on the way. For the next few hours, she worked on the software pitch until her brain began to fog and her eyes became bleary.

With such short notice, her presentation would be brief, but still, she felt it was compelling. Although she lacked technical knowledge—how did a person develop an app, anyway?—her expertise in human resources would carry the day. If the investors agreed to support her, she could slack off on new business long enough to develop the software. Then she could become financially successful without hiring a bunch of employees or building massive infrastructure.

She brushed her teeth, washed her face, and slipped into her pajamas. Tomorrow, Tuesday, she would work all day at the office with Ben's staff, getting the recruitment and internal processes started. In the evening, she would come back here and finalize her pitch. Wednesday morning would be blast-off time. She'd knock them dead and win funding. Celebrate New Year's at the St. Regis and then return to Key Largo to produce the software. In ninety days, she'd have an app, a fat paycheck, future Savannah business contacts, and the very real possibility of lifetime income…if she did everything right.

Slipping into bed, she wondered how she would ever get to sleep.

Chapter Ten

*O*n Wednesday morning, Karen dressed in her Superwoman outfit—the St. John's skirt, jacket, and heels—and walked out the door carrying her Gucci briefcase, a relic from her past.

Downtown at the Sherman Trust Building, she rode up to the eleventh floor and followed the receptionist, their high heels clacking in tandem on the cold marble. The woman left her at the doorway to a dark-paneled boardroom. The committee was there already, deep in discussion at the far end of the room. Ben greeted her and made the introductions. Six of them looked to be barely out of college. The two older people were Ted Natchez, a media mogul with silver hair and mustache, and Diane Florentine, a sharp-eyed blonde in her early sixties. Karen knew about Natchez, having seen his name on the annual list of top businessmen in America, worth almost a billion dollars. The knowledge made her very nervous as she greeted the investors. Operating on two levels, she saw herself making the appropriate facial gestures, her posture erect, and her handshake firm. On another level, she was quaking like a burglar about to get caught.

Ben led her to the front of the room where she would make her pitch. He'd provided a tripod for her one small display, a graphic portraying her app.

"This product is the answer to a prayer," she said. "Specifically, how to get more accomplished in less time. There's a story behind it." She began by describing a consultant, working hard to grow her business. She then told of the stressed-out executive of a large company, going through a complex process to find qualified employees. "Both those profiles are based on me. I'm constantly frustrated by the fact that so much of what I do is simple search. Why not automate it?" The investors rewarded her with slight nods. Karen continued with an overview of the software and its usefulness.

As she glossed over the technicalities, one of the younger men, Trevor, interrupted again and again to ask for details, details she didn't have due to the short notice. What about user engagement and stable revenue? What if she were tagged as a security threat under the new Atlantic protocols? How would she mechanize the validation of ROI?

His skepticism chipped away at her confidence, and it showed. After a few more questions that Karen struggled to answer, he clicked his pen closed and laid it on the desk. "It won't work for my business."

"Which is what?" Karen asked.

"We're developing a prototype for home-based water generation. My company's just getting started, too, and I need something that's further along. So I'm out."

"I understand. Thank you." Karen hoped her smile was convincing, although her heart was pounding so hard her upper body shook. "However, this idea is sound. In fact, it's crucial. I know this from my own background."

A young woman with thick glasses said, "I don't see how you can bring this to market without knowing more about it."

"I have several experts who've done this before," Karen said, "and I'll be relying on them."

"But how are you going to find enough public data to feed the machine?" said a third. "Most of that is private."

"Hard to imagine it working," said the girl with the glasses.

"Again, my experts would be capable—" Karen began, but Ted interrupted.

"Honey, the kids have a point," he said. "You can't expect us to front you a boatload of cash for putting together something that's just smoke and mirrors. That's not how you start a business."

"You did," she said.

"Well, that was me." Ted smiled. "Balls, young lady. That's what it takes. Let me tell ya a little story. When I was barely outta grad school, I went in and told the head of..."

Karen saw Diane, the older woman, pull a nail file out of her purse. The rest of the kids began thumbing away at their cell phones. She was stuck, like some altar boy being lectured by the parish priest. Ted rambled on about his lifetime in media, starting with service in army PR and working up to time served at the FCC in Washington. Twenty minutes later, as he began to wind down, Diane put away her nail file and the kids looked up from their phones. "So, bottom line," said Ted, "I think you oughta talk about how this sucker's going to get built."

"That's a waste of time, since she doesn't know anything about coding or programming." Diane turned to Karen. "Do you even know if there's a market for this product?"

"Yes, I do."

"Is that from your gut or based on research?"

"My own judgment and thirty years of HR experience."

Diane sighed, Ted smiled, and the young people frowned. Karen felt like an idiot. She'd known they'd be a tough sell, but she'd hoped to at least whet their appetites.

Ted stood. "I guess that's it, darlin'."

She had barely slept last night, done all this work, all this thinking and planning, and now they were dismissing her? It was unacceptable. "No."

"Pardon?" said Diane.

"I don't want you to miss out. If you cut me off without any more discussion, this opportunity will go elsewhere and you'll hate yourself. And you know what?" Karen's eyes bored into Ted's. "I'll hate myself, too, because my new friends in Savannah will see me drive around town in my Lamborghini, and I'll feel bad that you didn't get a slice of the pie."

Diane burst out laughing. "I'll give you that."

"Now maybe it's true," Karen continued, "that my answers fell a little short, but with about ten minutes to prepare, I think I did pretty well. However, I'd like a chance to answer your questions. I can promise you'll have them by this afternoon. Surely you'd wait that long."

Ted was grinning at her. "Better idea, come to the party tonight and finish your pitch there. See how I feel then."

"Thanks. I will."

As the investors filed out, Trevor came over and shook Karen's hand. "Sorry if I was hard on you. I don't like to risk my money unnecessarily."

"I understand." While the room emptied, she gathered her materials and snapped her briefcase shut.

"That was gutsy." Ben came over and sat on the edge of a table.

"I choked," she said.

"You may have pulled out a win, though. I'm proud of you."

"Tables turned, huh?"

"Yeah, boss."

Returning to the office, she had a full afternoon ahead, speaking with employees about their work, but she closed her door and fell into the chair behind her desk, a little weak from challenging the investors. What a departure from her career at Global. There, she'd painted within the lines. Now, the stakes were higher. She'd taken a shot and rescued the pitch.

A smile played at the corners of her mouth. *Way to go, Karen,* she thought.

Her intercom buzzed. She opened her door to greet the first of the afternoon's appointments, but her mind was on the app. When the programmers began to show up, though, she paid more attention, asking detailed questions.

"Do what?" The sweaty, pale boy in front of her stopped picking at his ear.

"You said you 'scrape API.' Tell me more about that."

"Uh, okay. So, you know how every website has an API code, and most of 'em aren't encrypted private. So what you can do then…" Karen ran forty minutes over, learning all about app development.

"Is this gonna help me get promoted?" the kid asked.

"I'll definitely talk to Ben about it. Thanks for your help."

"No problem."

Karen closed her door. She had learned so much her head hurt. Clearly, she needed to find a programmer right away, sooner than she'd expected. So much to learn, and so much to do.

On her way back to the hotel, she stopped in at the boutique and maxed out her credit card on a new party dress, earrings, and heels. She didn't like spending the money but considered it a business investment. Once the project was funded, she would reimburse herself.

In the few hours before the party, she researched Ted Natchez. In addition to his wealth, he had the reputation of being a playboy. Still, he was respected by the business community, although his ego was well-known.

Motivated, Karen put together a compelling response to their questions. She printed out a cover sheet and supporting data and tucked it into an envelope. Then she helped herself to the minibar and ran a bath, feeling like a warrior. She would make her case. Party or not, she would convince Ted Natchez and his band of investors to fund her.

Chapter Eleven

*C*urt rolled the barn door shut and crossed the yard, squinting at his phone. Not that he really expected to hear from her.

He hung his jacket on the hook in the mudroom and set his boots under the bench. A chill was seeping into the house. Snow had fallen last night, and the heater kicked on. Curt dropped into the leather sofa, thinking he should start getting ready, but he felt too tired to move. He didn't want to go to the party tonight. All that fake holiday joy. He scratched at his stubble. Didn't want to have to shave or get dressed up. For what? The woman he wanted was two thousand miles away, and he was losing her. Again.

It wasn't overt—nothing in actual words. It was her tone. Last time they'd spoken, she could have been ordering pizza for all the warmth in her voice.

Don't overthink it. She's busy, that's all.

In the library, the grandfather clock chimed softly. Curt put his hands on his knees but didn't rise. He looked around at the room,

remembering. They had such a good time together, and were so at
ease with each other, as if they had been together all their lives. He
thought of her that last night, resplendent in her nakedness, reclin-
ing on all the blankets and comforters and pillows he'd laid before
the fire. They fell asleep there, only waking when the fire went out
and the cold returned.

Curt went into the kitchen for a beer before going upstairs to
dress. He hated the idea of this party, but the house was silent, and
he hated that more. Might be a good idea to haul his sorry, isolated
ass to a function. The university president had already approved a
year's sabbatical for the gig in Spain, so Curt felt he owed them.
And he wouldn't be stuck in a corner; as one of the senior and most
accomplished instructors at the university, people would say hello.
Plus, the chancellor would be there, a guy Curt liked to talk fly-
fishing with, so it wouldn't be a complete waste. He tipped the bottle and took a couple of long swallows, wanting to feel the warmth
in his belly. For a long time, he stood at the kitchen window, looking out at the bleak winter landscape. He couldn't help but think it
would be a lot nicer in Florida right about then.

He emptied the rest of the beer down the sink and went upstairs.

Reaching into the closet, he pushed past Karen's wide-brimmed
hat hanging from a peg. She had wrapped a long blue scarf around
the band, trying to jazz it up. He'd bought it for her last summer,
prior to their setting out for a Badlands dig with his students. She
could probably use it now. He stopped for a minute, thinking how
it would look on her, lounging by the water, palm trees swaying
overhead.

Nah. Karen was probably inside working.

He pulled on a black T-shirt and sport jacket over his best faded
Levi's and cowboy boots.

The last time he had been inside March Hall was at the summer art festival, with Karen on his arm. It had been their first date,

and they'd danced nonstop to old and new songs spanning the years they'd been apart. After they had clung to each other through Dylan's "Like a Rolling Stone," Curt had taken her home, right back here to his family farmhouse. That night, they'd consummated their thirty-year love affair. In the weeks following, they'd been insepa-rable, until Karen's boss told her she was fired. Then all hell broke loose. The neighbor lady, Frieda, wanted to go to Denver and see her relatives. Problem was Frieda was ancient, so she talked Karen into driving her camper van. Curt hadn't liked the idea, but the women were out of town almost before he could express his opin-ion. When Karen got back a few months later, she was different. More than once he'd had to nudge her out of that thousand-yard stare. Then she got this crazy idea of buying a fifth wheel and haul-ing it all the way to Florida. Now she was there, and he was here.

When they'd talked, she hadn't been crazy about his coming to see her. Fine. He figured she was moving on, even if she didn't real-ize it. He pulled on the jacket and considered the Stetson but then hung it back on its peg.

Karen was a dreamer. He wasn't going to stand in her way, but now she had him thinking that maybe he should try something new before he got any older. The place was too lonely and quiet now. Maybe he'd like Spain so much he'd want to retire there. Isabel was still at the university—a fact he knew due to her occasional texts and e-mails. She'd always been friendly, and he knew she'd welcome him back.

He rolled his shoulders, trying to convince himself the party would be fine and he'd have a decent time, but Karen was raining all over his parade. The best predictor of future behavior was past behavior, and she'd left him once before. Bolted for the West Coast in her twenties and married some doofus stockbroker. Meanwhile, Curt had sewed his youthful oats, jumping from one relationship to another with inevitable consequences. He married the girl, dealt with the predictable divorce, and raised his daughter alone. But now Erin was on her own journey, and he needed to think about the future. Time seemed like it was passing faster every year.

Curt opted for the four-wheel-drive Ram pickup, its black paint reflecting the Christmas lights he'd strung along the porch. Climbing in, he connected his old reliable iPod, since streaming was iffy way out here in the country. As Chris Isaak sang about a woman he shouldn't have, the deserted highway rolled silently past snow-dusted fields of brown stubble. The heavy sky clung to the earth along a gray-blue seam at the horizon.

At the university, he parked his truck, waved at a couple of coworkers, and fell in with the girls from admin services. One of them, a zaftig thirty-year-old with chestnut curls, called out, "Hey, handsome."

Angela was a flirt, always joking about catching him in a dark hallway or the supply cabinet. Now she looped her arm through his, as if she were his date. Rene, on his other side, did the same, and the three of them waltzed up the steps. At the door of the ballroom, the head of life sciences scowled at Curt, but the rest of his colleagues mostly laughed and shrugged at the fact that he'd arrived with two women on his arm.

Eventually, Curt extracted himself and meandered over to the bar at the edge of the dance floor. He asked for a bottle of Grain Belt and listened to the warm-up band. A server came by with an appetizer tray, and he helped himself to a couple of mini pizzas and a melted-gouda/grapes/walnuts concoction that tasted pretty good. A couple of the guys from geophysics came over to shoot the shit, and they talked shop for a while until Curt got another beer and made the rounds. His mood didn't lift, and the beer didn't help. After an hour of working his way through the politics, he found a quiet spot as far away from the dance floor as possible, calculating how long before he could sneak out. He'd been seen by enough people to escape without repercussions. As soon as the chancellor took the stage, he'd ease out.

"Hey, Professor." The willowy brunette sidled up next to him.

His mouth went dry. He took a sip of beer. "Maddie. Thought you were in South America."

"I was, but UND offered me an adjunct, so I'm back here. I start Monday. How're you?"

"Good. Good. I'm, uh, good." He nodded. This couldn't be the same girl.

"Is that all you can say?" She smiled, and one side of her mouth turned up, the lip gloss catching the light—that witty sideways grin that surprised people who wrote her off as nerd-like. Maddie, the teaching assistant, was a quiet girl with a genius-level intellect, who usually wore baggy T-shirts, denim overalls, and field boots to class.

But now she wore a tight dress made out of some kind of copper fabric that caught the light and shimmered over every dip and curve of her luscious frame. Her glossy hair cascaded over her shoulders like black silk. He stole a sideways glance, wanting to look at her again in that dress. She caught him. With those skyscraper heels, she was eye level with him. Blue eye level. Blue like some alpine lake.

He looked away, trying to think of something witty to say…but he couldn't. Trying for urbane, he clinked his beer bottle against hers and drained it.

She set hers on a nearby tray. "Want to dance?"

"I don't know, I—"

"Come on." He barely set his beer down before she hauled him out onto the shiny parquet for a seventies disco tune. Thank God, or he probably wouldn't have known what to do. After that, it was Creedence, and he began to relax. Then Beyoncé and Taylor Swift, and he started thinking he could maybe get into this younger music.

He hadn't danced since last summer with Karen, but his feet woke up and did what they were supposed to, and Maddie seemed happy, shaking her hands over her head like that.

After a while the band took a break. Curt and Maddie sat at the bar, perched next to each other on tall stools with her leaning toward him. Sometimes they would touch—his shoulder against hers, her hip and thigh against his. He could smell her perfume, a light citrus and something else that interfered with his thought processes. Her shoulder was warm against his, and he wondered if she was crowding him on purpose.

He felt dizzy. He took a pull on the icy beer and turned to her. Maddie Hesse, who'd been a student in long, lazy classroom days gone by.

Sometimes life seemed stupidly random.

Maddie was pulling on his arm, wanting to dance again. For a minute he thought he should call it a night. She'd been his assistant. She was twenty years his junior. On the other hand, she was about to graduate with a PhD in chemistry.

So they drank beer and danced, fast, slow, and otherwise. In between, they took little breaks to catch their breath, until the band started up again and drew them back into the happy melee. Two hours later, when the party wound down and Maddie went to powder her nose, Curt took a breather outside. He hoped she took her time, because he was going to flat out have a heart attack or something. As he stood out on the patio, inhaling the icy fresh air of a Dakota winter evening, he realized he hadn't thought about Karen in these last few hours at all.

The crowd began to disperse. The parking lot was a madhouse. Red taillights punctuated the darkness on the roadway below. He went back inside and found Maddie. Tall and sleek, she reminded Curt of a blue heron, beautiful and elegant, poised to fly. He pulled her close. For one painful moment he thought of

Karen, but she'd made her decision. He would make his. He took one long ringlet of her hair and wrapped the strand around his finger. Their eyes met. "Can I give you a ride home?"

The girl answered with a deep, long kiss.

Chapter Twelve

When Karen arrived at the St. Regis just before nine thirty, glamorous revelers jammed the drive and filled the entryway of the building. She took the elevator to the tenth floor, where a private ballroom had been reserved for the corporate party. It was packed, and she was relieved to spot Ben almost immediately. "Come say hi to Yolanda," he said. They made their way across the crowded room.

"Yolie." Karen hugged Ben's wife. "So great to see you again."

"How've you been, girl?" The three of them made small talk until Karen spotted Ted standing in the center of the room, surrounded by a crowd of supplicants. She excused herself and walked up to him, looking like dynamite and feeling just as powerful. Ted turned toward her. "Ms. Grace." He took her extended hand and kissed it, his mustache tickling her skin. As he held her hand and looked into her eyes, the others drifted away. Karen gave him the envelope. He folded it into his breast pocket without looking at it.

"Aren't you going to glance it over?"

He patted his pocket. "It'll keep."

"That document represents my full and complete response to your questions this morning. I have absolute confidence you'll see the value of my software project. When can I expect you to take the time to read it?" Karen was tall, around five nine last time she measured, but in four-inch heels, she had to look up to glare at him, a fact that annoyed her.

He grinned, drew her to his side, and turned to greet another star-struck businessman, a man in a vest and party top hat. Ted and he spoke briefly, and the man moved on, to be followed by a couple and then a half dozen well-wishers. Unable to escape, Karen stood next to Ted, smiling mechanically at his supplicants. The line kept growing. Politicians, celebrities, and the regional elite lined up for a word with Ted. They met the mayor, a city councilman, and a collection of fat cats who bowed and scraped in front of the media oligarch. As much as he pissed her off, she was fascinated by the parade. And besides, there was his cologne, a combination of smoke and sandalwood. What was it about powerful men? They exuded pheromones like nerve gas.

Every now and then, Ted would give her waist a squeeze or whisper something in her ear that would make her laugh out loud. She was aware of the flash of cameras.

When the line dissipated, she stood in front of Ted, feet planted. "Just FYI, I intend to start building this app tomorrow morning. So if you want in, tell me now."

"How about a dance first?"

She wasn't going to let him use her as a prop all night. "It's been fun, Ted. Good-bye."

"All of Savannah's here right now. It'll be good for you to be seen with me. Kinda like your southern debut." He half bowed, sweeping his hand toward the dance floor.

"Oh, for God's sake." She let him lead her out to the polished marble floor, where couples whirled in three-quarter time. Karen said a silent prayer of gratitude to her mother for insisting on dance lessons in seventh grade. They danced two prim-and-proper waltzes, and then she told him she wanted a drink.

"Of course." He flagged down a waiter.

"Now, about my proposal."

"There's no quit in you, is there?"

"No."

The waiter brought over a silver tray with two glasses of champagne. Ted reached into his pocket, removed the envelope, tore it in half, and placed it on the tray. The waiter turned, preparing to walk away.

"Hey!" Karen grabbed the two halves of her envelope and jammed them into her clutch. She whirled on Ted. "What the hell was that about?"

"Champagne?" He held out one of the flutes.

"I only drink with friends." She snapped her clutch shut and turned to leave.

"Darlin', your idea has legs. It'll work."

"If you already knew that, why did you let me slave all afternoon to answer your questions?" Karen's face and chest flushed hot.

He eyeballed her cleavage and smiled. "Just trying to toughen you up. You were unprepared this time. Next time, you won't be."

"Next time?"

He waved a hand dismissively. "Inventors usually have more than one idea. You're smart. You'll be doing this again. But inspiration and development are only a part of the process. You have to run the politics, too."

"But what about the committee? They'll be expecting my response."

"Nobody's going to look at it anyway. They do what I tell 'em."

Karen stood there with her mouth hanging open. The man was pure arrogance, pure, unadulterated ego.

He chuckled. "You're an incredibly sexy woman."

"And you're a goddamn pain in the ass."

Ted threw back his head and laughed. "You're not a suck-up. I like that."

"I don't care what you like. Are you going to fund me or not?"

"Course I am. Didn't I say that already?" He pulled Karen back on the dance floor. This time, she went more willingly. They danced slow, and they danced fast, and she let down her guard and enjoyed herself.

Besides being a good dancer, Ted was funny, wiggling his eyebrows at some of the more remarkable dancers or outfits. More than once he had her shaking helplessly with laughter. She enjoyed his attention, and the pure feeling of movement was a blast after being stuck behind a desk for so many days. Ted was slick, maneuvering her through the flailing crowd, with a quick word, a smile, or a nod for just about everyone there. She kept pace, feeling as if she'd tapped into an overcharged battery. Her body tingled, and her brain felt euphoric. She never wanted to sit down. Finally the band slowed the pace, and Ted pulled her close. She felt the warmth of his breath against her ear.

"How long'll you be in Savannah?" he asked.

"I leave tomorrow."

"Me, too. Want to come to Hong Kong?"

"Sounds like fun, but I have work to do."

He smiled at her, the corners of his eyes crinkling in the way that made men of a certain age look better than when they were young. "Anybody ever tell you to lighten up?"

"All the time. But it's who I am."

"I already know that. Hey, remind me to give you the check before you go."

"What are your terms?"

He raised one eyebrow.

"I mean financial! I didn't mean—" she sputtered.

He laughed uproariously. "Oh, Karen, you are priceless, you know that? Hey, Jimmie, get on over here. Somebody you should know about." Ted waved to a local news reporter, who approached with a camera operator. "Want you to meet Karen Grace. She's going to be a celebrity in about ten minutes, so you better get hoppin'. Karen's a software inventor, and she's working on an app that's going to set the world on fire."

"Is that true, Ms. Grace?" asked the reporter. "What can you tell us about this project?"

Karen smiled into the blinking red light of the minicam. "We're in the very preliminary stages, but it'll be a game changer, as Mr. Natchez can verify." She tossed the reporter a few more tidbits, and then the bandleader led the crowd in a countdown to the new year. Cameras flashed as Ted leaned her backward in a cinematic kiss in the middle of the dance floor. When she straightened back up, people applauded.

Through the champagne haze, Karen thought of Curt and felt a twinge of guilt, but before she could think any more about him and wonder what he was doing on another quiet night in North Dakota, Ted took her in his arms. He drew her closer, and as they danced, she could feel the vibration of his voice, humming along with the music. She wanted to lay her cheek against his chest, his strong arms around her. His fingers played along her back, and she stifled a sigh. If she didn't leave soon, her defenses would definitely fail her. When the number ended, she pulled away. "It's been a long day," she said. "Remember where we started?"

"I remember every detail." He trailed two fingers lightly along the length of her upper arms. Goose bumps rose on her skin. "Are you cold?" He looked at her, smiling.

"I should call a cab." She didn't make a move for her purse or wrap, though.

"You might have to wait a long time, it being New Year's and all. Plus, I'm not sure about you riding around the city at this hour on this kinda night."

"You could ride with me," she said.

"Or you could make the call from my place upstairs. I'd ply you with refreshments while you wait in comfort and safety."

Safety being a relative term, Karen chose the latter of the two dangers, nodding slowly, her eyes locked on his. In the elevator, he put his key in a slot and pushed *P*. When the door opened, they stepped into a private foyer. Another door unlocked into a lavish living room where the fireplace crackled. A butler stood holding a tray with two perfect crystal snifters. "Port, sir?"

"Thank you, Alfred. And you may call it a night, my friend."

"Yes, sir." Alfred nodded and disappeared.

Karen crossed the room, her heels sinking into the plush carpets. At the corner of the living room, floor-to-ceiling windows revealed sparkling Savannah, far below. When she had lived in Newport Beach, many of her friends had lived in penthouses like this, with views of the harbor and the ocean beyond. Karen herself had owned a mansion in an exclusive neighborhood, but she'd lost it in the divorce. In the year since, she had struggled to make the best of things, but in truth, she missed the luxury of her old way of life. For a moment, she closed her eyes and permitted herself to believe she was home. "It's so beautiful," she murmured.

Ted came up behind her. His warm hands grasped her shoulders, and his voice rumbled in her ear. "Yes, you are." He turned her around, touching her lips with one finger. When she didn't object, he tipped her chin up and kissed her, exploring her mouth with his tongue. She felt the heat, from her breasts to her belly to the achingly soft place between her thighs.

"Do you still want me to call you a cab?" he asked. When she kissed him deeply in reply, his hands caressed her back, her waist, and the curves of her hips. Held tight against his chest, Karen felt his erection press against her and inhaled the fragrance of his cologne. He left a line of kisses from her earlobe to her collarbone and was rewarded with her soft moan.

He took her hand and led her to his bedroom, lit with candlelight and perfumed by the cherry aroma of the fireplace. She allowed him to unzip her dress, and it slid to the floor. Still wearing her heels, she kicked it aside, and he groaned with lust. Karen smiled. With her new push-up bra and thong undies, she felt like a wanton temptress, a she-devil in control of this powerful man.

With a growl, he eased her down onto the bed. The last thing Karen thought of as her bare backside hit the satin sheets was that she never did call Curt to wish him happy New Year.

Chapter Thirteen

*J*essie was going to a lot of trouble to prepare their holiday dinner. Since Lenny had to work over Christmas, he'd promised they would celebrate New Year's instead. There was a turkey in the oven already, all stuffed and draped with strips of bacon and covered in foil. She'd made a pumpkin pie last night, after he fell asleep on the couch.

As Jessie stood at the sink, peeling potatoes, she looked out the window. The dog's rope had wrapped around his water bucket sometime during the night, tipping the cheap plastic container and spilling most of the contents. She rinsed and dried her hands and went outside.

Booger stared at her, growling. Even from this safe distance, she could see his hackles bristling and the muscles quivering under his iron-gray coat. The dog had been Lenny's idea. He'd found him running loose in a dry creek bed and spent a day and a half trapping the half-starved animal, saying he'd be a killer watchdog and not to coddle him. Jessie turned on the hose full blast and aimed the stream at the bucket, intending to fill it from a safe distance, but the dog leaped into the water, snapping his jaws. He fell back, choking and coughing.

"Get out of the way, you dumb dog, and I'll fill it up," Jessie said, but the animal was relentless. "Okay, fine. Be thirsty." She gave up and went in the house to continue preparing the feast. The turkey would be ready by six o'clock. She hoped Lenny would come home on time. After hearing her plans to cook a traditional family meal, he and Kegger had bolted for the sports bar down the highway. Staying out of her way, as they put it.

"Let's see. Turkey, potatoes, gravy, cranberries, beans, rolls, butter, pie...that's it. Okay." Everything was cooking along just fine. Everything was on track. The aroma of turkey would soon fill the home, and she felt peaceful and satisfied. This must be what adulthood was like, having your own place and your own family. She knew from her psychology books that this was the beginning of her autonomy, that from here on out she would be making more and more adult decisions. Now if only Lenny could act more like an adult. But she felt sure that would happen eventually. She glanced at her watch. There was still time to do some studying.

When the baby began fussing, Jessie got her up out of bed and played with her for a couple hours while keeping an eye on the turkey. It was almost done. All she had to do was mash the potatoes and make the gravy, which could wait until later, when Sunshine was down for the night.

At six o'clock, Jessie fed and bathed her, read her a story from the new book she'd gotten at Christmas, and tucked her into her crib. Then, moving quietly in the bedroom, she put on a white blouse that looked festive and a decent pair of pants that might have worked for church, if she ever went. Her parents hadn't raised her in any religion, and she hadn't felt the need, but now with Sunshine her responsibility, it was probably time to find a congregation. The lady at the thrift shop had suggested the Baptist church down the street, and Jessie thought she'd check it out at some point. Maybe the three of them could go there and become part of the spiritual community. Plus maybe Lenny could make connections and find somebody to hire him.

She put her hair in a ponytail, placing a sprig of fake holly at the rubber band, and dug through her meager box of makeup for eye shadow, mascara, and lipstick. Then she went back in the kitchen and donned an apron. The oven door opened with a tearing screech, making Jessie wince. She stepped back from the wave of aromatic heat and then leaned in to check out the turkey. It had turned a gorgeous, dark honey gold, just like the picture in the cookbook. The thermometer told her it was finished, so Jessie, careful with such a heavy load, removed it from the oven and set it on a cutting board to rest. If Lenny didn't get home pretty soon, she'd have to cut up the bird herself, which would be disappointing since having the man do the carving was traditional. Jessie frittered away another hour straightening the house, replacing a couple of lights on the tabletop Christmas tree, and moving the mistletoe from one doorway to another—but still no Lenny.

Finally, she decided to tackle the carving, because at this point he probably wouldn't be that careful, and she didn't want him wrecking her beautiful turkey. She set a couple of serving plates near her workstation and opened the cookbook to page forty-seven. There, next to four illustrations of a bird in various stages of dismemberment, were Grandma Frieda's scrawly handwritten notes.

Jessie propped open the cookbook and began drawing a sharp knife through the meat. Grandma's funeral had been a total downer. At her age, Jessie hadn't gone to many, but this was the worst. Not only was it heartbreaking to say good-bye, but her mother was hysterical, babbling about keeping some woman from coming

inside the church because allegedly she'd kidnapped Grandma. *As if.*
Nobody could kidnap Frieda Richter if she didn't want to go. Jessie
was just happy she had gotten to do one last road trip—and at her
age! She was doing things her own way.

And who was the woman who took Grandma along anyway?
People mumbled about it after Sandy ran her off. Whoever she was,
this Karen chick must have been some tough bitch to put up with
Grandma Frieda all that time.

Looking back at the book, Jessie pulled on one of the drum-
sticks, cutting precisely between the two round circles of the joint.
The legs separated from the body with a satisfying crack of gristle
and bone. Then the wings. She set them on a plate and peered at the
directions. Karen Grace had had something for her at the funeral,
but Sandy had run her off before Jessie could get it. It looked like
an envelope, which could only mean one thing: money. And Jessie
could sure use it.

Jessie cut steaming slices of turkey with each pass. It was a big
job, and when she finished, she was amazed at the giant piles of meat
in each dish—one of dark, one of white.

And still no Lenny.

***

Dinner was two hours past ready.

At seven thirty, she'd had a glass of wine and a bite to eat, figuring it would hold her over for a while. At nine, she gave up and
ate, sitting by herself in the silent kitchen and thumbing through
the cookbook. At ten, when she was lying on the couch, watching *Miracle on 34th Street,* the headlights from Lenny's work truck
flashed in the living room window. Jessie aimed the remote at the
TV, and the room went dark. She watched from behind a curtain
as Lenny and Kegger staggered toward the trailer, arguing. The dog
barked and ran back and forth at the end of his rope like a frantic

pendulum. Stomping their feet on the wooden porch, they banged the door open and spilled inside, shaking the trailer with their noise and movements. "What the fuck," said Lenny. "Why's it so fucking dark—?"

A lamp clicked on. Jessie sat in a corner chair, silently eyeing the two men.

"Hey, look at you. All dressed up and pretty." Lenny belched. "Happy New Year, babe." He stumbled over, leaned on the chair arms, getting into her space and trying to kiss her, but she turned her face away, scowling. He straightened up. "So be that way. What's for dinner?"

"Like you care."

"I do. Me 'n' Keg are hungry, and it smells real good in here. So, we gonna eat?"

"Do what you want. I'm going to bed." Her special dinner, so carefully prepared over the course of the day, sat cooling in the refrigerator. All she'd wanted was a nice holiday meal with her family. Good food, a little conversation, and the beginning of a tradition. Now everything was ruined. He could feed his own damn self. She stood and turned toward the bedroom.

Lenny grabbed her by the arm as she passed. His eyes were bloodshot and watery. "I said, I'm hungry."

"Ow!" She pulled her arm back and rubbed the spot, sure to bruise purple by morning.

"Get in there."

"Lenny!"

He shoved her toward the dark kitchen, but she braced herself, resisting, incredulous. He pushed her from behind, propelling her, forcing her toward the stove. She grabbed the refrigerator door, trying to anchor herself. "Stop it! Leave me alone! Let me go—" Off-balance, Jessie threw her arm up, her fist connecting with Lenny's chin.

In the next instant, the trailer seemed to collapse around her, the sky landed on her, the roar of a thousand trains filled her head as she was flung to the floor face first, and in the next second, she was levitating upward, her throat aching with the angle, every strand of hair screaming from the roots as Lenny pulled her up by her ponytail, slammed her down, and then hauled her to her feet again. Steering her by the hair, he drove her into the counter, twisting her head so she had to face him. He breathed stale beer-breath into her face. Sweat and grease emanated from his pores.

"Fix. My. Fucking. Dinner." With a final yank, he released his grip.

Jessie collapsed against the sink, grasping the edge of the counter and holding tight to keep from falling. A single drop of blood rolled off the tip of her nose and landed on the white porcelain. It splattered and spread, caught a runnel of water, and raced toward the black hole of the garbage disposal. Jessie stared at it, gasping for breath, her heart pounding. Her first thought was to survive, to comply, to get Lenny to calm down so he wouldn't do anything that would hurt the baby. Her second thought was of her textbooks, the ones that spoke of domestic violence, and the stark recognition of it now. She had always presumed, with the certainty born of a middle-class birth and a peaceful childhood, that she would never be a victim. She had no frame of reference, no experience. This wasn't supposed to happen.

Lenny had a temper, sure. She'd seen the potential, seen him throw things at the dog or fling a tool when frustration overwhelmed him. But never this. Never violence. This was new, dark territory. Jessie needed to think, but her head pounded. She could barely figure out what to do next. In the living room, she heard his recliner squeak, the footrest extending. The refrigerator's door handle was cracked in two.

Jessie wiped her nose with her forearm and stared at the pink streaks on her sleeve. Her arm trembled. She held out both hands. They shook like she was a hundred years old, yet she couldn't feel them. Her hands were numb and cold.

"Later, man." She heard the screen door open and the outer door close. Kegger was only just now leaving? In what universe did a person stand by watching while his friend beat up a woman?

Jessie shivered, realizing it was now her, the baby, and Lenny.

"The fuck're you doing with my dinner?" Lenny yelled from the living room, where the television blared in the background, a man shouting about great deals on used cars, especially for people with bad credit.

"It's coming." Feeling as if her head was wrapped in layers of damp cotton, Jessie tiptoed to the refrigerator and began to pull out the leftovers.

Chapter Fourteen

On New Year's Day, Karen awoke alone in Ted's bedroom. She sat up, temples throbbing. Across the room, her cocktail dress had been hung on a hanger, her shoes neatly positioned next to her purse. She wondered if the butler did the honors, and if so, had he been puttering around in the room while she slept? She leaned forward, groaning and rubbing her temples, but the pain went deeper than blood and bone and tissue, straight to the place where humiliation lived. Was this who she was going to be now? Seduced by power and money, she had lost her head last night. She wondered if Ted had already left for Hong Kong or if she would have to face his smirk this morning. The penthouse was unearthly quiet.

She clutched the sheet around her like a toga, crossed the room, and pulled the drapes apart. Sunlight angled over the rooftops of Savannah, searing her eyes. With a moan, she let the curtain fall back. She found a robe in the closet and pulled the belt tight. The smell of coffee enticed her downstairs. Barefoot, she wandered into the kitchen. At a small round table in a nook overlooking the river, she found a fresh pot alongside a basketful of muffins. Fighting a wave of nausea, she filled a cup and carried it to the table, where a white velvet box sat atop an envelope bearing her name. It looked like a jewelry box, adding to the feeling she'd been bought. But you couldn't have a buyer without a seller.

She took a sip of coffee and swallowed, looking away from the table and down toward the city. If she left now, disturbing nothing, she would never have to know what the box and envelope contained. She would never have to work to erase from her memory whatever further humiliation lay waiting. She could leave Savannah forever. She looked back at the envelope.

On the other hand...

She set the cup down and, hands shaking, opened the box. Inside, a pair of diamond teardrop earrings shimmered. Her first emotion was excitement. They were worth ten grand if a dime. Her second was shame. There'd been times in her life when she'd felt as if she were prostituting herself for business, but never had it felt so literal until this moment.

She tore open the envelope. Inside, she found a scribbled note: *Left early for China. Happy New Year.*

The second piece of paper was a contract with a check for $15,000, a fraction of the amount she'd requested from the investors. She skimmed the document. It was brief and concise. With the least amount of funding, and in the shortest amount of time, the committee expected her to produce and deliver to them a toy, a bauble that they didn't appreciate or respect. On top of that, someone had stapled a law firm's business card to the document, in case she was so stupid she couldn't understand the wording or was too incompetent to secure legal counsel on her own. She folded the document and returned it to the envelope.

The check was a bone. Was she supposed to dive after it like some starving dog, happy to have a token from the man whose empire was worth billions? The check and the earrings felt like payment, and possibly the hint of a retainer, to a high-class call girl, nothing more.

Karen crumpled his note and left it on the table. She stared out the window, across the river to the rolling green grasslands on the edge of the city. If a guy offered you a couple hundred dollars after a night in his bed, you'd be insulted. But if he left you diamond earrings, what then? She knew what her mother would say, but it wasn't Mom she was thinking about right now, nor her Catholic upbringing, nor her father's ironclad sense of propriety.

No, she was thinking of Frieda. Karen could almost envision the little old woman sitting across from her at this small table, grinning.

Take the dang earrings.You earned 'em.

On my back, is what it feels like, Karen thought in response.

Don't be a fool.You see money down on the sidewalk, you pick it up, don't you?

Karen went into the bathroom, splashed water on her face, and ran her fingers through her hair. She put on last night's dress and lingered near the kitchen, considering. The earrings were hers to leave or take, depending on what story she told herself. Pride and ego warred with practicality.

When she allowed the penthouse door to click shut behind her, locking firmly, the jewelry box was still in the kitchen. Downstairs, she nodded at the doorman and walked slowly toward her truck, dressed like a party girl and feeling nauseated. Did Ted and the investors see her as a country bumpkin, come to town to be conned by the city slickers? Or as a desperate, washed-up professional, too long in the tooth for them to take her seriously? Was Ben in on this? He had steered her to them.

No. Whatever nastiness she'd stumbled into, Ben was her friend from California. He'd tried to help. It was she who'd failed. And as for the rest of them, it was just business. She needed to suck it up and stop whining.

At her hotel, she wandered through the hordes of hungover coffee seekers and took the elevator to her room. Inside, she showered for a long time, letting the cleansing spray of the hot water wash away yesterday. Then she put on her traveling clothes and checked out. Traffic was light as she drove through Savannah. The city was awakening slowly.

Savannah was beautiful, especially on a slow morning like this. She regretted that she hadn't had a chance to see the city, and on impulse, she parked near one of the city's iconic garden squares. This one occupied an entire block. In the center, a statue depicted a wartime general riding a battle-crazed stallion. The statue was surrounded by moss-laden oaks, dogwood, and azalea bushes.

She found a concrete bench and sat. The bucolic scene offered relief from the Greek chorus in her head, bemoaning her lack of brains, discipline, and strategy. In the distance, the sweet, aching notes of a solo violin reached her. Beautiful Savannah wore her gentility like a mask. She had surrendered to Union forces during the Civil War, a strategic decision to humble herself and thereby live to fight another day. Unlike other cities, Charleston for example, Savannah had escaped annihilation. Historic old homes and buildings still stood. Lives were saved, and businesses struggled on. The character of Savannah had been altered, but she survived and prospered. Today the city was a bustling waterfront, swarming with tourists and making money like crazy. Tough old broad that she was, Savannah had won in the end.

Karen felt her confidence seeping back, and the humiliation of last night subsided. It wasn't how she was brought up, but still. Things had changed. Her life had changed. The old strategies didn't work anymore, and she was ready to adapt—to learn. Times called for bold action, pride be damned. She would do what was necessary to thrive.

She returned to her truck and drove back to Ted's building. The doorman smiled, recognizing her. "Good day, miss."

Returning his greeting, Karen said, "I cannot believe how discombobulated I am this morning. I was in such a rush to get to church that I left my phone upstairs."

"I understand. That surely can happen. Person be rushing, and all."

She held out her hands, palms upturned. "Now it's up there and I'm down here, locked out."

"Yes, miss."

She plowed forward. "Can you please assist me in retrieving it?"

"I can't give you access, but I could call Mr. Natchez for you, though."

"Oh, shoot, that won't work. Ted's on his way to Asia." She screwed up her face in a pretty frown. "I desperately need my phone, and—well, maybe you could just let me in and stand by the door for the ten seconds it would take me to grab it? I know right where it is. It's on the kitchen table." She reached out and put her hand in his, as if to shake it.

He slipped the twenty-dollar bill into his pocket. "Well, we can't have you goin' through your day without a phone, now, can we?" They chatted companionably as the elevator rose to the top floor. The doorman waited in the foyer while she sashayed into the kitchen and retrieved the velvet box, which she slipped into her pocket. Then she ripped the check and contract in half and dropped them on the table. Brandishing her phone, she returned to the doorman.

"Here it is. What a relief. Thank you so much."

"You're very welcome, miss. Come back to Savannah soon."

Only when I can hold my head up again, Karen thought.

Chapter Fifteen

*C*urt awoke before dawn, his back hurting. He needed to get vertical PDQ, but first he had to lie there and look at her. There she was, in his bed, Madison Hesse, twenty-two years old and glorious. For just a moment, everything fell away in the giddiness of conquest—the cultural realities, the fact of their age difference, the expectation that they'd have nothing in common, nothing to talk about, nothing to say. Or worse, that he'd be unable to perform to her expectations. In fact, with his experience and know-how, he'd dazzled her. He grinned at her sleeping form. They'd talked and laughed and made crazy jungle love until a couple hours ago, and now here she was.

Madison Hesse.

In the kitchen, the automatic coffeemaker finished with a pneumatic wheeze. Curt turned over carefully and moved into a sitting position at the edge of the bed. Rolled his head around on his neck and listened to the crackling. After last night, he should feel like he got run over by his own tractor, but instead he felt like Superman. He tensed his legs and arms, ready to stand up without waking Maddie.

She rolled over. "Hey, lover boy."

He gazed at the stunning, earthy creature in his bed, with her dark hair, blue eyes, and sleep-puffed lips, and damn if he didn't get hard all over again.

"I was dreaming just now about all the things you could do for me." Her voice was gravelly from sleep, and her lips turned up in a wicked smile. "Unless you're too tired?"

Well, a man had to stand up for his rep.

Afterward, Madison fell back asleep and he went downstairs. Got a cup of coffee and the newspaper off the porch and headed out to the barn with a major spring in his step. Who said a May-December thing couldn't work? He'd always dated in his own age group, but now he wondered why. Maddie was perfect for him. It was like they were the same age. They were in tune on so many things—politics, geology, sex. Especially the sex! He couldn't believe her appetites. Jesus, she was an animal. He hoped she'd stick around for a while.

What the hell, maybe he'd even invite her to Spain.

Tucking the paper under one arm, he hauled the sliding door open and stepped inside. Feeding and stall-mucking had been Erin's responsibility while she was home during winter break, but she'd spent last night at a girlfriend's, partying. So it fell to him.

The dusty aroma of hay stung his nostrils, along with the warm fragrance of leather and livestock. Sleepy hens eyed him from their roosts, and Duke nickered in greeting. "Hey, boy." Curt scratched him around the ears. "Happy New Year." The horse blew a raspberry, and Curt said, "Let me get my caffeine fix. Then I'll feed you."

He went to sit down on a hay bale, slipped the rubber band off the newspaper, and began separating the readable sections from the ads. He was as tech savvy as his students, but he still liked to read an actual newspaper every morning. He set aside World and Local and was just getting to Entertainment when the photograph on the front of the section stopped him. He set his coffee down and squinted closer.

Yep, it was her. Karen, in a lip-lock with some guy whose face he couldn't see, but there they were in the paper, so it must be somebody big. He read the caption.

LOCAL WOMAN PARTIES WITH INTERNATIONAL PLAYBOY.

Curt looked up at the ceiling and then down at the photo. Took another sip, thought about Karen and that bastard Natchez, and then scowled at his self-righteousness. He folded the paper and set it on the bale, next to his coffee cup, grabbed a shovel and rake, and got to work cleaning up after the horses, his brain sifting through the realities.

It made sense. Karen was trying things, exploring the possibilities now that she was free and on her own again. That she would attract a man like Natchez didn't surprise Curt at all. Pissed him off, but didn't surprise him.

Well, he had no room to talk. Madison was still upstairs, sleeping off their New Year's Eve celebration.

Church bells pealed across the frozen countryside, announcing a brand-new year. He threw another forkful of shit into the wheelbarrow. His coffee grew cold.

The horses wandered out to the corral, kicking up their heels and nipping at each other. He refilled the water buckets and made sure they had plenty of feed. They were hardy, but the sky was clouding over, and they'd be back in soon. Curt worked fast, trying to put the photo out of his mind. It wasn't fair to begrudge Karen her fun. He'd had his own.

He tried to focus on the sexy young woman who slumbered upstairs, but the thought didn't make him feel any better.

He heard Erin drive up and stopped working, surprised. She was a day early getting back from the friend's house in Bismarck. Curt hung up the rake and hurried to head her off.

"Hey, Dad." Erin shot her chin at the Jeep in the driveway. "Whose car is that?"

"A friend." He reached inside her car and honked the horn twice.

"Why'd you do that?"

"We weren't expecting company. Did you have a nice New Year's?"

"I'm not company. And who is 'we'?"

"Sweetheart, before you go inside, there's something I have to tell you."

"Is Karen here? Hallelujah!"

"Wait." He tried to block her, but she slipped around him and had the front door open before he could explain.

Madison was digging around in the refrigerator when the kitchen door opened. "Babe, where's the eggs?" She turned, saw Erin, and straightened up, clutching Curt's robe tighter across her voluminous breasts. The two women stared at each other for a full minute. Finally Madison cleared her throat. "Good morning."

"Holy shit, Dad." Erin turned to Curt. "Are you guys, like, the two of you—I mean, holy crap."

"I was going to tell you."

"Tell me what? Did you and Karen break up?"

Maddie frowned. "Who's Karen?"

"And now you're dating somebody my age? Jesus, how gross." Erin spun on her heel and vaulted up the stairs. Her door slammed, rattling the windows.

"Erin, Madison. Madison, my daughter, Erin." Curt dropped into a chair.

Madison grinned. "Daddy's robbing the cradle," she teased.

"That's not funny."

"She'll get over it." Madison leaned down and kissed him, letting her robe fall open. Reaching down, she took his hands and applied them to her breasts, like ripe fruit, warm, the dark areolas right in his face. He let go and pulled her robe shut. She turned and tried to plant her ass on his lap, but he gently moved her aside. As much as her body had inflamed him last night, the feeling had evaporated.

"I need a little time to let Erin adjust."

"She's being a baby. I wouldn't coddle her."

"I never have." He turned on the kitchen faucet and began to wash his hands. "She's a good girl, Maddie."

"Well of course. I mean, she's your daughter. I wouldn't expect anything else." Madison wrapped her arms around him from behind and lay her cheek against his back. "I'm sorry."

He rinsed his hands, wondering how he was going to manage the day with both Maddie and his daughter in the same house.

Madison handed him the towel. "So what do you want to do today?"

"Hadn't thought about it."

"There's lots of football on today. We could go to the pub."

"We could." He said it without enthusiasm.

She made a face. "Or how about we go to the lake and have a picnic."

"It's pretty cold."

"God, you're such an old man."

That stung. "How about lunch and a movie?"

She pulled him to her and laid a fat kiss on his mug. When they broke apart, she leaned back, smiling. "Lunch, a movie, dinner, and a nightcap in front of your fire."

"Maddie." He raised his eyes, indicating his sulking daughter somewhere on the second floor.

"Tell her you'll be at my house tonight. Tell her it's a sleepover."

"Lunch, movie, the Holiday Inn, and dinner. How does that sound?"

"Boring." Now he had two sulking young women on his hands.

"Okay, how about we go to the pub, have lunch, and watch the game?"

"Better."

"Uh, and after the game, dinner at the Holiday Inn?"

"That place is so nothing."

"This ain't New York City, babe."

"Okay. But only if you agree to take me to the motocross championship in Fargo next weekend."

"Yes to motocross, no to the tractor pull the weekend after that."

"Cool, I'll go shower and dress."

As she scampered up the stairs to his room, he hoped Erin would stay in hers and not notice. Then he winced as Maddie's music kicked on, rattling the windows with a deep, vibrating bass. A door flew open, and Erin appeared at the top of the stairs.

"Really, Dad?"

"What?" He feigned innocence as the lyrics, if you could call them that, reverberated through the house. Something about boss, ass, and bitch?

The door slammed again.

Curt started up the stairs and then, remembering, pulled on his jacket and went back out to the barn. The newspaper article was still there, sitting on the hay bale where he'd been reading when Erin drove up. And Karen's picture was still there, too, with that jerk Natchez, his hands all over her. Curt wadded up the newspaper and shot it across the barn.

Chapter Sixteen

"Hold still, Little Squirmy," Jessie whispered, trying to sound as if everything was normal for her precious daughter. She managed to pull the baby's white tights up over her diaper, while at the same time pulling down the skirt of the black velvet dress. She finished off Sunshine's new look—courtesy of the church thrift store—with a white headband around her nearly bald head, a tiny rhinestone flower at the top.

Jessie had read of women who stayed, who put their children at risk, who suffered injury and even death at the hands of men. She'd always wondered why. Now she had an idea. Maybe they were scared to leave. Maybe they didn't have any money or a car or a friend who would drive them. Maybe after being hurt again and again, they couldn't think clearly enough to develop an escape plan and follow through. Maybe they were too scared to function.

Jessie held the baby in a standing position, inspecting her outfit. Such a precious little munchkin, and now in such danger. Or was she? Was that one extreme event, never to be repeated? How would a person know in advance how to decide, not staying too long or leaving too soon?

She heard Lenny moving around in the kitchen. He wasn't making a lot of noise, like throwing or banging anything. Maybe he was sorry, and it would never happen again.

Jessie's eyes stung as she kissed the baby's forehead, button nose, and cherry cheeks. Sunshine grinned, two bottom teeth shining through perfect pink gums, her innocence breaking her mother's heart.

"They're going to love you," Jessie said. When one of the thrift-store workers had invited her to attend Bountiful Baptist, Jessie had been drawn by the woman's kindness and by a longing for community. Besides, the church was right down the road. She'd passed it many times, wondering what it might feel like to belong to a congregation. Her mother—she had to stop calling her that—*Sandy* thought the value of church to be limited. But living out here in the country, a person got lonely, and Jessie hoped there would be kids for Sunshine to grow up with.

Now, that rosy picture was in doubt. Jessie still couldn't believe it had happened. She'd barely slept last night, she was so scared. Only the fact that the dog would sound the alarm kept her from sneaking away in the darkness, Sunshine bundled in her arms.

Jessie carried the baby into the bathroom and with her free hand dabbed a last bit of extra concealer to her face. She wore her hair long this morning, hoping it would hide the evidence. As she closed the concealer, her hand shook. She didn't trust her own judgment at the moment. She felt rattled and skittish, and Sunshine was fussing, no doubt picking up on the fact that she was upset. Church would be a relief, a calming influence where she could organize her thoughts.

Jessie fought back tears as she remembered Lenny's aggression. Surely this was an aberration. He'd always treated her decently, and she expected him to show remorse this morning.

They could maybe go to counseling. If not together, she would go alone. Did she feel strongly enough that counseling would be a condition of her staying with him? Lenny needed help. She could be quietly supportive as he worked to get to the bottom of this new thing, this rage he was feeling. She didn't understand it, but she was sure that, with the right guidance, they could untangle the cause, find a solution, and make it work. Jessie leaned in for one last look, pulling her hair forward.

With the baby on one arm and the diaper bag on the other, she opened the bedroom door and walked softly down the hall to the living room. Lenny sat in front of the TV, already drinking beer although it wasn't even ten o'clock—a bad sign.

Jessie put the baby down and slipped into her jacket. "I'll be back in an hour or so." He didn't answer. "Lenny?"

When he continued to stare at the television, she figured he was ashamed. According to her textbooks, this would be a natural reaction the first time a young man raised his hand in anger against his loved ones. Alcohol would do that, but there was hope. If the church had counseling services, she'd sign them up right away and then tell Lenny about it later. She would be gentle but insist. They had to. Their future depended on this never happening again.

Jessie lifted the baby in one arm and shrugged into the shoulder straps of the diaper bag and purse. Overloaded, she tried to open the door, but both straps slipped off her shoulder and down to her elbow, forcing her off-balance. She fell against the wall, catching herself and muttering a curse.

Still no sound except the TV.

"Could you at least open the door for me?"

He took his time turning to look at her. His eyes were blood-shot. "Where you going?"

"Church."

"It's not Sunday."

"New Year's is a church day. The service starts in a few minutes. So can you help me get out the door, please?"

"How you getting there?"

Jessie sighed. "I'm taking the car." She waited. He wasn't happy when she went somewhere alone in the old Honda. He said he was afraid it would break down, and she'd be stranded. She hoped he wouldn't insist on driving her, as usual.

"You want to go, fucking go." Lenny belched and looked back at the TV. He raised the can and took another swig. "Don't expect me to help you after the way you acted."

She couldn't believe it. *He* was mad? He was the one who hit her, not the other way around. She juggled the baby to get a more secure grip and reached for the door. "Fine. Be that way. Don't trouble yourself."

He was up and out of the chair in an instant, pushing between her and the door, his barrel chest blocking her. His face was almost red, and the veins on his neck pulsated. "You want some more?"

The baby began to wail. Jessie found it hard to breathe. Her whole body shook as she stepped back, away from him. A knot formed in her solar plexus, and she fought to maintain control in order to protect Sunshine and escape. Struggling to slow her breathing, she looked down at the floor. "I didn't mean anything."

"What?" He pushed at her sore arm, the one he'd bruised the night before. "I didn't hear you."

"I said I'm sorry."

"Fuckin'-A, you're sorry." His head bobbed like a proud rooster.

She tried to think of evasive action she could take or what she could do to protect herself if he escalated. The most important thing was to get through that door and away without aggravating him further. Utilizing every shred of acting talent she possessed, she dropped her shoulders, averted her eyes, and spoke in a soft voice barely above a whisper. "Is it okay if I go?"

He moved a couple inches to the side. "Don't be whining to people about your problems."

She nodded, looking down in what she hoped he saw as submission. Fear struggled with growing anger. If not for Sunshine, Jessie would say what she really thought. But now she was a mother, and if he did anything to hurt the baby, she would flat go crazy on him.

"So keep your mouth shut."

"I will," she mumbled.

"What?" He put his face right into hers, noses almost touching. She shook her head.

"That's right. Don't say *anything*." He blocked her for another ten seconds then stepped aside.

Jessie hurried out, afraid he'd give her a shove on the way past, so murderous was the rage emanating from him. Her hands shook as she buckled Sunshine into her car seat. Jessie swung the back end of the Honda into the bare spot by the dog's tree. Booger raced to the end of his chain, barking furiously. Shifting into drive, she stepped on the gas. The tires chirped when they hit the blacktop. She hoped Lenny hadn't heard it. She watched her home grow smaller in the rearview mirror, realizing he could do whatever he wanted now: get drunk, put her clothes in a pile in the driveway, or wreck everything she owned. He could burn the trailer to the ground.

She concentrated on the road as it wound through the countryside, past broken-down bungalows and rusting trailer homes, past a small pond and a pasture, and past a feedstore, until she found the church.

Bountiful Baptist Fellowship, a white clapboard building nestled between two ancient willows, was doing brisk business on the first day of the new year. Although the church was small, the parking lot was packed, and a choir was in full voice. She almost turned around and left, but she didn't know where else to go. Lenny had scared her so bad she couldn't think straight. She felt numb. As she wove through the parked cars, carrying the baby, she heard rather than felt the gravel crunching underfoot.

An usher stood at the top of the steps, holding the front door open. A thin frizz of salt-and-pepper gray topped his dark skull, and his suit was shiny with wear. "Just go on in, dear. There's plenty of places left to sit."

"Thank you." Jessie turned her face to hide the bruise. Inside the second set of doors, she stood looking for a seat, but the church was packed. Not one seat was empty. At that point, her courage failed her. She turned to leave, but to her horror, an usher called out from the front row.

"Come sit up here, child." He looked at the people who were already seated. "Can you scoot over a bit for the young lady?"

Jessie blanched. Now the whole congregation would see her face. Behind the pulpit, a robed choir began singing a gospel song. She was trapped, exposed before the entire community.

A kindly old gentleman appeared at her side. "I'll take you." He held his arm out behind her like a shield and escorted them to the front pew, where a beaming grandmother patted the seat next to her. She wore a hat adorned with purple, green, and blue sequins, topped by a fake songbird. As she moved her head, the bird bobbed and wobbled. Sunshine was entranced. "Welcome," the woman said. "Today is my lucky day. What a precious baby girl." She spoke to the man next to her, and he got the rest of the row to shift to the right. "There. How's that?"

Jessie gulped and nodded.

The reverend had ascended the pulpit and stood waiting. "Is everybody good now?"

"Yes, Reverend, we are just dandy, thank you," said the woman.

Jessie felt both trapped and embraced. Even if Lenny had followed her here, no way could he hurt her now. The fear she'd been holding at bay began to dissipate, leaving her weak. It was all she could do not to cry. She glanced at Sunshine, who was studying the hat. The choir began a new hymn.

"Aren't you the most adorable little thing?" the woman said.

Sunshine began to fidget. She leaned away from Jessie, squirming toward the woman, wanting the stranger to hold her. Jessie tried to distract her, jiggling and whispering, but Sunshine wanted to go, so her mother gave up and handed her into the eager embrace of the lady with the bird hat. The baby, now shy, rested quietly in the woman's arms as the hymn continued. The woman hummed along with the music, rocking back and forth, beaming and cooing at Sunshine.

The choir finished, their robes rustling as they sat down. The pastor checked his notes and looked up, studying them all for a moment. "We fall into routines," he began in a sonorous voice. "Routines that take us reliably through our days. Routines that help us take care of business, that help us keep our lives under control and running smoothly. Routines are useful. They help us. They are good." The congregation murmured assent.

"But routine can be deadly. Because sometimes"—he grasped the edges of the pulpit and looked out at them—"sometimes routine can lull us. It tricks us. Seduces us. We become hypnotized by our little routines, which are so useful and effective." His voice strengthened. "We become complacent. We miss what is happening around us."

"Amen."

"Yes, brother."

The reverend leaned forward, glaring. "*And that's when Satan grabs us!*"

Jessie flinched, and the grandmother patted her arm, chuckling. The members of the choir were smiling, too. Apparently this was an expected part of the pastor's act, a move designed to shake them up.

It worked. Jessie's brain cleared, and she began to focus on her situation. Whatever love she had for Lenny was unimportant. He had turned into a scary asshole. She sent a silent apology skyward, but it was true. She had to keep herself and her daughter safe.

And that meant she couldn't go back. Tears stung her eyes as she saw the reality. She would have to leave with the clothes on her back.

The preacher finished his sermon and let the choir take over. As they sang "Since I Have Been Redeemed," Jessie made her plan. The first step would be to clean out the bank account—what little there was—and find a cheap hotel for the night. That was the easy part. She would also have to get as much cash from the credit cards as possible, before Lenny noticed and canceled them. First thing would be to fill up the gas tank.

If she was going to run, she'd have to run far. Otherwise, Lenny would find her. In fact, he might be looking now.

She could barely sit still, waiting for the service to end, but when it did, she grabbed Sunshine back from the hat lady and, with baby wailing and bags bouncing, ran to the parking lot and fled.

Chapter Seventeen

*T*raffic was light as Karen left Savannah, deep in thought as to her next move. She would pawn the earrings and bank the cash. Savannah was nothing more than a memory now, a fading image in the rearview mirror, but it had clarified Karen's intentions. If she'd been focused before, she was now a heat-seeking missile. She knew what she had to do.

The CRS ladies would be a challenge. With their retiree mindset, she'd have a hard time getting anything done, short of pulling down her shades and turning into a hermit. They'd never go for that. In the month she'd been at the campground, they'd refused to believe her when she said she needed peace and quiet. Oh, they acted like they were on board, but then something would always happen, and they'd be pounding on her door, demanding her presence at this party or that outing.

The ladies were good friends, but they were impossible when it came to her work. And for the long term, the app was critical, because if she couldn't figure out how to work smarter, she'd never get further than where she was, right now. She drove southward, deep in thought.

An hour later, nausea had been replaced by hunger. At the next off-ramp, she followed a sign that indicated hotels and restaurants at a place called Jekyll Island.

The lone roadway onto the island narrowed down to a bridge over the Intracoastal Waterway. Down below, yachts and pleasure craft stood at anchor, and pennants flew from the spires of a grand old building. She drove past tidal grasslands and mossy oaks toward a historic area. Grand Victorian homes adorned with slate roofs and gables, and shaded by stately magnolia trees, lined the drive to the Jekyll Island Hotel. A driveway, shaded by massive live oaks draped with silvery moss, curved around to the front of the hotel, a three-story gingerbread-style mansion. Karen handed her keys to the valet and ascended a flight of steps. A veranda, decorated with hanging baskets of ferns, led to the lobby. Lush with leather wingback chairs, a marble fireplace, and a hand-carved cherrywood staircase, it spoke of a lavish life in days gone by.

The hostess led her to a table in the center of the dining room, which was adorned with crystal chandeliers and white linen tablecloths. A massive fireplace anchored the far end of the room, and candlelight flickered in the center of each table. "Welcome to the Jekyll Island Club." She handed Karen a menu and wine list and departed.

Outside the window, a pair of Adirondack chairs posed under a willow tree on a lawn that sloped gently down to the banks of the Intracoastal. Boats, both leisure and working, passed each other heading north and south. A sigh escaped Karen's lips, and in spite of the prices, she ordered cheese crepes and a mimosa.

The hostess came back and handed Karen a brochure. "You may want to look around a bit. There's quite a lot to do."

Karen unfolded the map. Jekyll Island wasn't huge. She could check it out in less than an hour before hitting the road and heading back to the challenge of Key Largo.

After paying her bill, Karen drove past a collection of sprawling, multistory mansions. Some had been converted to fine-dining establishments or B&Bs. One, the old infirmary, now housed gift shops and a bookstore. Horse-drawn carriages waited in front of a sleepy museum. It was all very quaint and would make a nice vacation spot if Karen could ever take the time. She rolled down her windows and inhaled the balmy sea air.

The road looped around the island. On the southern end, modest homes lined the shoreline, affording million-dollar ocean views. A sign in front of a small craftsman bungalow read *For Rent*. Couldn't be much—the house was faded and worn and needed a new roof. Then she slammed on the brakes and backed up. Down the long gravel driveway, a shiny, new Airstream stood perched on a rise overlooking the ocean. The retro aerodynamic shape looked like a thirty-footer, plenty of room for one person.

Karen parked and scanned the yard, but all she saw was a few hens, clucking and pecking at the ground. She walked down the drive for a closer look.

What a perfect place to stay. You'd have solitude, but if you needed supplies or a nice meal, you could drive a couple miles to a shopping village. And all around were sweeping views of the ocean. Karen knocked on the door of the house.

"Just a minute, please."

The door opened, and an old black woman smiled at Karen. She wore a hand-embroidered apron with oversized pockets.

"I saw the sign. It refers to the trailer?"

"Yes, it does. Are you looking for a rental?"

"I might be. Can I see the inside?"

"I'll get the key." The woman came down the stairs, leaning on a cane. They walked together toward the Airstream, parked on a concrete pad that looked as if someone had just swept it. Thirty yards beyond the trailer, the property ended, bordered by a low-growing hedge of palmettos. The land sloped away to the water's edge, closer than the length of a football field. A couple of patio chairs were tipped against a table, and the umbrella was closed and covered with a canvas sleeve. Twin pots of geraniums bracketed the door. The woman inserted a key, pushed it open, and labored up the step. Karen followed.

The interior was laid out like a barbell, with the living room at one end, the bedroom at the other, and a narrow hallway down the middle. A queen-sized bed filled most of the bedroom, with windows on both sides and storage over the headboard.

The kitchen was monochromatic stainless and ivory, with a new coffeemaker on the counter. "There's silverware and such," the woman said. "Go ahead and open the drawers and cabinets."

"Okay."

The kitchen was fully equipped, even to the extent of napkins and condiments in the cupboards. The appliances gleamed. Karen felt a surge of excitement as idea took shape.

In the combination dining/living room, a large window occupied the back wall of the trailer. Karen opened the curtains to a glimmering view of the ocean. She could work here. It would entail extra expense, since she'd want to leave her rig in Key Largo, but with the earrings in her purse, she felt as if she could afford it.

"How much are you asking?"

"How long would you want it?"

"A month," said Karen, "depending on the price."

"Two fifty a week," said the woman. She was old. Her milky eyes were glazed with age.

"Would you take eight hundred, cash? I could give you two hundred today as a deposit."

"I would." The old woman reached out to shake Karen's hand. "I'm Ida. This is my daughter's trailer. They live out in LA, but they never use it, so I decided to rent it. You're my first customer."

Karen gave her a business card. "I'll be back tomorrow night."

Ida nodded, studying the card. "See you then."

Back on the road, she slid a disc into the CD player. This was just what she needed—a lovely secluded place from which to work on all of Ben's new projects, plus the app. She would need to find someone to do the coding. Maybe Curt knew of someone at the college? Or cousin Lorraine, or her friends back in North Dakota? She would call around tomorrow, in between all the other chores necessary to pack and secure the trailer. She could ask Fern and Bell to keep an eye on it, once they got over being mad at her for leaving.

Karen couldn't believe her luck in finding the Airstream. She would be free to avoid distractions and work, work, work until she'd built a foundation for her new life.

Everything was coming together perfectly.

Chapter Eighteen

When Jessie sped from the church, she'd been fueled by fear and determination, but as the miles passed, the enormity of her endeavor began to sink in. She had no idea where she was going, and she had a baby to care for.

Lenny would be furious, but once he calmed down, what would he be thinking? Would he be sorry? Would it ever be safe to return, and if not, what would she do? She had a couple hundred dollars in her wallet, from cleaning out their checking account. That wouldn't last long.

Sunshine had only needed attention a few times, once when her diaper had to be changed and a couple times to be fed. Other than that, Jessie mostly drove without interruption for four hours straight, and that gave her time to think.

In midafternoon, she found Valdosta and a crappy chain hotel that didn't look too scary, right off the Interstate. She handed the clerk her credit card, acting brave until it went through and then slumping a little in relief. It might have been smarter to pay cash, but she didn't want to part with it. Besides, Lenny hadn't called yet, so probably he was sulking and expecting her to come crawling back—like that was going to happen. In the morning, she'd move on, once she figured out where.

The hotel room was depressingly bleak. She wadded up the germy floral bedspread and stuffed it into the closet. The baby wanted to get down and explore, so Jessie took her for a walk, holding her. Cars whizzed by on the Interstate, and people drove in and out of the parking lot, loading and unloading, slamming doors and yelling. After a while, Jessie took a seat at the hotel's café, fed the baby, and picked at a salad for herself. Back at the room, she locked them in and tipped a chair against the door. Using towels as bumpers to keep the baby from getting too adventurous, she fashioned a little corral on the bed for Sunshine. Then she watched TV and wondered what the hell she was going to do.

Once Sunshine was down for the night, Jessie had time to second-guess herself. Where exactly was she going? And with what? Everything she owned was back at the trailer. School books, clothes, dishes, housewares, baby stuff, and her life. Doubt arose, threatening to swamp her. Was she overreacting? If she was, this would be like starting a war for no reason. Lenny had been under a lot of pressure lately. It wasn't like him to drink so much. Maybe there was something going on with him. Had he been hurt at work? Was he sick?

Or worse?

Lenny had been a star running back on his high school football team. He was a hero to the school, racking up hundreds of yards and winning all kinds of awards, but he'd been injured a lot, too. He had sustained several concussions that they knew of. In her classes, she'd learned that brain trauma could lead to personality changes. Her feelings bounced back and forth between compassion and anger, but certainty eluded her. If she could only know the future. Was this a onetime thing? Was he sorry? Could he be helped, or was this it?

And what about Sunshine? What was the right thing to do, even under the circumstances?

She put her face in her hands, wincing as the pain reminded her of last night. However, the pain was a blessing. It clarified her options. Even if she was overreacting, she was a mother. She had to protect the baby. Surely, Lenny would understand that, after he calmed down. Maybe, after a few weeks of her being away, maybe even a month, he would agree to go to counseling and learn how to control his anger. Or maybe she would get him to open up about the real reason he'd acted so mean. She just needed a little time away, to figure things out and to give him time to think. She fell asleep, one arm draped protectively over the baby.

The next morning, the rumble of eighteen-wheelers on the nearby freeway woke her. Sunshine slept deeply, barricaded by a berm of towels at the edge of the bed. The baby was on her stomach, knees drawn up, face smooshed against the sheet. Her face, expressive even in sleep, changed from frown to smile as she dreamed.

Jessie sat up, gently so as not to awaken Sunshine. She looked around the gray hotel room. Her only option was to go home to her parents in Denver. Go back home with her tail between her legs and ask her asshole parents to take her in.

No. Regardless of her crappy circumstances, she'd come too far for that.

She had no place to go and very little cash. But Grandma Frieda had intended to help her. All Jessie had to do was locate Karen Grace and ask for the envelope. Maybe Karen could send it via Western Union or something.

Jessie rinsed her face and made a cup of hotel coffee. Maybe Karen would be good for something more than just the envelope from Grandma. Her outlook brightened as she considered this new idea.

Jessie needed to hide out for a while, and she couldn't keep paying for hotel rooms. Older people usually had more house than they knew what to do with. Probably Karen had an extra bedroom. Maybe even a yard. She would be happy to see them. Her psychology book said that old people lacked purpose after their kids were grown and needed somebody to take care of in order to feel useful. Jessie would be doing this Karen Grace a favor.

And Lenny wouldn't be able to find her until she was good and ready.

After breakfast, she put Sunshine and a couple of toys in the middle of the bed, surrounded by pillows. Then she called her mother. Surprised, Sandy sounded happy at first, but then when Jessie asked if she knew how to get in touch with Karen, she got mad and started yelling. Pretty soon they hung up on each other, as expected.

Option two was to search the Internet, where she quickly found Karen all over the place, but none of the links led to anything personal. It was all very corporate and businesslike. She was about out of time—Sunshine was getting fussy—when she got the idea that the church in Dickinson might know how to contact Karen's aunt, and maybe that would lead to Karen.

"St. Joseph's. This is Father Engel." He sounded out of breath.

Jessie explained that she was Frieda's granddaughter, and the priest said, "Ah, you're the Larsons' daughter, Jessica."

"Uh, yes." She was surprised he knew her name. "Yes, Father, that is me."

"How are you, Jessica? The last I heard, you've become a mother yourself. A little girl. Congratulations." When she didn't answer, he said, "Hello?"

"I'm sorry. I'm just blown away that you have those facts at your fingertips."

"Your grandmother was a wonderful person. She and I would visit often, and she told me how much she was looking forward to seeing you and your daughter in Denver last summer. I'm sorry for your loss, but she died doing what she wanted. She was happy."

"I'm sorry I didn't get to see her before she passed." Jessie closed her eyes, hating her mother with everything she had.

A phone began ringing in his office. "Excuse me. Just a—oh, for the love of God." The phone rang and rang, and she heard fumbling and banging as he tried to get to the second line. Then he cut her off.

She called back.

"I am sorry, Jessica. I'm not the most adept secretary sometimes. How can I help you?"

"Actually, I'm trying to get in touch with Karen Grace, the woman who took Grandma on that last camping trip."

"Yes, I have her number. I call her every time my employees quit."

"Sounds like you'll be calling her again soon."

He laughed. Jessie took down the number, promised to relay his greetings, and hung up. She baby-talked at Sunshine while getting ready mentally, because her next call would be a lot more difficult.

Chapter Nineteen

*B*y sunrise Friday morning, Karen had packed for the move, cleaned the fifth wheel, and emptied out the refrigerator. When that was done, she went over and knocked on the screen door of Fern's RV. Inside, a recliner snicked shut and heavy footsteps shook the trailer.

"Thought we'd see you today." Fern held the door open. "Let's sit in the kitchen. How was Savannah?"

"Good. I got reacquainted with an old business colleague, saw the city. Relaxed a little."

Belle poured coffee and joined them at the table. "Did you accomplish what you set out to do?"

"Absolutely. I landed a whole new load of projects."

"Congratulations."

"Except I'll need to be leaving again."

"Oh, no. We've hardly seen anything of you," said Belle.

Karen put the mug down and began her speech, her best sales pitch, the one she'd practiced on the drive home from Jekyll Island. "It's such an opportunity. If I could focus for a month on nothing but my business, I could lay the groundwork for the rest of my life."

"You know they won't hold your space," said Fern. "This is high season, and there's a waiting list. Once you roll out of here, it's gone."

"That's why I'm leaving my trailer here."

"And rent someplace else? Must be nice to be rich."

"I received a grant from an investment group." It was sort of the truth.

"Yeah, that's great. Good for you." Fern blew on her coffee. "Just so you know, Eleanor's gotten worse."

"I haven't been over to see her yet. You were my first stop."

"It's stomach cancer," said Belle. "There's nothing they can do."

Karen's shoulders sagged. "How long does she have?"

"Couple weeks, maybe," said Fern. "We're going over there in shifts."

"We don't want her to have to do anything," said Belle. "She won't have to cook or clean or be alone one minute of the day or night."

"This is awful," said Karen.

"Yes, it is," said Belle. "She was always so nice."

Fern set her mug of coffee down with a thump. "Eleanor was a hard-ass who can't stand people. But she was her own person, by God. *Is* her own person."

"You know what I mean," said Belle. "She's so smart and well-traveled. She always had something interesting to say."

"She's an amazing woman," said Karen.

"How long can you stick around and help?" asked Fern.

"Please don't hate me, but I'm leaving in a couple hours. That's why I came by."

Fern stared at her. "I thought when you joined us that you wanted to be a part of things."

Karen stared back. There were almost two dozen CRS ladies in the camp. Regardless of Karen's feelings of guilt, the group didn't really need her. Fern was the one who needed her...to rally around the flag and show respect for her leadership. She saw the resolution in Fern's jaw and the lines in Belle's forehead. Part of her felt horrible for abandoning them, but she also chafed at the obligation. Might as well be honest about it. "I do want to be part of the group, but this is work, and I have to go. Will I be welcome back at the end of next month?"

"Why wouldn't you be?"

"Because...I—you said—" Karen shut her mouth. "Thanks for the coffee."

Belle looked away from the window, her eyes red. "Do you still want us to watch your rig while you're gone?"

"If it's not too much trouble." Karen laid the spare key on the table.

"We'll be here when you get back," said Fern. "Gimme a hug."

"Just be sure you see Eleanor before you leave," said Belle.

"Of course." Karen wished they knew how hard it was for her not to cave. She'd been raised to put other people first, but last summer, on the road trip with Frieda, everything had changed. Even if she had to fight for it, Karen loved her new sense of independence, though it scared her at times. She refused to be trapped, ever again, by anyone.

At Eleanor's RV, Gina answered. "Thank God you're here. I'm going to be late for my manicure." She grabbed her purse and ran out the door.

In the bedroom, Eleanor lay quiet under a pile of blankets. Karen sat in a black folding chair next to the bed. "I go away for two days, and look what happens."

Eleanor held out a thin hand.

Karen took it between both of hers, trying to warm it. "They tell me you're under the weather."

"Feeling a mite poorly."

"Are you in a lot of pain?"

"I have some very good drugs." Eleanor's voice faded.

Karen looked around the cramped bedroom, which was filled with mementos from across the globe. Mirrored embroidery from India, a blue-and-white vase from China, and a miniature totem pole from the Pacific Northwest sat atop the dresser. A Japanese silk panel adorned one wall, an African mask the other. Elongated, with bland features, it wasn't pretty or striking in any way.

"If not for that mask, I'd be dead," Eleanor rasped. "Look at the cheek."

Karen went over and peered at the mask. The hardwood bore a gouge on the left side of the face. She turned to Eleanor.

"We were in west Africa. This was around 1960. There was a coup, and our tour guide deserted us. We bribed a man with a car." She stopped, grimacing. Her hand rested on her belly. "At the airport, the mask was in my backpack. We made a dash for the terminal doors. Somebody fired at us. I saw a bullet hit the cinder block in front of me. Then we were inside. When I got home, I realized what happened."

"Quite a trophy," Karen said.

"My husband bought it for me at the start of the trip, in Sierra Leone. The small mouth and eyes symbolize humility. Funny man."

"When did he pass on?"

"I don't know." Eleanor's eyes closed. "We split up after traveling the world together. Got divorced but stayed friends."

"I have to tell you something," Karen said. "Tomorrow, I'm leaving for a month. It's related to work, and there's no alternative. I know everybody's going to be helping you, but still, I feel bad that I won't be here."

"For Pete's sake." Eleanor labored to rise up on one elbow. "Fern probably tortured you over that, didn't she?"

"I should be here to help."

"I knew it would come to this. Sometimes I wish I'd just left a note in my RV and drove my truck off a pier." Eleanor fell back and stared up at the ceiling. "What good is it going to do if you hang around? Nothing will change the outcome."

"We'd feel better."

"Exactly. But I wouldn't."

Karen smiled. "It's all about us."

"They're hovering around because that's how they manage. They feel bad. But I'm at peace. I—" She stopped, gasping.

"What's happening?" Karen knelt on the floor next to the bed. "What can I do?"

Eleanor waved her off. Karen sat at the edge of her chair, ready to bolt for the phone, but the older woman's breathing returned to a calmer, steadier rhythm. Sunlight beamed through stained-glass panels hung in the windows.

Eleanor sighed. "I will admit to being surprised at the rapidity."

"Me, too." Karen turned back to the bed and took Eleanor's hand again. "It doesn't seem fair."

"Speed of decline is a blessing. I don't want to die—what idiot would? But I'm curious about the next place." She withdrew her hand and tucked it under the blanket. "Don't let those old biddies hold you back. I never did, up until yesterday."

"They mean well."

"Yes, and that's the problem. You can't hate them for it." Eleanor opened her eyes and smiled at Karen. "Save yourself."

Karen watched her drift back into silence. Humility wasn't the first word that came to mind when she thought of Eleanor. Yet the woman was quiet about it, living a strong, peaceful life without pissing off her community. Karen wished she could have gotten to know her sooner. What a mentor she could have been.

An hour later, a light tap on the door told her the next shift had arrived. Karen locked up her trailer and headed for Jekyll Island. It was what she wanted, she told herself—plenty of room to spread out and the silence to hear herself think.

As she headed north on the Overseas Highway, her phone rang. She didn't recognize the number but figured it might be related to work, and anyway, it would be a good distraction, regardless. So she answered it and got a surprise.

Chapter Twenty

"This is Jessie. Frieda Richter's granddaughter?" Jessie hoped Karen wouldn't freak. "I saw you at my grandma's funeral. We didn't have a chance to say hi."

There was silence on the other end. Then a soft voice said, "That was because your mother pretty much chased me away. How are you?"

"I'm sorry about that. I would have liked to talk with you."

"Frieda wanted to see you and the baby."

"I know." Jessie struggled with what to say next. On the hotel-room bed, Sunshine, playing with her toys, laughed and babbled inside the pillow walls of her makeshift baby jail.

"Frieda left you an envelope. Can I mail it to you?" asked Karen.

"No! I mean, the problem is, our mailbox is wrecked. I mean, we're having problems with our mail delivery right now. It'd be great if you could hang on to it until I get that resolved, and then I'll call you back."

"That would be fine. You have my number."

Jessie couldn't let her hang up yet. "Wait, Karen? Can you tell what's inside it? I mean, can you get any kind of an idea, by feel or holding it up to the light?"

"No, it's one of those superpadded jobs. It's not heavy, but it is a little bit thick. Could be her memoirs." Karen chuckled.

"Would her memoirs be funny?"

"It's not that," Karen said. "You didn't spend much time around Frieda, did you?"

"Not since I was a little kid."

"That's a shame. She was a wonderful human being."

"So you live in Florida?"

"I do, in Key Largo."

"That must be nice. Whereabouts?" Jessie grimaced. She sounded like a stalker with a bad script.

"Paradise Shores. Why?"

"Well, maybe sometime I could bring the baby and we could visit."

Just then, Sunshine chortled at a toy and said, "Mama."

"She sounds adorable," said Karen.

"She's an awesome little kid. I am so lucky. I just wish Grandma could have met her."

"She really wanted to. That was the whole point of our road trip." Karen paused. "But don't feel bad. She had a great time. It was like she was starting her life all over again. At ninety, she was curious about everything and excited to see things and go places."

"Thanks for saying that. I've felt guilty ever since. And I hate my mother for her part in this."

"Don't spend your energy on that," said Karen. "Maybe you could come visit sometime. I could meet Sunshine, and we could share stories about Frieda."

"I would love that."

"Okay. Well, you have my number."

"I'll stay in touch." Jessie hung up, a smile threatening to crack her face in half. The call had gone better than she expected. She found Key Largo and programmed it into her GPS. In eight hours, she'd be at Karen's.

Chapter Twenty-One

*A*s Karen left the Keys behind and crossed to the mainland at Homestead, the clouds opened up with a tropical downpour. She'd secured her luggage under a tarp, so she wasn't worried. With the wipers on high and traffic light, the only thing missing was music.

She slid Fleetwood Mac into the CD player and advanced to "Landslide." The CD had been a going-away present from Curt, and the song made her a little sad, but it couldn't compete with the excitement over her next moves. Breaking away from North Dakota and fleeing to Key Largo had clarified her thoughts. She still had a fire in the belly, one that demanded freedom of movement. Her marriage had faltered, due in large part to her focus on work. Until she figured out how to do business and pleasure together, she wouldn't commit to a relationship.

Although she and Curt shared a common history, one that made her nostalgic for her childhood, she wondered if she could ever make a long-term relationship work. In her younger years, she'd tried to be everything to everybody. Now, in the second half of her life, she had the power to decide. Getting older meant taking the reins, making a decision, being assertive. This was what Karen told herself by way of justification.

Of course, Curt wouldn't understand this if she never told him, and she couldn't tell him if she never called him. She imagined him back in North Dakota, moping around and pining for her, and she swore she'd call him as soon as she arrived at Jekyll Island. She pressed down on the accelerator, trying to leave the guilt behind.

***

Curt opened one eye and tried to focus on the nightstand clock. When he saw it was almost noon, he cracked a grin. Next to him, Maddie slumbered on.

They'd started out yesterday the same way, sleeping almost until lunchtime. After a lovers' brunch, they'd dressed and spent the afternoon riding Duke and Missy all over hell and back and then taken a tub bath together to wash off the trail dust. Which of course led to Maddie climbing on top of him in the bathtub, a big claw-footed number overlooking his property.

He took her out to dinner at the Cowboy Country Club, and they topped that off with drinks and dancing in town. The way Maddie danced, she lit him up all over again, and they got home and hung from the chandeliers until after midnight.

He rolled over and stretched, noting that nothing seemed broken. In fact, he didn't feel the least bit achy, which surprised him. Fifty-five years of living, half of it spent in the field—both farm and geologic—had delivered a few dings and damage, but Maddie's magic must have been unlocking his joints and sending his blood flowing through his veins at top speed.

In fact, that was the best part. He didn't feel old anymore. Maddie was giving him his youth back.

He reached toward her and was rewarded with a generous handful of backside, followed by a soft moan. She turned to him, all floaty and warm, and reached for his cock.

Off to the races.

***

The narrow highway to Jekyll Island was little more than a raised strip through a broad reach of salt marshland. The tide had receded, revealing muddy channels through the lowland grasses. In the golden light of late afternoon, Karen crossed the Intracoastal Bridge and headed for the southern end of the island. She parked in front of Ida's house and climbed out of the truck, stretching her aching muscles as she walked. Halfway to the porch, the sound of jungle birdcalls reached her from inside the house.

Ida opened the door. "I was beginning to think you weren't coming," she said, reaching for a set of keys in her pocket.

"I got a late start." Karen cocked her head. "What am I hearing?"

"It's a recording a friend made for me when she visited the Amazon. I like to listen while I'm knitting." Ida held out the key. "The bed is made, and I turned on the refrigerator this morning. Let me know if you need anything further." They wished each other good night, and the door closed.

Karen hit the lights inside the Airstream. Everything was as clean, bright, and sleek as she remembered. In spite of fatigue, she felt a rising sense of promise. To think of all she could accomplish here, working without interruption! She opened the refrigerator (cold), checked the burners (they worked), and went around opening and closing cabinets, taking inventory. Ida had stocked the kitchen with everything she would need except food. It was either make a meal out of decaf and sweetener or go to the village for groceries. Darkness fell and she turned on her headlights, but met no other cars on the road.

In the village, she found a diner. Through the windows she could see only two people inside, a waitress and one customer. Karen ordered chicken soup and an order of cornbread to go. She stopped at the nearby market for milk. The place was closing up, although it was only eight o'clock...and Friday night yet.

After finishing off the soup and cornbread, Karen unpacked enough of her luggage to get through the night. She brought in her expensive electronics, retied the ropes, and hoped everything else would be there in the morning.

She locked the truck and secured the door of the Airstream, brushed her teeth, and washed her face at the granite sink. After checking the windows and making sure the door was locked, Karen climbed into bed. She stretched, fluffed a pillow, and let out a long breath. In the darkness, she listened to sounds reaching her through the air vent over her bed—intermittent raindrops, the soft hooting of an owl, and the wind rustling through the loblolly pines.

I'm here at last, she thought, all alone to focus on my work and not worry about anybody but myself. I should sleep like a baby.

She refluffed the pillow and turned over. And then turned over again. An hour later, she was still awake.

It wasn't that she was nervous. The place had to be safe. Ida lived alone, and she'd probably been here fifty years.

And it wasn't that she missed the CRS ladies or Curt or Aunt Marie. Or even Steve. So what was this unease she felt? She closed her eyes, hoping to get drowsy and fall asleep, but her senses were on high alert, and she noticed every sound and smell. It was the strangeness, of course. In the past year she'd lived like a transient, moving from California to North Dakota to Florida, and now here in Georgia. The distant whisper of the surf crept in her window, along with the salty tang of coastal dampness. She missed the security of home, but she had no home. Karen pulled the covers up around her chin and waited for sleep to come.

Chapter Twenty-Two

*I*n the waning light of Friday afternoon, Jessie, exhausted and skeptical, crept along behind a long line of cars on the highway into Key Largo. She had expected a house in a community, but the GPS had brought her all the way down to this skinny strip of land with touristy shops and campgrounds. The chance of finding an actual neighborhood on this island seemed remote. She drove on and on, increasingly desperate. Where would they sleep tonight if she couldn't find Karen's house?

She'd driven nearly five hundred miles since talking on the phone that morning, stopping only to feed and change Sunshine and let her toddle around a bit. Fear of Lenny kept her moving, fear of him finding them, hurting them, and making her come back. Jessie had used a big chunk of her remaining funds on food, gas, and the motel. Luckily, the Honda held together, and Jessie wondered fleetingly why Lenny had always acted worried that if she went anywhere in it by herself, it would break down. That at least gave her satisfaction. She'd beaten the odds on making it here.

But this? Instead of the gated community she'd expected, Paradise Shores was an RV campground. She pulled in and parked in front of the office, rested her head against the steering wheel, and fought the urge to cry. Karen Grace lived in a trailer park. No house, no spare bedroom, no yard, and no lonely retiree grateful for company. Karen was probably a cranky old woman with Chihuahuas, with no room for a runaway mother and her small child.

Sunshine whimpered, and Jessie lifted the baby out of her car seat and went into the office.

The mannish old lady behind the desk looked up. "We're full."

"I'm visiting someone who's staying here." Jessie jiggled Sunshine to keep her from fussing. The baby was tired and hungry, too.

"What's the name?"

"Karen Grace. I was told I could find her here." Fatigue made Jessie tentative. She could hear the sound of fear in her own voice.

The woman shook her head. "You're out of luck."

"What do you mean?"

"She left this morning. Won't be back for a month."

Jessie's knees sagged. She felt as if she might drop the baby.

"Are you all right?" The woman hurried out from around the counter. "Come here and sit down. I'll be right back." She returned with a granola bar and a soda.

"Thank you."

"Where're you from?"

"Atlanta."

"You drove all the way with her?" The woman looked out the window at the Honda. "In that?"

Jessie took a long swallow of the soda. This woman looked like a bulldog, but she'd fed them, so she had a soft side. "Karen Grace is my aunt."

"I'll be damned." The woman held out a calloused hand. "I didn't think she had any family. I'm Fern."

"I'm Jessie."

"I don't remember Karen mentioning any brothers or sisters."

Jessie thought fast. "They had a falling-out. It was years ago. Actually, I haven't seen Karen since I was a baby."

"Okay." Fern raised an eyebrow.

"Aunt Karen said if I ever needed anything I should call her." Jessie turned her face to show the bruise. "So when this happened, I panicked and jumped in the car and drove here. I thought she could hide me."

"Jesus Christ. Husband?"

"Not exactly. And I used up all my money getting here. I'm trying to think of options but—" Jessie stopped when Sunshine began to fuss.

"Yeah, there's nowhere in town. It's high season. The place is full up." Fern studied her. "If you want, you could follow me to my place. My wife's making dinner. We'll have a bite to eat and figure out what to do with you."

Jessie wondered if that was safe, but short of sleeping in her car, she was out of options. She would have to trust this Fern woman. If things went bad, she had a small canister of Mace in her purse. She buckled a squirming, cranky Sunshine back into her car seat and waited for Fern's vehicle to appear. When she saw the new black-and-tan three-quarter-ton pickup truck wheel around from the back of the office, she relaxed a little. Most ax murderers would be driving a junk heap. She followed the truck into the campground, hypnotized by the red taillights.

At Fern's massive fifth-wheel, a woman held the screen door open, a look of puzzlement on her face. Her gray hair was pulled back in a long ponytail, with tendrils framing her face. Jessie opened the Honda's back door and unstrapped Sunshine. The woman gasped. "A baby. Come in, come in."

Jessie climbed the steps. The woman seemed mesmerized by Sunshine. Fern, standing inside, said, "Jessie, this is Belle."

"Hello, dear. We're just about to have dinner." Belle stepped aside. From the kitchen wafted the aroma of dinnertime. In the living room, a scented candle flickered on the coffee table, and a new-age melody played quietly.

"This is Jessie, and the little one is Sunshine. The two of them drove all the way from Atlanta to see Karen."

Belle's eyes widened. "But she left this morning. You just missed her."

Jessie nodded. "I know. Fern told me."

"The kids're hungry." Fern put her arm around Belle and gave her a squeeze. "Got enough for everybody?"

"Of course I do," said Belle. "Can the baby eat solids? I can give you a bowl to mash it up."

"They're going to need more than dinner," Fern said. "She's on the run. I'm afraid this is a case of domestic abuse, plain and simple."

"I'm sorry," said Belle.

"I don't want to impose," said Jessie.

"Not at all," said Belle. "It's our pleasure. Not that many young people come to visit anymore."

Fern stood in front of them, her arms folded. "They don't have anyplace to stay tonight."

"They can stay here." Belle smiled at Sunshine, who stuck a thumb into her mouth and hid against her mother's breast.

Jessie felt limp with relief. She could stop running, at least until morning. "I would be so grateful," she whispered.

"The sofa folds out, and we have lots of extra bedding. Do you have something in your car for the baby to sleep in? A playpen or something?"

"I had to leave without it." Jessie had found a thrift store on the way south, bought a few items of clothing for herself and Sunshine, and continued down the highway. At the motel this morning, she'd barely showered, worried about Sunshine climbing off the bed.

Belle looked around the room. "Maybe we can roll up some blankets, find some pillows, and use the sofa cushions to make up a little bed for her."

Fern retrieved her truck keys from the hook near the door. "Why don't you finish getting dinner ready, get them settled, and I'll be right back." She jumped into the truck and backed out of the driveway.

"What do you think she's doing?" asked Jessie.

"Fern has a mind of her own." Belle stood up. "Do you like meat loaf? We're having that, with mashed potatoes, gravy, and a salad. What do you think the baby might eat?"

"I still have a little of her food left." Jessie spread a blanket on the carpet and set Sunshine in the middle. The baby sat and watched, her face grim.

"Will she stay there?" asked Belle.

"Not for long. She's a little nervous right now, so she won't move right away. Then she'll get brave and start to explore." Jessie offered the baby a couple of toys and a clean pacifier. Returning to the bag, she fished out several jars and a can. "I have green beans and pears, but no protein or liquids."

"We have string cheese you could chop up. And apple juice."

"That would be good," said Jessie. "I have a sippy cup." The two women worked side by side in the small kitchen, Belle peeling potatoes and Jessie preparing the baby's dinner. Then she gathered up Sunshine and, holding her on her lap, used a plastic spoon to feed her. The hungry baby gobbled her food, opening her mouth like a baby bird. When she finished, Jessie returned her to the blanket and played with her while Belle cooked.

A half hour later, Fern drove up. She shut the truck door with one hip and carried two bags of groceries into the house. "Diapers, baby food, a bunch of other stuff." Then she went back outside and returned with a big cardboard box, grinning at the look of surprise on Jessie's face. "I asked the lady at Walmart for a playpen, and she looked at me like I was some kinda idiot and said they don't call 'em that anymore. So this here is a play yard. The lady said she can sleep in it, too." She set it down in the living room and began to unpack the box in front of Sunshine, who watched, her eyes big. "You are gonna love this, little one."

Chapter Twenty-Three

*I*n the middle of the night, Belle awoke to the sound of a baby crying. She thought it was a dream, but it seemed so real a knife twisted in her heart. The trailer jiggled, and Jessie's voice carried through the darkness as she soothed her baby. Belle wondered about the big bruise on her face. If the animal who did it lived in Atlanta, there was little chance he'd find them here. Jessie and the baby would be safe for as long as they stayed.

In the morning, the baby pulled herself into a standing position and jabbered at Fern, who sat on the couch, reading a newspaper. Jessie sat at the table, wearing a pair of Belle's pajamas and checking her phone for messages. In the kitchen, Belle mixed onions, bell peppers, and cheese into an omelet. She filled three glasses with orange juice and blotted the grease from the bacon. The ritual, so simple, brought her a rich feeling of peace. "Who's ready for breakfast?"

Fern folded the paper, caressed Sunshine's head, and sauntered into the kitchen. "Load me up."

Belle placed one strip of bacon on her plate.

"Is that all?"

"I'm just thinking of your cholesterol, dear."

Fern made a face and slipped past her, reaching for the eggs.

"Thanks again for letting us stay here last night," said Jessie. "I don't know what I would have done."

Stay as long as you like. Belle bit her tongue before the sentiment escaped. "We have salsa, if that's your thing. Help yourself to toast, and we have spray butter, because we're getting too darned fat."

"Speak for yourself, darlin'." Fern speared three additional pieces of bacon and winked at Jessie. "What's on the agenda today?"

"Gina's having a planning meeting for the Valentine's Day fashion show," said Belle. "That's at ten."

Fern groaned. "My back still hurts from last time, moving all the furniture and decorations around."

"You do too much," said Belle.

"If I don't, who will?"

"You have a big heart." Belle smiled at Fern. The two of them shared a look. "And this afternoon we should stop by Eleanor's."

Jessie stopped to wipe the baby's chin. "You have a lot of friends in the park?"

"We're an RV travel group," said Fern. "We drive all over the country, depending on the weather. Like snowbirds. We'll be here until it gets hot, probably the end of April."

"And Karen is part of your group?"

"Yes," said Belle.

"No," said Fern at the same time. "Well, she sort of is. She's a strange one. Wants company, then doesn't. Ran off to some island in Georgia so she can work. If you ask me, she could just close her door and work right here. I don't know what the problem was."

"She's a very private individual," said Belle. "Not everyone wants to share their personal business."

Fern shot a look of frustration at Belle. "Sometimes it's necessary."

"So is tact." Belle loved Fern, but sometimes she plowed straight into people without realizing it.

"Tell me again," Fern said, "how it is that Karen didn't know you were coming?"

Jessie chewed slowly. When she was done, she reached for a glass of milk and took two long swallows. "She told me she had something for me. Something from my grandma Frieda's funeral."

It wasn't an answer, Belle noticed, but given the purple bruise on the girl's face, her evasiveness was understandable, and it posed no threat. She hoped Fern would drop her line of questioning. She followed Fern's glance at the window, where campers were beginning their morning walk. "Your granny was a real straight-shooter. If Frieda had something to say, she said it."

"Fern." Belle shook her head.

Jessie added salsa to her eggs. "You knew her?"

"We met in Moab," Belle said. "She and Karen came to our camp for lunch. We had a wonderful meal. Pasta and garlic bread. Lots of wine."

"Then we played poker," said Fern. "I won, but your grandma made me work for it."

"Frieda stayed for hours," said Belle. "She was so funny and wise we couldn't get enough of her. At first, Karen was overprotective. Something terrible happened on their journey through Wyoming, but we never heard the story. She was very good to Frieda."

"My mother said Grandma wanted to go home, but Karen wouldn't let her."

"No, honey, it wasn't like that," said Belle. "They were traveling to California. Frieda wanted to see the ocean, and Karen planned to rent a beach house. They were very excited."

"That totally contradicts my mom's story," said Jessie. "In fact, I was a little afraid to come here because she made Karen sound like such a witch."

"Not at all," said Fern.

"Karen doted on Frieda, waiting on her every need," said Belle. "We were surprised to find out they weren't mother and daughter, because they were so attached. Maybe they were close because Karen had so recently lost her mother and dad."

"And by the way, Jessie, she didn't have any siblings," said Fern.

Jessie exhaled. "I might have exaggerated."

"So how do you know her?"

"I only know her because she was the person driving Grandma to Denver. They were coming to see me and Sunshine, because my mother lied and said we were there with her. But we never were. My mother wanted to see Grandma, and used me and the baby as bait."

"That's a shame," said Belle. "Poor Frieda."

"So when I heard Karen had something for me, I started thinking she could solve my problem, at least for a little while."

"What about your parents?"

"As far as I'm concerned, they don't exist."

Fern cleared her throat. "Thank you for answering our questions."

"We're sorry for your troubles." Belle pushed away from the table and began clearing.

Jessie went in the bedroom to change the baby.

Fern helped in the kitchen until it was clean, and then Belle hung up her apron. "Let's go for a walk."

Outside, Fern said, "I don't know if I believe everything she said."

"She's on the run and needs help." Belle took off down the lane.

Fern caught up. "What if she's a con, working the neighborhood? What if she got Karen's name off stolen mail?"

"And hit herself in the face to make it look convincing?"

"Maybe her pimp did it."

"How can you say that?"

"How do we even know she's Frieda's granddaughter?"

"I don't care who she is! She needs our help. They both do. We can't just leave that baby homeless."

Fern reached for Belle's arm. "Stop. Honey, please."

Reluctantly, Belle slowed. She swiped a lock of hair out of her eyes and glared into the distance. Most of the time she deferred to Fern's stronger personality, but not today. Today she would stand her ground. The kids were too important. She had to protect them.

"I'm sorry for all the mess this is stirring up inside you," Fern said.

"You don't know anything."

"Having Jessie and Sunshine here won't change the past, and it could put us at risk."

Belle shook her off. "I'm not an imbecile."

"I know. I didn't mean—cripes. I'm not saying this right at all."

"This isn't about me," said Belle. "This is about Jessie."

"Who I don't trust. She already admitted to lying once."

Belle threw her hands up. "Oh, honestly, Fern! She's making it up as she goes along."

"That's obvious."

"She's desperate for a safe place to hide until she can figure out her next move." Belle dropped her arms. "And here's how we're going to help her."

Chapter Twenty-Four

On Saturday morning, Karen awoke to the raucous crowing of a rooster and remembered that Ida kept chickens. Perfect. The birds would serve as her alarm clock for the thirty days. She jumped out of bed, pulled on a robe, and opened the curtains in the living room to see if she'd imagined it, but no. In the near distance, the gray-blue Atlantic Ocean rippled, practically in her backyard. A man walked along the shoreline, tossing a stick for his Lab. A couple of joggers passed him, making side-by-side tracks in the wet sand. Clouds parted, and the horizon shimmered. The sun broke through overcast that had blanketed the sky.

Karen padded into the kitchen. She found coffee packets in one drawer and sweetener in another. As she set the coffeepot to brew, she thought about Jessie's phone call yesterday. Something didn't feel right, but maybe it was her imagination.

She poured a cup of coffee, pulled on a sweat shirt, and went outside to savor the morning. The rooster had quieted, and Ida's kitchen light was on. Karen unfolded a lawn chair at the top of the slope. The dog walker and joggers were gone. It was just her, a gentle breeze, and the small waves breaking softly on the sand, smoothed from the night's high tide. No chatty walkers threatened to intrude on her solitude. No self-appointed group leader pressured her to commit to the day's social calendar. Karen sipped the hot brew, joyful over her decision, immersed in the sounds of the island and nothing more.

When the cup was empty, she thought about going for a walk, taking either the shoreline or the bicycle path along the road. She yawned and stretched, deciding on the latter, saving the beach for another time.

As she passed Ida's backyard, the hens busied themselves finding breakfast while the rooster, a colorful fellow, eyed her with malice. A pink bicycle with fat, beachy tires leaned against the house. Across the road, the bike path circled the interior of the island, which resembled a jungle. Easing into a trot, she turned east, momentarily reaching for her headphones, but the day was awakening to a chorus of birdsong with a backdrop of surf, a composition more glorious than anything electronic. Her sneakers trod silently along the bike path, careful to step across the cracks buckling from the roots of giant oaks and ancient pines.

Presently she discovered the sweeping lawn of a soccer field, deserted now except for a gardener kneeling over a sprinkler head with his tools. On the far side of the playing fields, a pathway cut through thick vegetation. Following the path, Karen found a boardwalk leading across sand dunes and followed it to its end, a viewpoint spanning the eastern coast of the island. She leaned against the wooden railing, inhaling the salty, damp air. Gulls wheeled and cried overhead while long-legged shorebirds played tag with the surf. Pillars of golden light beamed from breaks in the clouds as the sun rose up out of the calm, gray Atlantic. The placid waters stretched to the horizon, as featureless as her beloved Dakota prairie, and as deceptively placid.

The clouds began to dissipate, leaving the sky a bracing blue, and Karen turned back. As she walked up the driveway, Ida waved to her from the kitchen window.

Karen propped the door of the trailer open, untied the cargo net, and began to move in properly. Everything inside the trailer was small—the closets, cabinets, and refrigerator—but having lived in an RV for the past couple months, she was used to traveling light. In fact, she'd pretty much emptied the trailer in Paradise Shores, except for her plants. She hoped Belle remembered to water them. The basil in particular was important to keep alive, having been grown from a cutting out of Frieda's garden.

Soon, three business outfits hung in the small closet, shoes lined up under them, and a couple of purses fit on the overhead shelf. The queen-sized mattress raised up on a hinge to reveal storage space underneath, where she stashed the empty suitcases.

The bathroom's small medicine chest filled up quickly with her personal items. The rest went in the cabinet under the sink, alongside a roll of TP, a box of tissues, and some cleaning products.

In the kitchen, she opened a tall, skinny cupboard to a vertical row of pullout shelves. The shelves contained paper napkins, condiments, and spices, all new and unused. Other cabinets held cups, cookware, and utensils. The silverware matched, the pots and pans all had bright copper bottoms, and the cups and glasses were lined up in the cupboards in even numbers, as if no one could trouble to use them.

She hummed as she worked. The sun rose, sending a warming breeze in through the screen door. The overcast had burned off, leaving a bright blue sky. Back at Paradise Shores, the campsites were close enough that one could hear the neighbors talking, but here Karen heard nothing but birdsong, wind, and surf.

When the truck was unpacked and the Airstream had started to feel more like home, Karen set her computer and files on the dinette; laid out her pens, pencils, and charts; and propped three small whiteboards against the back of the sofa. Each whiteboard represented a project, and each completed project represented a significant paycheck. She wrote a bulleted list on each board, indicating the necessary progress from start to completion.

Her first project would be the employee handbook for Ben's young company. Although most of the work could be done on the island, Karen planned to take advantage of her proximity to Savannah and drop in on Ben weekly. She also wanted to reassert herself in town so it wouldn't look like she'd been run off.

Karen gazed out at the ocean as the laptop booted. Unbelievable that this would be her office for the next four weeks. The sun, well up now, lit the deserted beach, the sand sparkling as the tide receded. A driftwood log, weathered silver gray with time, would serve as a picnic bench when she broke for lunch.

She glanced back at the screen and frowned. Her mobile Wi-Fi unit wasn't picking up a signal in this remote end of the island. Apparently, perfection had its limits. She locked the trailer, threw the laptop on the passenger seat, and headed for the village. She circled around the small shopping area, looking for someplace that might sell electronics, but nothing looked promising. She would have to drive to the mainland.

At the main highway, she turned north toward Brunswick, crossing the river and wetlands. The soaring white cables of the Lanier Bridge resembled a line of tall-masted sailboats chasing each other across the sky.

In town, she was assailed by signs trying to entice her to play the tourist. In one direction lay a seaport that predated the Declaration of Independence. In the other, the highway branched toward the Golden Isles, with shopping, restaurants, and resorts. Directly ahead, the road led to the historic HB Plantation. Faced with so many intriguing choices, Karen made a mental note to return at some point and explore the town.

She located a big-box electronics store and found a salesclerk. "I need some kind of Wi-Fi reception booster for my trailer," she said. "I think it's supposed to go on the roof."

"What kind of trailer do you have?" When she told him, the man chuckled. "I don't think that'll work. In case you haven't noticed, the Airstream has no ladder, and the outer skin will dent and scratch if a mosquito lands on it. So you'll need a scaffold to get up there."

Karen didn't see that happening. "What else would you suggest?"

"Instead of a roof mount, how about this?" He reached into a nearby display case for a box containing a device the size of a paperback. "This is an antenna. You connect it to your computer, and it pulls in a signal. Now you're in business for less than three hundred bucks."

Karen winced. She had barely arrived on the island and was already in the red. She thanked the man and completed her purchase.

Back at the trailer, she followed the instructions and was rewarded with Internet reception. She logged onto Ben's network, more determined than ever to make money, given the hole she was digging. After a couple hours of work, she would have lunch, go for a rejuvenating walk, and then dig back into her projects. Her business would fly. One way or another, good things were about to happen. She could feel it.

The phone interrupted her thoughts. "Hey Fern. How's it going?"

"Are you sitting down?"

"Why? Is something wrong?" She listened while Fern explained, and realization grew. This was why Jessie had tried to find out where Karen lived.

"So if you wouldn't mind," Fern said, "it would just be for a couple weeks—maybe three. Long enough for her to find an apartment nearby."

"Can't she stay with you, or with someone else? I'm not sure I'm comfortable having someone who I don't know stay in my RV."

"In a way you know her, being she's Frieda's kin."

"And besides," said Karen, "the trailer isn't really set up for a baby. There are probably a lot of hazards."

"You're trying to make excuses. Look, they need shelter, your trailer's empty, and I'm here to keep an eye on things. It'll work out fine and you'll feel good about helping."

Karen stood looking out the window. What a crazy idea. Why hadn't Jessie sought refuge at her mother's house in Denver? Now she knew why Jessie's phone call had felt so odd. She'd played Karen for the information, planning to go and see her, no doubt expecting Karen to give her shelter.

"Are you still there?" asked Fern.

"Let me call you back."

Karen went outside to think. Other than the fact that they had Frieda in common, there was no connection. And Karen had the envelope, but when she'd offered to mail it Jesse had practically flipped out. Well, probably the girl didn't have an address at the moment. But still. She was a stranger. Karen didn't want her living in her RV.

Like it's so special. Your precious trailer.

Karen sighed. *Don't interfere, Frieda.*

I let you live in my Roadtrek for six weeks, and that was a lot more special to me than that old fifth wheel you call home.

It's not my problem.

Sure, go on. Let that little baby head on up the road with no place to go. Maybe they can sleep in their car. There's an idea.

Dammit, Frieda. Was this your idea?

A few weeks. That's all they're asking.

Karen sighed again, put both hands on her knees, and pushed herself up. She went back in the trailer and called Fern, who was overjoyed.

"But you're responsible, Fern. Anything happens to my trailer, it's on you."

Karen hung up. She knew she should get back to work, but as usual, human drama and all its tentacles of logistics and worry were dragging her down. She went outside and sat in her beach chair, staring out to sea, trying to find her motivation for business. Instead, thoughts of Key Largo bounced around in her head. The audacity of Fern and Belle, the horror of domestic violence, and the need for refuge—Frieda, Jessie, Sunshine. On the one hand, she was happy. On the other, a virtual stranger would be sleeping in her bed, using her bathroom and kitchen, and entertaining the CRS ladies in her home. And a one-year-old would be toddling around, finding all kinds of loose things to get in trouble with. She wondered what the child looked like and felt a weight on her chest at the thought that Frieda never got to see or hold her.

The least Karen could do was let Jessie use the trailer while it was empty, until she found another place to live. And Fern, for all her arrogance, would make sure Karen's RV was well-maintained. Still, Karen decided she needed to talk with Jessie soon and get a sense of the girl. She rubbed her face and then stared out to sea, thinking of Frieda. *Are you happy now?*

A raven, riding a branch in the giant eucalyptus overhead, began to laugh.

Karen chuckled. It was too ridiculous to believe, but it made her happy nonetheless. After a while, she went inside, fired up her computer at the dinette table with a view of the Atlantic, and began to build her future.

Chapter Twenty-Five

*J*essie put the baby in the playpen and did the dishes. As she finished wiping the last spoon, there was a knock on the door. Every morning since she'd moved into Karen's trailer, that knock had occurred—the CRS ladies coming to play.

"Are we too early?" asked Patti.

"I saw a family of ducklings over by the pond this morning," said Doc, "and we thought Sunshine would enjoy seeing them."

"She's already dressed."

They strolled off down the path, the scientist and the retired firefighter holding the baby and pointing out a line of pelicans flying overhead. Jessie watched them go. She and Sunshine had lucked out. From the first day, someone was always offering food or clothing or baby clothes and toys. Not to mention they practically begged to be able to come in and play with the baby.

Later today, the ladies were coming to take her and Sunshine for a picnic on the beach. Jessie felt a little anxious. These old women were retired, their own kids long-since grown. They would expect to enjoy an adult conversation while the baby played quietly. Which would never happen. Sunshine was much too busy to let anybody complete a sentence.

And what would she say to them? She had nothing in common with the ladies. Old people didn't have much going on, which was why they were starved to have young people around. So the afternoon would be totally boring. A couple days ago, Jessie had gone with Belle to see Eleanor, but after five minutes, the older woman had fallen back asleep. Jessie didn't understand the point of the visit, except maybe that Eleanor half-smiled at the baby. It was all very sad. Jessie personally didn't want to live past sixty-five, maybe seventy, tops.

On the other hand, no matter how boring their company, it would be good to go somewhere. Jessie was beginning to develop a bad case of cabin fever.

The first couple days in the RV, in which she always awoke fearing Lenny had found her, Jessie had felt restless and unsettled. When she confessed her fears to Fern, the older woman went and bought reinforcing locks for all the windows and doors. Then, Fern took her to the hardware store and helped her install child locks on all the cabinets. Rita, the trucker lady, bought her a slow cooker for meal preparation, and Doc helped her construct a bunch of mobiles to hang in front of the windows and catch the light.

So the trailer was beginning to feel more like home. She had watered the little plants in the kitchen window—basil and thyme—and now they were thriving, and Fern and Belle lent her a laptop so she could see about restarting her classes. Most days, she sat outside at the picnic table under the awning while Sunshine napped, and she carried the baby around the camp a few times, but that was exhausting, so they didn't go far.

She had snooped around, looking for the envelope from Grandma. She hadn't found that, but she did manage to unearth a sewing machine—a total score, because Jessie was an ace seamstress. In high school she'd won a 4-H competition by sewing a winter coat, complete with three layers of underlining and interfacing.

When Patti and Doc brought Sunshine back, she gaped a happy smile at her mother. "We saw bunnies and lizards and birds," said Patti. "And she wanted to grab the ducklings and play with them."

"That's so cool. Thank you," Jessie said.

"See you down at the beach."

Jessie took the baby inside. At five minutes to ten, she answered the door to two women who, except for the fact that one was white and one black, could have been sisters. Candace, the blonde, wore blinding diamond earrings and a visor with *Pebble Beach* stitched on the edge. Margo wore a red straw hat accented with a purple and gold scarf. Gold hoops adorned her ears. Both women wore rhinestone CRS pins on their bright pastel T-shirts—or maybe they were actual diamonds.

Margo grasped the handle of a shiny new stroller with balloon tires and a sunshade with a colorful fringe. "We assumed you could use this. You can go four-wheeling with this sucker. I had it custom-made to use in beach sand, but my grandkids never visit. It's yours if you want it."

"Are you serious? This is awesome!" Jessie lowered the baby into the stroller. "Look, she loves it." The four of them set off toward the beach, Margo pushing the stroller. On the path behind them, Rita hurried to catch up. She held a shopping bag full of plastic measuring cups, bowls, and spoons to use as toys.

Down at the beach, Fern anchored an umbrella deep in the sand. Belle hurried over. "How's my baby this morning?" She bent to kiss Sunshine. Jessie lifted her out of the stroller and set her on a blanket next to a pillow and a teddy bear.

Fern gave the umbrella one last twist and wiped her hands on her shorts. "Anybody thirsty? I made a pitcher of Bloody Marys."

That was another thing Jessie had discovered about the group. They sure did like to drink. Jessie did, too, but she figured by the time you were old, you'd probably stick with iced tea or water.

The women arranged their chairs around the blankets, forming a wall in case Sunshine headed in the wrong direction. The baby toddled from chair to chair, accepting pats and hugs and fingering bracelets and buttons. Occasionally, she let herself be held.

With the ladies fawning over Sunshine, Jessie was free to enjoy herself. She inched her chair to the water's edge and dug her toes into the wet sand. A sailboat carved a path through the sparkling waters, and a pelican dove for fish. She leaned her head back and closed her eyes, lulled by the melody of birdsong and splashing water. After only a couple days in Key Largo, she already knew she never wanted to leave. With its soft, fragrant breezes and tropical beauty, Paradise Shores was unlike anyplace she'd ever been.

Of course, her experience was limited to Denver, where she had grown up in a gated, self-important community, and the outskirts of Atlanta, where she'd lived in a single-wide with her abusive boyfriend. Her situation was bad now, but there'd been a time when Lenny was good to her. They'd met while snowboarding in Colorado, Jessie on Christmas break from college and Lenny— well, Lenny was hanging out. But he'd offered to buy her an Irish coffee at the top of the lift, and they'd smoked a little pot behind the warming hut. Then she'd thrown up. He'd helped her get back down to the base and given her his number before they parted in the parking lot. She stopped by the drugstore on the way home.

Sure enough, she was pregnant, thanks to homecoming and all the partying she and her friends had enjoyed a couple months earlier. Her mother was on her practically before Jessie flushed the test strip. Sandy made her life intolerable, so Jessie called Lenny, and a week later he was out front with a U-Haul truck.

At first she was excited. Well, as much as she could be while throwing up all the way to Georgia. When they pulled in his driveway, her heart sank at the sight of his beat-to-shit trailer home, but she made the best of it.

Now that situation had gone bad, too. She was out on the streets again, this time with a baby. Honestly, sometimes she thought she was brain-damaged or something. As smart as she'd been in school, she kept messing up her life. What was she supposed to do now? Where would she go? How would she support the two of them?

"Are you Jessie?" The voice clawed into her reverie, and Jessie opened her eyes. A twig-thin woman with a huge rack stood in front of her, holding a bundle of cloth.

"Somebody said you sew. Can you fix this?" The woman unfurled a brushed suede jacket. "It doesn't fit me anymore since I got my latest boob job, and I'm heartbroken."

Jessie took the jacket, turned it inside out, and examined the seams. "Put it on, and button it."

"Right now?"

"Unless you want to wait until after I'm through with finals."

"Well, gosh no. And hi, I'm Gina." She pulled the jacket on over her swimsuit and stood obediently as Jessie tugged and pinched the fabric, assessing it.

"It needs letting out in the bodice and the shoulders, and it could be more fitted in the waist. Plus, if you want, I could do something with the cuffs. They're pretty ragged." She helped Gina out of the jacket. "I could have it for you in a couple days. At my rate and the number of hours it will take, I can do it for eighty dollars."

"I used to pay my girl ten dollars for a little job like this!"

Jessie held it out to her. "Maybe you should have her do it, then."

"All right, fine. But I want it by Thursday." Gina walked away.

"Cool." Jessie nodded and sat back down, her sunglasses hiding her shock. The old chick went for it. Eighty bucks! She fought not to smile, to laugh out loud. Fern caught her eye and gave her a subtle nod of approval.

Two hours later, after snacks and plenty of attention, Sunshine got cranky. While the baby drifted off in her playpen, Jessie checked her voice mail. Lenny had left dozens of messages, some filled with vitriol, threatening to report her for kidnapping. Then he turned maudlin and weepy, begging her to come home. The angry ones were tapering off in favor of self-righteousness.

"You know I've been working my ass off," the first one said. "It's not easy, putting you through school and taking care of the kid." Jessie scowled. All she wanted was an apology and some acknowledgment of his behavior, so they could go to counseling and work their way past this, but he sounded as if everything was her fault. Hers and the baby's.

His messages continued. "I probably should have said it sooner, but I was burning out. Work's been a bitch."

That was a laugh. If it weren't for his unemployment pittance and the occasional sale of weed, they'd be living on Jessie's thrift-store resales on Craigslist. On top of that, she kept house and took care of the baby. And worked on getting an education, so one day she could obtain a good job and make money. Lenny acted like he was the only one doing anything. She clicked on the next message and the next. He never once mentioned the fact that he gave her a black eye, and he never, ever, said the word *sorry*. He didn't ask where they were or express any worry or concern. Not that it would have made a difference.

That evening, she fed and bathed Sunshine, read her a story, and tucked her into bed. Then she warmed up a couple of pork chops Belle and Fern had given her, along with instant mashed potatoes and a green-bean casserole from Rita. She opened a bottle of Riesling that had been a gift from the ladies, poured herself a glass, and took a bite of her meal.

She was peaceful and happy here. Why couldn't she and Lenny have that? They had, when she'd first moved in with him. When she suffered with morning sickness and puked in the toilet, he'd asked about her with kindness in his voice. When the baby was born, even though he was too squeamish to be present in the delivery room, he'd sat in the waiting room all night. True, he never changed a single diaper, and he'd started complaining about all the time she spent on schoolwork, but all couples had their problems. A child added pressure, especially one that wasn't his.

She checked her voice mail again, playing the last six or seven, trying to read into his words the truth of what she should do. There was a new one—from Karen.

At first, Jessie didn't want to have to talk to the woman she'd tricked. Then she remembered Grandma's gift and called Karen right back. "Before you say anything, please understand how sorry I am, and how grateful."

"I'm doing it for your grandmother," Karen said. "How's my trailer?"

"It's great. Thanks for letting us stay. How's Georgia?"

"Peaceful. Do you have any questions about how things work?"

"No, Fern showed me.

"Good. And you know I'll be home at the end of the month, right? In about three weeks? At which time you'll need to have found another place to stay. Sorry, I know that's blunt, but the trailer's not big enough for all of us, and that's when I'm coming home."

"We're looking for a place. Everybody's keeping an eye out."

"Good," Karen said again. She seemed at a loss for words, so Jessie dove in.

"You know that envelope from Grandma you were telling me about? Is it here?"

"There's a key under the coffee tin in the first cabinet. It unlocks the outdoor storage compartment by the trailer hitch. Look there."

Jessie got off the phone in a hurry, went outside, and found a plastic file box. Inside, she found a fat envelope with her name on it. She tore it open.

Inside was a rubber-banded bundle of black-and-white photographs. In the top one, standing in front of St. Joseph's church in Dickinson, were Grandpa Russell; Grandma Frieda, holding infant Jessie in a flowing white baptismal gown; and Jessie's mom and dad. Her mother wore long, straight hair and granny glasses and a floor-length dress she'd made herself, held up by a drawstring that tied behind her neck. Her dad, skinny and with lots of hair, wore a three-piece suit, complete with vest.

Jessie fell back on the bed. She needed money, not pictures. Maybe it was Grandma's way of trying to get them all back together again, but Jessie would never return home. She would never speak to her mother again. Her dad had sided with Sandy, so Jessie was done with him, too.

She put the envelope back in the compartment, where it could stay for all eternity as far as she was concerned.

Chapter Twenty-Six

*A*t the end of the seventh day on the island, Karen emerged from the trailer like a hermit coming out of her cave. Her cupboards were bare, so she drove to the village for dinner at the café, to be followed by a trip to the grocery store. Windows rolled down, she took in deep breaths of the salt air, happy to be out and away from her self-imposed isolation.

Every day on Jekyll Island consisted of eating, sleeping, and working. The only variation was a daily walk, at which time she waved at Ida twice. Once on the way out, and once on the way in. That was the extent of her social life.

It was fun for the first few days. She'd really made progress—on everything except the app, which was proving to be more of a hassle than she'd expected. And she hadn't heard from Curt, which disappointed her, but guilt over New Year's Eve kept her from calling him.

At a patio restaurant on the wharf, she ordered shrimp creole and a salad, along with a glass of wine, and enjoyed her meal in the company of a half dozen tourists. For an introvert, it was enough, and her spirits lifted, but she missed Curt. She'd made gentle overtures, texting him photos of island sunsets, live oaks draped with moss, and the glittering coastline in the brilliance of sunrise, but he hadn't responded with so much as a thumbs-up or happy face. Maybe that was the way it was supposed to be. For all their chemistry, she respected that he had a life in North Dakota, and she had her work. Maybe he was as independent as she was. Maybe they weren't meant to be anything more than old friends, getting together from time to time for hot sex and fond memories.

She paid her bill and parked in front of the grocery store.

You can pick things up with him after the work is done, she told herself, pushing a basket through the deli section. *This is only temporary. You're a big girl. Suck it up.*

And the work was paying off. Already her commitments were expanding. She had contract agreements stretching into the next ninety days. Soon her bank account would expand as well. She was accomplishing so much. The degree to which she could focus, living alone in the trailer with no social life, was thrilling. It was also somewhat depressing.

Back at the trailer, she unloaded the groceries and sat down on the sofa with her phone and another glass of wine. She edited a photo of last night's sunset and began trying to compose a text message.

You should be here with me.

She frowned and hit *delete.*

Miss you.

DELETE.

Thinking of you.

DELETE.

This is every night from my place. Not bragging ;)

DELETE. DELETE. DELETE.

Hope you are well.

DELETE.

In the end, she sent it without words, hoping he would respond with some kind of clue.

Chapter Twenty-Seven

*C*urt was having the best sex of his life, and it was about to kill him.

Erin went back to UC Davis right after the New Year's Day debacle, and right afterward, Maddie practically moved in. She had a tendency to run around the house wearing his T-shirts with nothing underneath, her taut, smooth flesh calling to him, her thick, jet-black hair with nary a gray strand falling to his chest as she sat astride him last night, rocking, rocking—

He felt himself grow hard in spite of what must surely be sprained limbs and slipping discs. Maddie lay beside him in the morning light, her hair arrayed on the pillow, her face innocent and clear. So young. He calculated, and proximity to his daughter's birth year came up fast. He grimaced and went flaccid.

In the kitchen, he poured a cup of coffee and drank it black, staring out the window at the sun coming up over the steaming gray shingles of the barn roof. His mouth tasted bad from last night when, mellowed out from after-dinner cognac, he'd smoked a cigar while they sat on the veranda and looked at the stars. Maddie had crawled into his lap, talking about Hemingway and calling him Papa.

Seemed okay last night. This morning, not so much.

Today they were going to play racquetball. Since everybody would be in church, they'd have the courts to themselves. She meant to sharpen up his game after that first lamentable effort. Curt had held his own for a while but then flopped on the bench, gaping like a landed fish and trying to understand. After years of trekking around the Badlands with students, he'd thought he was in the best shape of his life. His friends couldn't keep up with him. And yet, he felt ready to keel over at the feet of his young lover.

And the dancing—Maddie would go out every night if not for him. The other night, he'd seen one of his professor colleagues heading for a lecture on increased intuitive awareness in the aging brain, but Curt had had to duck the guy and get home to Maddie, who wanted to try out some new edible lube she'd bought.

That was a highlight.

But most nights, she stuck around Curt's house, watching stuff on her laptop while he worked in his office. It distracted him, having her there, but she seemed to want to be around him all the time. She sat in the big chair in the corner of his office, her bare legs tucked up under her bare bottom, staring at her computer screen. She had to be aware of the neural traffic jam she was creating in his head. His work was falling behind.

And hers—when did she study? She had a dissertation to finish. It would mean the difference between a tenure-track position and the life of an adjunct. The difference between a profession and a job. Yet he rarely saw her work on it. The most time she spent on her computer was doing social media and ordering stuff from Amazon.

It's like living with a teenager, he thought. He poured another cup of coffee and sat at the kitchen table, staring into the near distance.

He heard her making noise upstairs, and she called to him. When he didn't answer, the shower started in the upstairs bathroom. Eventually she came down, dressed for the gym. She eyeballed his faded jeans and T-shirt.

"You're not coming?"

"I got a call from an old friend. I need to check on her." He got up to pour her a cup of coffee. She went in for a hug, and he held her close, resting his chin on her head.

Maddie looked up at him, concern in her eyes. "Who is she?"

"My friend's elderly aunt."

"Oh. Okay."

They sat in silence, him reading the paper and her drinking coffee and checking her phone. "Hey, you know what?" she said. "The rodeo ends today. So this afternoon, let's go see the bull-riding finals."

He folded the paper. Glanced out the window.

"You don't want to."

"It's not that I don't want to. I just have a ton of stuff to do before tomorrow. Can you get a couple of your friends to meet you there instead?" He felt like her old dad, trying to find ways to amuse a bored child.

"I was hoping you'd come with me. Are we still on for tonight?"

"Sure," he said. "I'll defrost some leftover pork chops and open up a can of sauerkraut."

"Hmm. Maybe I'll see what my friends are doing. See you later, okay?"

He pecked her on the lips, not giving her a chance to start anything. When the door closed, he stood alone in his kitchen. The sauerkraut ploy had worked, but now silence settled over him like a cold blanket. He started the dishwasher, and its familiar swishing and humming helped restore a sense of normalcy. He straightened the living room and cleaned out the fireplace, brushing the ashes into the metal bucket.

He knew Maddie was too young for him, but over the years he'd dated plenty of local women his age, and none compelled him. He sank into the couch cushions and stared at the fireplace. It stared back, implacable.

He rolled his head around on his neck, releasing the tension. Soon, he'd travel to Spain for a short visit. The administration wanted to meet with him and talk about what to expect when he arrived later in the summer. He needed to get things ready for the year ahead, and once there, he'd probably look up Isabel. They'd had fun that last time. Sure, she smoked, and she was loud, and she was a night owl, but she was closer to his age. Well, forty, maybe. Maybe they could pick up where they left off, once he settled in Barcelona.

The idea didn't excite him.

He glanced at the clock. Marie would be home from church by now, and he'd promised to stop by. He wished he could climb on his Harley and tear around the flatlands for a couple of hours, but the weather wasn't good for it, and besides, he'd promised to bring her some jam.

***

Curt tucked his sunglasses in his breast pocket and limped down the sidewalk toward Aunt Marie's front door. After a cold night of rain and sleet, the skies had cleared, and the sun reflected blindingly from every surface. Moisture dripped from the eaves, from the ancient branches of the tall spruce, and from the holly bushes next to the house.

Standing on her porch, holding the screen door open, Aunt Marie waited, a quiet smile on her pale, lined face. He followed her through the door, the floor squeaking beneath his feet. Inside, the air was thick with the aroma of baking. "I made a coffee cake this morning. I'll cut you some."

"Just a small piece." He handed her a couple jars of his renowned chokecherry jam and sat down at her kitchen table, wincing.

"You have a hitch in your git-along."

"Comes and goes." Curt pointed at the purple bruise on Aunt Marie's elbow. "What happened to you?"

"It's nothing."

He savored the warm cake, melted through with brown-sugar crumble. "How are you managing these days? Everything good?"

"As much as can be expected," she said. "What about that limp of yours?"

"Too much fieldwork."

"In January?"

When he didn't answer, Aunt Marie shrugged. "In my case, it was ice on the sidewalk. It's not the first time, and probably won't be the last." She looked down at her table and found a chip in the Formica to worry with her fingertip. Her nails were neatly filed, and her knobby joints reflected her age.

"Marie."

"That's my name. Don't wear it out." She looked up, smiling.

The childhood taunt made him laugh. "Do you need me to do anything around here?"

"Like what?"

He looked around the kitchen. "I'm pretty good at replacing lightbulbs."

"I can do that myself."

"You need a new roof. I can find a contractor for you."

"I'll wait until Karen comes back."

"You sure she is?"

"I believe so," said Aunt Marie. "It gets hot in Florida."

He carried their empty plates to the sink and rinsed them.

Aunt Marie said, "I told her if she didn't, I'd get distracted and maybe fall or something. I laid it on pretty thick. You know how stubborn she is."

"Yeah." He dried his hands.

"To tell the truth, it is getting harder." Aunt Marie held out her coffee cup, and Curt filled it. "Lorraine and Jim have been hounding me enough that I guess I'll move into their cottage."

"That's smart. You'll be a stone's throw from each other."

Marie's gaze lingered about the kitchen. "This house is all I have left of Lena. Everybody's dying."

"You seem to work through it, though," he said. "You're always busy."

"People stay busy out of desperation. Anyway, I'm slowing down. I'm not so busy anymore, because there's less and less I can do. My fingers don't work as well, and I can't see. I've got a big magnification light where I sew, but aside from that, it's a chore. I already decided I wasn't going to put in a garden this year. I'm too darned old to be getting down on my knees to pull weeds."

"I can build you a container garden on the porch of the new place. I'm good with drip lines."

"That would be appreciated. Then I could work outside from a chair. No more crawling around in the dirt," she said.

"All right." He rubbed his aching leg. "Did you tell Karen you're moving?"

"She didn't want to hear it."

"Typical." He leaned down and kissed her on the cheek. "Call me when you're ready to move, and I'll come over with some guys and help."

That evening, Curt fried a hamburger for dinner, but it didn't have much flavor, so he threw half of it in the garbage. Then he poured himself a drink, bundled up, and went outside to sit on the porch in the dark and cold. Christmas lights still adorned a neighboring ranch house. In the distance, a cow mooed. Curt took a sip of bourbon and flirted with the idea of lighting the cigar, but the thought reminded him of Madison, and he let it be.

The temperature suited his mood. He watched his breath fog out in the frigid air. Did Karen know what was going on with her aunt? While she worked her ass off, did she even see it? Deny it all you want—nobody lived forever. Yet she was out there in Florida, running around trying to start a new business like she was still a kid. He thought about answering her texts—she'd sent a lot of them lately, but they were chatty and superficial little blurbs like, "How are you?" and "How's everything in ND?" Nothing that made him feel like it mattered if he responded.

Eventually, the cold was too much. Curt eased his gimpy leg around and levered himself up. He went inside and lit the fire, wondering why he was still here. Erin had already told him she would remain in Davis after graduation. Aunt Marie was in good hands. There were plenty of people standing in line to take over his professorship. When he got back from his year in Barcelona, he could retire. Do a little contract work, enough to write off travel expenses.

He stood warming his backside against the flames, a glass of whiskey in his hand. The fling with Maddie had been fun, and educational, too, because now he remembered why he liked being in his fifties, and it didn't have anything to do with racquetball or late-night barhopping. He was happy with his quiet life, living on his family's land in the farmhouse he'd grown up in. North Dakota was home. He loved it, loved the openness and the wind and the rolling fields, the deep rich smell of turned soil and the fragrance of rain on the dry earth. The warmth of the people who made their lives here. As long as he could get away once in a while, his little farm was as close to perfect as a place could be.

And as much as he hated to admit it, he was growing old. It didn't scare him, but there were ups and downs to that reality. For the most part, he was satisfied with the way his life had gone, and he was ready for new adventures. He looked forward to experiencing Spain, but there was only one woman he wanted to enjoy it with.

But she didn't want him.

Chapter Twenty-Eight

*J*essie bit a thread and held up the floaty summer dress, a castoff from the back of Gina's closet. A week ago, when she'd delivered her updated jacket, the old lady was so jazzed she went through her whole wardrobe looking for other things to rehab. Jessie went back to the RV with her arms full of work, but Gina also gave her the dress, a couple of blouses, and a coat. Jessie would fix those up and sell them.

She clipped a couple of leftover threads from the dress, a gauzy pastel that would be perfect for evening cocktails. After narrowing the back with a couple of strategically placed darts and adding decorative stitching at the neckline, the dress was ready to be sold on Jessie's new website. This afternoon when the light was right, she'd get Doc to come down to the beach with her fancy camera. The first time they did a photo shoot, Patti had arranged a couple of Adirondack chairs, their white paint peeling to bare wood, at the waterline. Lit by the rose-colored hues of the setting sun, Doc captured the flowing lines of a floor-length swimsuit cover-up that Jessie enhanced with spaghetti straps and buttons shaped like Japanese fighting fish. When she'd sold it for sixty-five bucks, her business was launched. After that, the three of them partnered on all the photography. Jessie wanted to give them a cut, but Doc shook her head. "I enjoy it, and it's good practice."

"Like you need it," Patti said. "She'll never tell you this, but she's won awards. Her work is in galleries."

"Come on." Doc pulled her field hat low over her eyes.

Jessie laughed. She'd never seen Doc blush before.

When Sunshine awoke, Jessie changed and fed her and then pushed the stroller through the campground, stopping to say hello to people. At the clubhouse, she found the CRS ladies working on crafts. Fern was whittling, Belle had a coloring book and several dozen specialty pens and pencils, and Patti was building a bird feeder made of empty tuna cans. Margo and Candace had a quilt spread between them, stitching from opposite ends.

Jessie left Sunshine with them and ran back to the RV for a blouse, her next project. At first, she'd had to borrow sewing notions from the ladies, but after her first two sales, she could afford her own, which she kept in a shoe box.

When she returned, Belle was holding Sunshine, who basked in the attention. Jessie sat down and got to work, as happy as she could remember being. She'd never had the company of a circle of women like this. They were funny and generous, and every day the age difference seemed less and less important. She settled in, repairing a cuff that had begun to unravel.

The clubhouse door opened, and Rita, the trucker, came in. She went around the group, complimenting the various projects. Then she leaned down near Jessie. "Can we talk, outside, privately?" she said in a low voice. The other women kept their eyes on their projects.

"Sure." Jessie laid her sewing on the chair and followed Rita out. They sat on a bench under a shady clump of palm trees. "What's up?"

Rita sat up straight, hands on her knees, perched on the edge of the bench. "There's something I need to say to you." She looked away from Jessie, and her jaw muscle twitched. "Back when I was working, I was assigned to a county court school, you know, where they teach kids in juvie."

"Okay."

Rita cleared her throat. "I taught English and creative writing for ten years at this facility, and I never felt like I was in danger. They were just kids. Troubled, but still forming, and I wanted to help them find a better path."

"Good for you. Teachers can change a kid's life for the better," Jessie said. A breeze rustled the palm fronds overhead.

"So they say. Anyway, it was a tough environment. I knew some defense moves. The faculty were all trained and aware of how to protect ourselves, so I was careful, but you can't think of self-defense twenty-four seven. Day in and day out, it was just teaching. I guess you let your guard down. It's natural.

"But then we got this new kid. Well, not a kid. He was, like, six feet; I'd guess two-twenty. He was like a man. And he used to look at me."

Jessie felt ill at ease. Rita had to be fifty, at least, yet she seemed so vulnerable right now.

"One day he followed me into the ladies' room. I guess I wasn't paying attention, and he trapped me there. Even before I could scream, he broke my nose and then shoved me face first into the sinks and raped me from behind."

"Oh my God."

"Yeah, pretty much." Rita still looked straight ahead.

"I'm so sorry," Jessie repeated. She struggled to know what to say. The two of them sat quietly for a few moments.

Rita cleared her throat again. "I was a mess for a couple years. Finally my brother, Ernesto, taught me to drive his truck, and then I bought my own. Now I'm a long-haul trucker. I go all across the country. I have a sleeper, like a little RV, with a kitchen and everything. It's my home."

"And you're okay now?"

"Yes."

"Good." Jessie reached over to give Rita a tentative pat on the forearm.

"I was suicidal, a nutcase, for years. It shouldn't have happened. I should have known better." Rita hunched her shoulders, her arms propped on her knees. "So I'm asking you to think long and hard before you go back to him."

"Why would—"

Rita whirled on her. "It's not worth it, Jessie. And the baby... Jesus Christ."

Jessie let out a breath. The ladies must all be talking about her going back to Lenny. She hadn't mentioned it to anyone, but she had considered it, because she needed a place to live for a couple of years. If only she knew this thing with Lenny was an aberration. If only she could see the future. She turned to Rita, a fake smile on her face. "Don't worry."

"I will be worrying. I have to leave tomorrow. I'll be back on the road when you do whatever you're going to do, and I won't be able to help."

"I'll be careful."

"Promise you won't go back to him."

Jessie stared at her hands.

"Fine." Rita jumped up and stalked away, not even going back into the clubhouse. When Jessie stood up, she was shaking.

"You look like you've seen a ghost," said Belle.

Jessie took Sunshine and buried her face in the baby's neck.

Chapter Twenty-Nine

*O*n Monday morning, Karen was reading the *New York Times* on her laptop while she ate breakfast. Messages kept popping up in the lower corner of the screen. Peggy wanted her to return to California to interview with a board of directors, Ursula had another project, and a couple of Ben's supervisors needed to meet with her. She told Ben's people that she'd be in Savannah in a few hours and would see them then. She showered and dressed, loaded her small suitcase into her truck, and headed for the big city.

At Savannah Health Solutions, she waved at the receptionist and stuck her head into Ben's office to say hello. At her own temporary cubicle, Karen unpacked her briefcase and lined up her files. A voice boomed down the hall, and she feared it was Ted. They hadn't spoken since she'd torn up his check and ran off with the diamond earrings.

But it was only a supervisor arriving for his meeting with Karen. The hours rolled by in a sequence of employees and note-taking as she learned more about the operations of SHS.

By noontime, she was famished. She grabbed her purse and walked with Ben a couple of blocks north to a rooftop restaurant overlooking the city. In the shade of umbrellas, they ate and talked shop, with Ben excited about another project he wanted Karen to take on.

"I was talking with Diane a couple days ago. She's looking to expand. She needs my help, and it would be a great opportunity for you." Ben bit into a shrimp po'boy. "You've got her contact info, right?"

Karen nodded. Diane Florentine, one of the investors she had pitched, ran a caregiver agency with franchises all over the state of Georgia. On one hand, it was a great lead. On the other, the work would soon be too much. Karen would either have to start hiring help or declining business. The HR app seemed dead in the water. She couldn't figure out where to go next with it.

"You could open an office here in Savannah." Ben was a realist. He could see what she was mulling over.

"It's tempting."

"You'd love it here. There's plenty to do. The people are great. You could put down new roots." He looked past her and grinned. "Hey, look who's here."

Karen was reaching for her glass of sweet tea when a couple of strong hands gripped her shoulders from behind. She froze.

Ted pulled out the chair next to her and sat down. "Heard you were here. Thought I'd come up and say hi." He turned to Karen with a smile. "Hello, Gorgeous."

"Hello, Ted." Karen flushed, remembering the things they'd done to each other in the candlelit darkness of his rooftop penthouse.

Ben said, "I thought you were in Hong Kong."

"Got back last night. Met with the guy who started Chinese Facebook. He wants to partner on some stuff with us." Ted ran a hand over his mustache, smoothing it. "So, you freezing me out or what?"

"I'm sorry?" Karen said.

"You must be mad at me. You never called."

"Ted." She narrowed her eyes in warning.

He peered at her. "How come you're not wearing my earrings?"

Ben grinned. "You two need some privacy?"

"Excuse me." She folded her cloth napkin, exited the dining area, and disappeared around the kitchen area. A discreet walkway took her to the far end of the rooftop, well out of sight of the restaurant. There she found seclusion, and the chance to gather her thoughts.

Of course she had expected to have to face him again. She'd assumed he would pretend nothing happened, and her shame would be internal and private. Instead, true to form, Ted was having his fun, announcing her humiliation to anyone within earshot. In this case, going so far as to take over a business conversation with her client.

And Ben, laughing, as if he were delighted.

She stood straighter and took a deep breath. She would go back to the table and explain she had an urgent phone call and would see them both later. Karen straightened her jacket and reminded herself she was a grown woman. Hopefully, by the time she returned to the table, Ted would have ridden his high horse out of there, but if he hadn't, she would be polite and cool.

She turned around, and there he stood, hands in pockets, head lowered, a guilty grin on his face.

"You doin' anything this afternoon?" he asked.

"Yes, I'm working. I have a full afternoon and, as a matter of fact, was just leaving. Nice to see you." She forced a smile and tried to walk past him.

"So that means you don't want to go to Buenos Aires with me?"

"No, thank you."

"Do the tango? I bet you'd be good at that." He held his arms in the classic position and shook his narrow hips.

She stifled a smile. "No."

"Okay, but, well, I also want to apologize."

"You had to chase me across the roof to tell me that?"

"I'd chase you anywhere, for no reason at all," he said. "But I would like a minute."

She folded her arms.

"I didn't mean to embarrass you."

"Don't flatter yourself."

"I enjoyed our evening very much, and I wished I coulda taken you with me to Hong Kong the next day. I know it bothered you that I ran off like that."

She groaned inwardly. The man was ridiculous. "Fine. Great. Now please move."

"One more thing." He held up his hands in a gesture that was half traffic cop, half conciliatory. "I know you were pissed about the app, but it wasn't ever going to be worth anything."

"It was to me," she said.

"But commercially, it's a nonstarter. Apps are all over the place now. Little kids're making them. You had a good idea, but it was five years too late."

"Thanks so much for clarifying."

"I'm trying to be straight with you."

"Then why the contract? And why leave that tiny little check? It was an insult."

He lowered his hands. "Worse than if I just left the earrings on the nightstand the next morning?"

Karen looked away. Contract or not, she'd felt like a whore. And then she'd kept them. She closed her eyes.

188

He grasped her gently by the arms. "Hey, listen. I screwed up, okay? I'm sorry."

She nodded.

"Something else. I had my guy do some research after I got back from Hong Kong. He said you could build that app yourself at a couple of DIY websites. You could probably look around and find one already made."

"I did look, and there's nothing like it anywhere."

"So maybe it's not feasible."

"That can't be true," Karen said. "In my own situation, that app would let me do the work of ten people—while I'm sleeping. Without it, I can't grow my business. I'll be plugging along in my little trailer forever, working myself to death and staying poor."

"Then try this." He scribbled something on a business card. "Here's their website. It won't cost that much, and they'll copyright it for you."

"Really?"

"Yes."

"Thank you, Ted." When she reached for the card, he took her hand, raised it to his lips, and kissed it. Then he turned and walked away.

She stood there, holding the card, knowing he would always be her friend.

When she returned to the office, she opened an account on the Do It Yourself app-development website, submitted her specs, including application for copyright, and paid the analysis fee. The site confirmed her payment and promised to deliver a preliminary assessment within seventy-two hours.

That afternoon, she drove back over the bridge to Jekyll Island, the yachts below gleaming in the late afternoon sunlight. She was pleased with her work, but she was tired of her singleminded focus, and felt the need for company. She thought she might drop in on Ida but dismissed that thought. Except for the occasional friendly wave, the older woman kept to herself—two introverts living next door to each other.

Instead of going home, Karen headed for the historic district. She dawdled past the millionaire mansions and the sprawling lawns of the Jekyll Island Club and pulled up in front of the island bookstore. Inside, she wandered the aisles. Every cover that attracted her ended up being a romance novel. Her conversation with Ted had upset her equilibrium. His masculinity and self-assurance had reawakened the need in her. She picked up another novel and stared at the cover without seeing it. What the hell was going on with Curt anyway? Why hadn't he answered any of her texts? Sure, she'd been standoffish but not rude or anything. It wasn't like she'd told him to leave her alone. Besides, if nothing else, she'd made overtures. It didn't make sense.

On the other hand, maybe he was shrugging her off. Maybe he'd found someone else. She knew what it was like back in Dickinson. Women flocked around Curt like sea gulls around a fishing boat.

And she'd been neglecting him, doing the workaholic thing as usual. Same old story, she thought. My special brand of magic applied to a relationship.

It was part of the reason her marriage had ended—neglect. Apparently she would never learn, and for the rest of her life, she would spend her evenings alone.

At the register, the woman smiled at the stack of romance novels. "Looks like you're a fan," she said.

"It's more like I need to study," Karen said. She left the store with a bagful of paperbacks.

At the trailer, Karen changed into sweats and went down to the waterline. The shoreline was deserted as far as she could see, and no footprints marred the smooth sand. She walked on the beach at sunset, as romantic a scene as a person could ever hope for, and yet she was alone. Peach, pink, and purple hues brushed the clouds, changing by the minute, and the setting sun lit the ocean with gold. Karen took a dozen new photos and trudged back up the slope to her trailer.

She poured a tall glass of wine and started a smooth-jazz playlist on her iPod. As much as she appreciated time alone to focus on her work, tonight the solitude felt leaden.

Maybe Curt hadn't dumped her. Maybe he was waiting for her to make a move. After all, she was the one who'd run off to Florida and Georgia.

She scrolled through tonight's photos, chose the best one, and composed a text.

I'll only be here another week. Come see me.

DELETE.

I'll be here another week. Come see me?

DELETE.

I miss

DELETE.

She took another slug of wine. *I'll be here another week. It would be great to see you.* She crossed her fingers and clicked *send*.

Outside, clouds rolled in from the east. Karen opened a package of ground beef into a frying pan. While it browned, she chopped onions and tomatoes, grated cheddar cheese, and heated corn tortillas. When the tacos were ready, she set the table, closing the curtains against the darkness. The meal reminded her of California. Maybe when this was all over, she'd go back to Orange County. Peggy would throw her plenty of work. The thought didn't do anything to lift her gloom.

She finished dinner, cleaned up the kitchen, and opened one of the new romance novels. This one, the first in a series, was about a woman leaving her law practice and buying a fixer-upper named Annalise, a decrepit mansion on a tropical island. The story seemed the height of impracticality, yet Karen was soon riveted. Hadn't she done the same thing, in a sense? Leaving everything behind and starting a new life on a shoestring? She drained her wineglass and went into the kitchen for a refill, glancing at her phone for any sign of a text message arriving.

What if Curt called back? What if he accepted her invitation to visit?

She would love it.

She felt hot—either from the novel or the wine. Yes, he would definitely be welcome in her bed.

The wind picked up, coming in off the Atlantic, rocking the trailer. Thunder rumbled in the distance, and then raindrops fell—softly at first, then hitting the roof in such profusion it sounded like pebbles landing. In the deluge, Karen almost missed the sound of her phone ringing.

"You want company?" His sexy gravel voice was deep and compelling.

She smiled into the phone. "How soon can you get here?"

***

The next morning, Curt strode down the hall of the geology building, whistling a Fleetwood Mac tune and inhaling the aroma of freshly brewed coffee. He tapped on his boss's door.

Dan looked up from a pile of paper. "You're looking chipper."

"I wanted to let you know I'll be gone next week."

"Is Madison going to cover your classes?"

"I'll probably ask one of my other assistants."

"Good idea. She's been moping around the halls like a twelve-year-old girl." Dan shook his head. "I warned you."

"Yeah, I should talk to her."

"Saw her in the cafeteria."

"Thanks." Curt found Maddie frowning at a thick textbook propped in front of her and writing in a three-ring binder. When he pulled out a chair, she closed the book and started packing up.

"Wait. Can you give me a second?"

"I have a class." But she stayed.

Curt ran a hand through his hair, trying to think of how to say it.

"Don't bother," she said. "I know how things are."

"You do?"

"Do you think I'm stupid?"

He put on his most earnest face. "I didn't mean to hurt you."

"Don't give yourself that much credit." Maddie fastened her backpack. "We had fun, but you're too old for me."

Curt grimaced. "The thing is, we're at different places in our careers, our lives, everything. You're at the very start of yours, while I'm—"

"Done." She stood.

"I was going to say my life is changing in ways I'm still figuring out…"

"Keep telling yourself that. See ya, Professor."

Regret mixed with relief as Curt watched her walk away. Then he hurried back to his office to book a Saturday flight to Georgia.

Chapter Thirty

*K*aren put on lipstick and brushed her hair. She turned this way and that, inspecting the light summer dress she'd picked up in the Keys, wondering if it hugged her curves too tightly. She considered changing but didn't have many choices. Besides, Curt would be here soon.

Her stomach churned from nervousness. She tried to think about what would happen when he arrived. She would give him a tour of the trailer—that would take two minutes—and suggest that place on the wharf for dinner.

But that was nerves talking. All she really wanted was to get him into bed.

She wandered around, looking for things to clean, but the place gleamed like a new coin. She'd hidden her whiteboards, stashed her folders, and stuck her file boxes in a storage space under the bed. She didn't intend to take them out again for the next few days.

Tires crunched in the gravel driveway, and a new black Corvette pulled in. Heart pounding, Karen stepped outside. Curt unfolded himself from the low-slung seat and leaned against the car, staring at her with a squint, as if he were studying a mirage.

She caught her breath. He wore a T-shirt and Levis, his long legs ending in a pair of attractively beat-up cowboy boots. He removed his reflective aviators, tucked them in the pocket of his shirt, and opened his arms.

She walked toward him slowly, incredulous that he was really there. When she reached him, he leaned down and pressed his lips against hers, muffling her words. She kissed him back with equal fervor, and he groaned. "Wait a second."

He reached inside the car and brought out a wide-brimmed hat with a long blue scarf wrapped around the band. "I thought you could use this."

"My hat." She clasped it to her head as he wrapped his arms around her.

"Let's go inside," he said, his voice rumbling in her ear.

She led him up the step and through the door. Without a word, he grabbed her by the waist and pressed her against the kitchen counter. His hands ran up and down her back and hips, his touch hot through the thin fabric of her dress. Then his hands slipped under her hem, and she was the one who moaned. He trailed hot kisses along her jawline and throat, and when he paused, she led him to the bedroom. She tossed her hat across the room, and when she turned back to him, he grabbed her by the shoulders and pressed his mouth hard against hers. He turned her around and unzipped her dress, letting it fall to the floor, his hands roaming. Her bra fell open, and she gasped as he kissed her breasts, first one and then the other. She unzipped his Levis, sliding them down over his hips, the fabric catching on his erection. They fell onto the bed, skin against skin, his hands burning her. She wanted to kiss and taste every inch of him, and for him to do the same to her, yet she couldn't wait another second to feel him inside her.

On his knees, he balanced over her. Her nails sank into him as she pulled him down onto her. He covered her, blocking the light, his hot breath singeing the skin of her neck, her lips. His body moved, pushing her. She closed her eyes and moaned, feeling the rhythm, rocking beneath him until she began to float in time, losing any sense of up or down, losing herself in him as she began climbing, lost in sensation. And when she had peaked and peaked again and finally began to slip back to the present, she became conscious of her breathing and her heartbeat, both slowing, leaving her with the greatest sense of peace. She opened her eyes and found him looking into hers. Then he smiled, and his grin turned into laughter, and she laughed with him, caught up in his delight.

"Oh my God, Karen." He wrapped her in his arms and held her, still chuckling.

She pressed her cheek against his chest, closed her eyes, and savored the warmth of his skin. She breathed in his cologne, a woodsy fragrance with a hint of citrus. She must have dozed, because when she next noticed the light in the bedroom, it had changed to the grays of dusk. One of his arms encircled her shoulders. The other was flung upward, resting on his pillow as if in celebration. He slept quietly, his mouth closed, his lips curved as if smiling in his sleep. With tenderness, she reached over to brush a strand of dark hair from his eyes.

He woke, grasped her hand, and kissed her wrist. "You're here."

"You're here." She sat up, raising the sheet to cover her breasts. Smiling, he pulled it back down and touched her breasts, cupping their weight and squeezing the nipples gently. She closed her eyes. "We should get up."

"I already am." He pulled back the sheet to reveal his erection.

"You're insatiable," she exclaimed.

Laughing, he turned her around so her back was to him and slid inside her warmth while using his fingers to pleasure her.

When they finished, he held her in his arms, his face against her cheek, his front against her back. Lost in her own thoughts, Karen wondered if she was fooling herself when she proclaimed that life without him was possible, that she belonged anywhere in the world where he was not, or that her work, which kept them apart, even mattered. Making love with Curt restored something to her psyche, balanced her. She felt the greatest sense of peace.

She half turned, to be able to face him, and touched his lips with her index finger. He smiled and pretended to bite it.

"Hungry?"

"Starved." He rolled out of bed and held his hand toward her. She took it, and naked, they padded to the kitchen. He opened the refrigerator, studying its contents and letting the cool air out. "Nuts and berries? Is that it?"

She elbowed him aside and came up with a handful of provisions. Sitting on the couch, they polished off a box of gourmet crackers slathered with a tub of pâté and washed it down with a bottle of wine. As Karen took her last sip, she saw him eyeing her. She set down her glass and reached for him, and he knelt on the floor between her knees. She twined her fingers through his hair, smiling at the idea that she could even consider coming again, and then the smile turned into an *O*, and her head fell back.

Afterward, they lay on the sofa, fitted together like a couple of spoons. Karen rested her head against his bicep, the length of his body warming her from shoulder to calf. They fit perfectly, her backside tucked against his abdomen, her back against his chest. "I can't believe you're here," she said.

"I can't believe you invited me."

Eventually, they dressed and walked down to the beach. The moon rose, painting a glittering path to the horizon over a peaceful Atlantic.

***

In the morning, he awoke when Karen slipped out of bed. She pulled on a robe and tiptoed into the kitchen. Moments later, he heard the coffeepot begin burbling, followed by the beep of her computer starting up.

He rolled over onto his back, laced his fingers behind his head, and studied the room. A scarf hung from a light sconce, and three small whiteboards leaned against the opposite wall, but nothing else personalized the small space.

Of course it was temporary, but it seemed too austere. He'd never seen the inside of any home she'd lived in. When she returned from California, she'd stayed with Aunt Marie. Then she drove to Florida in her fifth wheel, and now this. For all their closeness, Curt didn't fully understand this mature version of the girl on whom he'd had a crush in high school—no, it was more than a crush. He knew that now.

But after all the years apart, they'd both changed. He wanted to know her better—to fully understand her—and a person's home would be a good start, but the Airstream revealed little.

He'd have to work harder.

In the quiet of the morning, he heard her fingers tapping against the keys, then silence, then the sound of a heavy mug setting down.

"Karen?"

A chair scraped the floor. Then she entered the room, stood by his side of the bed, and dropped her robe. He drew in a breath, slid over, and pulled back the blankets so she could climb in. He reached for her breasts and ran his hands, warm from sleep, up and down her thighs and hips.

They were slower this time, with him moving gently to her rhythms as she guided him to give her what she needed. Afterward, they lay quietly, snuggled under the warm blankets. When Karen traced his lips, he kissed her fingers then grasped her hand and held it to his chest. He didn't say anything. He knew what she was thinking.

* * *

But he was wrong. Karen was thinking of another man she'd loved, a man who'd pledged to love her forever—her ex-husband.

In the early years, they'd loved each other with the passion of youth. They saved enough money for their first house and joyfully made love in every room. They celebrated their advancements at work and took vacations together. Sex with Steve was hot and frequent, and she'd quickly gotten pregnant, and they'd celebrated, delirious with happiness, until the first miscarriage. The cycle repeated itself, and after each tragedy, they experienced shock, heartbreak, recovery, and a tentative reaching out for each other—but with each death, the scar tissue thickened over her heart. Eventually their relationship became platonic, neither willing to risk the heartbreak. They drifted away from each other, and he found solace elsewhere.

She no longer felt anger over his infidelity; the grief had receded. At this age, Karen was more adept at navigating life's deadly shoals. Her challenge now was to begin again, to renew herself. She thought that with Curt, she might have a chance, but it would require her to trust him, to give herself over to him completely, and for him to accept that at this point in her life, she needed to be her own person. If he was secure in himself, they could grow alongside each other. She thought he was. She hoped he was, but time would tell.

Karen sighed.

"I feel the same way," Curt said. "Making love with you is unbelievable. You're amazing. We're so good together."

She hugged him, glad he wasn't a mind reader.

Curt pulled her close, and they fell back asleep, skin to skin but a million miles apart.

Hours later, they awakened in each other's arms. He leaned up on one elbow, his other arm flung across her rib cage.

"Hmm?"

"It's almost ten. Assuming we get vertical sometime today, what do you want to do?"

Karen laced her fingers across her waist, thinking. "There's a historic district, bike rentals, beaches—whatever you want."

"Golf?"

"Three full eighteens. But I haven't played yet."

"We'll have to remedy that." He moved his arm and kissed her belly, his whiskers making her laugh. Then he moved lower, and she stopped laughing.

Chapter Thirty-One

*I*t was time. Lenny was supposed to call at ten.

Candace and Margo had promised to watch Sunshine for a couple of hours. Now Jessie headed for the gazebo at the beach, glad to see it was deserted. She pulled her phone out of her back pocket and climbed atop the picnic table. The capricious wind rippled across the bay, appearing and disappearing, leaving the water as it was before. On the surface, anyway.

Over the past couple weeks, Lenny had left dozens of messages each day. In spite of the fact she never responded, he continued with a barrage of entreaties. His wording was the same each time: some variation on how much he loved her and wanted her to come home. He never apologized for giving her the black eye or scaring the hell out of her on New Year's, and he never mentioned Sunshine. But still, she knew he was suffering. It was apparent in every syllable of his statements. He said he had hope for their future together. That they were each other's best friends, that they knew each other better than anyone else, deep in their hearts. They'd had fun before, he said, reminding her of fishing along the Chattahoochee and camping in lake country. They could have fun again. He'd buy her a regular house. He begged her to have faith in him.

After a while, she'd relented a little, agreeing to speak with him.

Car doors slammed, and a couple of families approached, hauling towels and coolers and fishing poles. Laughing and chattering, they headed toward a patio boat tied to the dock. Kids bounded around wearing bright orange life vests, while the mommies, in chic cover-ups, shouted directions. The dads, wearing tank tops and reflective sunglasses, struggled like pack mules, hauling beach paraphernalia to the boat. The two groups stowed their gear as the boat rocked against its ties. Somebody turned on the music, loud.

Jessie felt a twinge in her heart, wishing she and Sunshine and Lenny, and maybe a couple of friends and their kids, could get together and have a simple, fun day at a lake. She couldn't see it, at least not for a long time. In her current reality, it would be Kegger, Lenny, and their dog, Booger, on some beat-up skiff where the wearing of a life jacket would be mandatory, and Sunshine would have been left with a sitter. If they could afford a boat. Which they couldn't, even to rent.

Jessie wasn't sure what she would say when he called. Naturally, he'd beg her to return to Atlanta. She desperately needed a home for herself and Sunshine, and all their things were back at the trailer. It would be so simple to decide to return, but it could also be a hideous mistake, endangering them both.

She didn't know what to do. If they were older, Lenny would have more of a track history. Was his behavior established, or would it change—and if so, for better or worse? She had to decide whether to risk going back, and hope it would work out for the better, or stay away, which meant possibly leaving a good man behind. If he *was* a good man.

She closed her eyes. She didn't even know that. Was one incident of domestic violence enough to condemn a person? Could she excuse him for any reason? The stakes were too high for her to be wrong.

Jessie knew from her sociology classes that one important factor would be whether or not Lenny was willing to go to counseling, preferably in her absence. Because if he were motivated enough to meet with a therapist even while she wasn't there threatening and haranguing him, that would truly show intent to improve.

She would insist on that. And maybe if she could avoid going home for a little while longer, she could see whether or not he followed through.

The boat motor fired up, and she opened her eyes. A couple of adults threw off the lines, and the boat puttered at wake speed out of the marina and into the bay. Jessie watched until they disappeared into the sparkling, blinding distance.

She had choices. Just not good ones.

The phone rang.

Chapter Thirty-Two

*K*aren slid into the seat of the Corvette, excited at the prospect of exploring the island in such a beautiful ride with such a handsome driver. They stopped first at the Jekyll Island Club for lunch. On the way through the lobby, she snagged a couple of brochures, determined to finally do the tourist thing.

They started at the museum, opting for a tour in a horse-drawn carriage. Their guide, a natty gentleman with a broad-brimmed hat, explained that Jekyll had been developed in the late eighteen hundreds by people who collectively owned one-sixth of the world's wealth and who protected their private island with armed guards. "That's the Rockefeller cottage over there." The guide clucked at the horse. "Twelve thousand square feet. Next door were the DuPonts, and the Carnegies were across the way."

"This was where the workaholics came to relax." Curt elbowed her gently.

She elbowed him back. "If I had that kind of money, I'd have no problem relaxing."

After the tour, they got back in the car and drove north, winding around the periphery. She rested her head against the seat back, the Corvette's power rumbling beneath her.

Curt pressed her arm. "What's this?"

They parked in front of a crumbling building, its paint faded to a dull terra-cotta. Nothing remained except the walls, with doors and windows open to the sky. A mighty oak leaned over the roofless structure, shading the inside. "Horton House. It was built in the eighteenth century," Karen said, running her fingers over a wood-framed windowsill. A family had lived here, a family with no idea that far in the future, people would be poking around what was left of their home. The thought of life being so transitory caught her by surprise, and she turned away.

"What's the matter?" Curt asked.

"Everything's great." She kissed him. "Let's go see Driftwood Beach."

At the northernmost point of the island, whole trees had washed up on the sand, lying on their sides, roots pointing skyward. The tropical sun had bleached the wood white, and the effect was of nature's art gallery, fantastical shapes brought in by the tides.

Back at the trailer, they arranged beach chairs at the top of the slope and watched the light change over the water. Karen felt more peaceful than she had in years—and also more confused. If all it took to be happy was a good man and plenty of sex, why was she killing herself for work?

Of course, the answer was that she needed more than that.

In the morning, she opened the refrigerator, looking for something from which to make a meal. She hadn't fixed breakfast for a man in a long time. With yogurt, blueberries, honey, and granola, she conjured a couple of tasty parfaits while humming along to her iPod. She had slept like a baby and was brimming with energy.

The shower turned off. She folded napkins, laid cutlery on the table, and arranged a sprig of flowers in the center. Curt came in, pulling a polo shirt down over his wet head. He eyed the breakfast and then reached around her into the fridge and pulled out a pound of bacon. "Do you have any eggs?"

"What's wrong with what I fixed?" She put her hands on her hips.

"Woman, after last night, I need sustenance." He wiggled his eyebrows and went looking for a skillet.

"You've been living in North Dakota too long."

"Probably right." He peeled off a few strips of bacon. "Want some?"

Without the slightest hesitation, she nodded.

***

At the pro shop, they rented golf clubs, checked in with the starter, and drove up to the first hole on the Pine Lakes nine.

Curt strode to the tee box, his posture confident. His shoulders were as straight as those of a much younger man, and his waist was slender. He lofted the ball into the air, and it soared through the sky.

Karen took her turn, and her shot was precise, though not as long. They returned to the cart, excited to be together, and at the sheer joy of being outdoors doing something they both loved. Oak trees, draped in gray Spanish moss, lined the fairway. Tall, skinny pine trees leaned with the breeze. Somewhere off in the distance, a woodpecker drilled into a tree and a club struck a ball with a metallic clank.

While Curt strategized his next shot, Karen snapped photos of elegant white egrets nesting in the trees at the edge of a pond. A marshal drove up in a golf cart, gesturing at her. "I wondered if you missed the signs. There's gators in that water."

"Yikes. Thank you." Karen moved back.

"You folks enjoy your round."

Although Karen had plenty on her mind—Jessie, Ursula, Ben, the app, and work—she put it aside to focus on her game. Over the next four hours, they competed fiercely; he took the lead at first, and then Karen caught up. The day was gorgeous, with occasional cool breezes stirring the palms.

Karen played for enjoyment, whereas Curt was more competitive. At times, he offered suggestions, recommending a particular angle or strategy. At first, she was amused, but after the fourth or fifth time, she said, "You know, Curt, I'm a fifteen handicap."

He was sticking a club back into his bag, but he stopped and looked at her, his brows knitted.

She smiled. "So I'm pretty sure I can figure out what to do."

He pushed the club in and sat next to her, one hand on the wheel, the other arm behind her on the back of the seat. "I'm sorry. That was insensitive of me. Forgive me?" When she nodded, he pecked her on the lips and drove off. "But just FYI, I'm a six."

She whacked him on the arm, and he laughed. Six or not, they were pretty evenly matched. Whereas his drives and fairway shots were longer, her short game was more precise, and by the sixteenth hole, a three par, they were even. At the tee box, she pulled the rental driver out of the bag.

"It's only a hundred and forty—oops. Never mind," said Curt.

"Thank you." She addressed the ball, took her shot, and landed it on the green.

"Good job."

She gave him a flirty little smile, and he put his hand behind her neck and kissed her hard.

On the eighteenth hole, her shot flew into a bunker, but she almost didn't mind because the sand was beautiful, a sparkling ivory color, well-raked and pristine, and if she hit the ball just right, it would land on the manicured green with a clever spin and a light spray of sand. Which it did—and then it rolled neatly into the cup. She gave a shriek of delight and a fist pump.

Curt tapped in, retrieved his golf ball, and walked toward her. "Where next?"

"Picnic."

They stopped at a deli for sandwiches and drove to Wanderer's Beach, where they found a park and picnic tables. In the distance, a gentle surf lapped against the shore, and the wind rustled in the trees.

"Weird how quiet it is," said Curt. "You'd think a place this beautiful would have more tourists."

"It's the off-season. Too cold for swimming, and it still rains a bit. So it's quiet, but I like it."

They ate their lunch and spoke of home, which for him was North Dakota and for her was California, at least for now. Afterward, they paid for a Segway tour and rode around the island with a guide and six other visitors. Karen loved the feeling of gliding effortlessly along coastal bike paths and through the jungle-like interior. It almost felt like flying.

After the tour, they picked up a few staples from the grocery store. At the Airstream, Curt held out his hand for the key. His old-fashioned gesture caught her off guard, but she liked it.

Inside, they showered and kicked back on the sofa, checking their phones for messages. A text from Ben reminded her of a few loose ends she needed to address, but Curt's hands were traveling up under her blouse. She laughed and let him kiss her, Ben and work forgotten as her body warmed to his touch. He slowly undressed her, leading her to the bedroom in incremental degrees of nakedness. When she was completely bare, he laid her on the bed and pleasured her, and she marveled that he could reawaken her like this, again and again; in her youth, she'd assumed older people never had sex. Instead, sex at this age was more intense than at any earlier time.

While Curt napped, Karen booted her laptop and began work-ing. She answered Ben's questions and then checked her e-mail, looking for a response from the app-building website, but there was nothing. She logged off and sat back, chewing on a fingernail. Maybe they didn't see the value either, but she knew it was feasible. More than that, it was critical. If she couldn't increase productivity, she had two choices: status quo or hire staff. Neither one appealed. She looked up at the ceiling, frustrated, wondering if she could in-vent a Plan C.

Chapter Thirty-Three

*F*or the first three days of his visit, Curt and Karen indulged every whim. They made love, played tourist, dined on the waterfront, and took long, romantic walks on the beach. In the evenings, she sat at the kitchen table catching up on her e-mail and a bit of work while he stretched out on the sofa, already halfway through her John Sandford novel. One night, she looked over to see a new recliner in her living room. Curt had found a button that released a footrest from a section of the sofa. She hadn't even known it was there. That made her laugh, having forgotten what it was like to live with a man.

The Airstream was small for two people, but they managed to find their way around each other, employing patience and humor. They learned that the kitchen could only support one cook at a time, and they had to take turns getting dressed, because the bedroom and bathroom were tight. What could have been stressful was relieved by their good natures and a mutual desire to please.

But on the fourth day, Karen was on edge, waiting for the results of the app. Picking up on her mood, Curt escaped to the fishing pier to see who was catching what.

In the late morning, she received an e-mail from the DIY site. The app was ready for testing. She typed in typical requirements for a nurse recruitment in a major metropolitan area and was stunned by the results. Not only did she receive dozens and dozens of names, the results included contact information and a brief bio about each person, all culled from information made public by the candidates. She'd been right. The app was brilliant. Karen danced around the kitchen, thinking about the implications. There was one person she had to tell right away.

"Ben, it works!" She couldn't hide her enthusiasm as she explained what the new tool would mean.

"So now you can stay in Florida indefinitely."

"Hmm." Karen sat back down. Ben still didn't realize Grace and Associates was based in a travel trailer. She glanced around the Airstream, full of her belongings and, now, Curt's. "I'm not sure that's the plan," she said.

"If you're going to move, there's no better place to combine business and pleasure than here."

"You sound like a chamber of commerce guy," she teased.

"But it's true. Yolie and I have never been happier, and you'd love it, too. In fact, every day on the way to work, I drive past this office/apartment combo that's for lease. It's beautiful, in the historic district. Centrally located, close to downtown. Want me to check it out?"

"That's a pricey area," Karen said.

"I'll find out what they're asking. And congratulations again. It looks like everything's coming together."

She hung up, grinning so much her face hurt. Ben texted her back a short time later. The combo unit was a bit out of her range at the moment, but her business could easily double or triple now that she had the capacity. She contacted the leasing agent and, after a lengthy and detailed discussion of the property, started the process.

When Curt came in the door at noon, she wrapped him in a hug and made him sit at the kitchen table. "It works! My app is live," she said, angling her computer toward him and demonstrating. "This is what I needed to grow my business. Isn't it fantastic?"

"Amazing," he said, but he didn't sound that impressed.

That afternoon, they drove to the far side of Brunswick, to the HB Plantation, where they toured the farmhouse and grounds. The docent described the last owner of the rice plantation. Ophelia Dent was a successful businessperson, as well as a sophisticated, glamorous world traveler, and she attracted many offers of marriage. "But she rejected them all," the docent said. "Had she married, the husband would have controlled her assets. Miss Ophelia was a bit of a feminist."

Curt nudged Karen, who poked him back.

"We see that a lot," the docent said.

After the plantation, they stopped for barbecue, sharing a dinner of juicy ribs. At one point he reached over and dabbed a bit of barbecue sauce from her chin, causing her to blush. "I eat like a hungry wolf," she said. "It's a bad habit."

He crunched a French fry. "They say you can tell how much a woman enjoys sex from how she relishes a meal."

The two of them were good together. Karen didn't want that to end, but how would it work, long term? Her immediate future was in Savannah, but his career was in North Dakota. She doubted he'd want to start over, being only a few years from retirement. Lots of couples maintained long-distance relationships, though. Surely they could, too. At least for a while.

It could work. She would make it work.

That evening, they sat outside to watch the sunset. Karen's phone beeped, indicating a text. She glanced at the display. It was Ben again.

"That your boyfriend?"

"No." She put the phone away.

"That guy in Atlanta," Curt said. "The one you were kissing on New Year's."

Karen stared at him. His jealousy was flattering for about five seconds. Then she thought about the logistics. How—and what—did he know?

Curt stared back. "It was in the paper. The social page of the *Dickinson Press*. I believe the headline was, 'Local Girl Parties with Ted Natchez.'"

"Oh, no." Aunt Marie would have seen it and all her friends and relatives in North Dakota. Not to mention the Dickinson clients she'd worked with, like Father Engel and the governor. Karen groaned. "It was nothing."

"It looked like something."

She sat quietly, gathering her thoughts. Although the past few days had deepened their relationship, they had no claims on each other. "Is there a problem?"

"Not at all. You're a grown woman, free to do whatever you like. It's not up to me to judge your private life."

"And yet you are. How do you want to deal with this?"

He shrugged. "To be honest, I guess I'm not comfortable with the idea of you being with other men."

"Okay," Karen said. "Then what are you going to do about Maddie and Isabel?"

Chapter Thirty-Four

*C*urt, gathering his thoughts, shifted in the beach chair. It creaked as if it might break. To the east, the full moon rose, its cold white light illuminating Karen's face.

"You have Isabel's picture at your house. I saw it our first night together. And Madison sent a text, suggesting I leave you alone."

He figured Maddie must have gone through his phone contacts. "When did she text you?"

"A couple weeks ago. Right after New Year's. Look, why don't we leave it alone? You don't have to explain. I was just angry for a moment. Your private life is none of my business."

But he wanted it to be. He stood and held out his hand. "Let's go for a walk." He waited until she took it and allowed him to pull her to her feet. They fell in step along the shoreline.

"I met Isabel when I did a semester at the university in Barcelona. She worked in the bookstore. We went out a few times." That was an understatement. Within days, he was living at her place, but Karen didn't need to know that.

"You like her enough to have her picture on your desk."

"And Maddie is one of my teaching assistants."

"A student?" Karen stopped walking.

"She's not a kid. She's a doctoral candidate, and she's in her twenties."

"Your daughter's age."

He winced. "I had a midlife crisis. It lasted a few weeks."

They walked in silence as Curt battled conflicting feelings of pride and embarrassment. Pride that he'd bedded such a hot young thing. Embarrassment because it had been hard for him to keep up. Yet his time with Maddie had made him appreciate Karen even more. They were contemporaries, and it deepened their relationship. He knew what he wanted. Curt slowed his pace. "I'm going back to Barcelona. They offered me a teaching assignment for a year."

"Very cool for you." She stuck her hands in her back pockets and gazed up the beach.

"Karen." He took her by the shoulders. "Come to Spain with me."

"How can I do that? I'm right on the verge of my business taking off."

"Can't you do some of your work remotely?"

"Some, not all."

"You do most of it from a trailer on a Georgia island. Who would know if you were e-mailing them from Spain?"

"Part of the reason I'm here is because I go into Savannah weekly. Sure, some of it I could do remotely, but there's the fact of being seen, being around town, meeting people, making connections, going to different offices and speaking with groups. It's more complicated than you understand." She shuffled her bare feet in the sand.

"Which is why I put down a deposit on an office and apartment suite in Savannah. I'm selling my truck and trailer and moving at the end of the month."

"When did you decide this? Ten minutes ago? Get your deposit back."

"I'm tired of living like a transient. I need stability."

"What do you think I'm offering you?" He ran a hand through his hair in frustration.

"A year in Spain, and then what? My work would dry up. At the end of the year, I'd have nothing."

"You'd have us. Karen, think of it. We'll eat tapas, swim in the Med, dance on Las Ramblas."

She shook her head. "You make it sound so beautiful, Curt, and I'd love to, but I can't do both."

"So you'd choose work over me?"

"It's more than just work. It's my profession. I love what I do. I want to be successful again, make a ton of money, and ensure my future. I've spent most of the past year building the foundation. It's just starting to take off, and you want me to toss it out the window so I can keep you company in Spain? What did you think I'd say?" She turned and walked away. The damp sand showed two trails of footprints in the moonlight: both of them coming out, and one going back.

Maybe it was really all about that guy, that rich asshole she'd danced with on New Year's Eve. Karen was right. Curt didn't understand. He picked up a piece of driftwood and hurled it into the surf. He trod the shoreline, up and back, thinking and arguing with himself. Pissed off, because now he saw that he was too late. He should have made his move sooner. Karen was driven and motivated—her energy was one of the things he loved about her. She wasn't going to hang around waiting for him to make a move. She'd made hers.

He glared out at the ocean. The whole time she'd been on the road last summer with Frieda, he should have been telling her every night—every morning, too—how he felt. But he hadn't. Curt set off down the moonlit beach, unsure he could salvage this mess.

A mile down the beach, he found a washed-up log and sat watching the starlit waves lap at the shore. He shouldn't have been surprised. In a sense, Karen had left him once before, right after she finished college. She'd left for California before he had the chance to tell her how he felt. She'd gone on to marry someone else, and made a life for herself. He'd never expected another shot.

Curt glanced up as a voice reached him. A man and woman approached, talking softly in the darkness, and he felt the cold prospect of solitude settle over him. His wife had run off years ago, chasing after an acting career, leaving him to raise their daughter alone. Curt was a good father. He doted on Erin, arranging his teaching schedule to accommodate her needs. He'd dated discretely, but he'd kept the women at arm's length. Now he was free to create a new life for himself, and miracle of miracles, Karen was back.

Except she was poised to run off again.

Did she not care that much about him? Or was she so mad for money or recognition or ego or whatever the hell it was that she couldn't tell how much he felt for her? He was offering love and security and a lifetime together. He rubbed his chin, feeling a spot where he'd hurried the razor.

His hand stopped. He hadn't said anything of the sort. All he'd said was—

Curt stared down the beach, in the direction she'd fled. He needed to explain how he felt, to make it clear he loved her.

Back at the trailer, she was sitting in the beach chair, huddled against the damp, waiting for him. "I'm sorry," she said. "I don't like fighting."

"Let's get married."

Karen's hand went to her throat. She stared at him without speaking and then rose. "I'm freezing."

He followed her inside, where she got a bottle of water out of the refrigerator. Cracking the seal, she took a couple of gulps, looking at him while slowly twisting the cap back on. "You're really asking me that?"

"Yes, I am." He kissed her, tasting the water on her lips. He knew he couldn't live without being able to wake up with her every morning for the rest of his life. When she broke away, her eyes were smoky with what he took to be desire.

He kissed her hand and held it to his chest. "How about tomorrow morning, we drive over to St. Simons Island and find a jeweler? I'll buy you the biggest chunk of ice—"

"Curt."

He stopped talking, gripped her hand harder. Felt her slipping away from him.

She looked into his eyes, her gaze steady. Loving. "I was married for almost thirty years. I'm only now learning to be alone."

He scowled. "I've been there. It's overrated."

"I love being with you, but I love being able to get up every morning and decide what my day is going to look like. I like making decisions about my business, seeing what works, trying new things. My work consumes me at times. I lose track of time, and that's fun for me. I can work into the wee hours, totally focused on what I'm doing, without feeling guilty about shortchanging the man in my life."

He couldn't believe she was that much in love with work, but worse than that was her assumption that he'd be dependent on her. "I don't need babysitting. If we were together, you could do whatever you wanted. Why is that so hard for you to understand?"

She sat down on the couch. "This time of my life—it feels so rich, so promising. I don't mean to exclude you from it, but if we were together, I would feel like I had to dial myself back, to make sure your needs were met. We'd be a couple, and it would be wrong for me to act like you weren't there. So I couldn't be as intense about what I want, or as single-minded."

"It wouldn't be like that at all."

"It was in my first marriage, and that's one of the reasons it failed."

"I don't want to go to Barcelona without you."

Karen held out her hands. "See? It's already happening. You want me with you in Spain so you don't have to be alone."

"I'm capable of finding company if I want to."

"And I'm sure Isabel will be happy to see you."

They glared at each other. Karen broke first. "I'm sorry. That was childish."

"When I watched you walk away on the beach, I felt like it was thirty years ago and you were leaving me all over again."

"I know, and I feel terribly guilty for that."

He hugged her as they stood in the kitchen, silently holding each other. A gust of wind rocked the trailer. "We should have been together from the start."

"But the minute I left for California, you married Janet," Karen said.

"She wanted me, and you didn't. You were gone before the ink dried on your diploma."

"Let's not fight. We did our best." She continued in a soft voice. "When I went to California, I missed my family and friends. It was all so big and unfamiliar, but it was exciting, too. Like now, after all the turmoil, losing Mom and everything, I'm excited again. There's still so much I want to accomplish."

"Accomplish it with me. I could help you. I'm in great shape financially. I could give you a springboard."

"I need to do it myself."

"Nobody does it all on their own." He studied her face. "I don't even know why you invited me here."

"I missed you."

"Then marry me. Come to Spain."

She groaned. "I can't."

"Karen, I can't wait another lifetime. You have to trust somebody. Let it be me. You say you want security, but life is unpredictable. If we were together, we could help each other. Look out for each other. Don't you want that?" He saw her struggle with it, pacing the kitchen, picking up the water bottle and putting it back down without drinking, staring out the window at the blackness beyond and her own reflection.

***

For a long while, they sat together on the couch, not speaking. She felt as if her entire life had led her to this point, culminating in a choice between two passions: for him and for her work, and her great failure was that she couldn't find a way to reconcile the two.

He sat forward, elbows on knees, staring across the room. It was almost midnight, but she didn't want to be the first to go to bed. So she waited.

When she reached for the water, his arm shot out, and he took her by the wrist, turned her toward him, and kissed her, sweetly... then passionately. The fire rose in her belly, and she returned his kiss with the same fervor.

They dragged each other into bed, and their lovemaking was intense, fierce, and primal, but when she climaxed, she turned her face away so he couldn't see her tears.

Later, she lay in the darkness, staring at the ceiling, the covers up to her chin. She could hear him breathing softly, and she wanted to put her hand on his back, press her face to his neck, and tell him how much she loved him. But she didn't dare wake him. He would want more, and that, she couldn't give him.

It was after two. In time with his breathing, she counted slowly backward from one hundred. Finally, she slept.

In the morning, she heard him stirring. "Curt."

He leaned over and kissed her on the forehead. Then he rose, and the shower started. When he returned, toweling off, she said, "I'll come visit you. We can do all those things you talked about."

"I don't think that would be a good idea." He dressed and stuffed his things into a duffel bag. "For me, anyway. I'm sorry."

"But what about in the future?"

"This is the future." He hoisted the bag over his shoulder, looked at her, and shrugged. "Good-bye, Karen."

She pressed her face into the pillow as the rumble of the Corvette faded in the distance.

Chapter Thirty-Five

A light drizzle streaked the windows of the Airstream. Karen stared out at the gray, monochrome world. The coffee tasted bitter this morning, or maybe it was her mood.

She tossed the coffee into the sink, but the brown liquid shot out the other side, coating the backsplash. Sighing, she reached for a dishcloth and attacked the mess. Today, she would sign the contract that would bind her to Savannah for a year. With any luck, longer. She was tired of living out of a trailer.

She needed a change. Needed to throw herself into her new life and try to forget about Curt. She'd hated the look of pain on his face last night. Hated the thought that it was all or nothing between them. He was gone, and that was his decision. She had made her own, and would learn to live with it.

Savannah would show her how to survive.

After meeting with the rental agent today, Karen would return and pack up the Airstream. Tomorrow she would leave for Key

Largo, to prepare the truck and trailer for sale. In the past three weeks, Fern and Belle had said little about Jessie's plans or any new developments. Later this morning, Karen would call Jessie, ask about her progress toward moving out, and let her know they'd be roommates for a few days.

She filled the kitchen sink with soapy water while glancing at the sky for a break in the clouds, but the overcast remained. After washing all the dirty dishes, she got out her suitcases and folded whatever clothing and personal items she could. Then she cleaned the bathroom and straightened the living room. As much as she had enjoyed staying here in Jekyll Island, its ending cast a pall over the beauty of the experience.

She dressed and left for Savannah. On the highway, she phoned Jessie. After exchanging pleasantries, she got down to business. "I'll be coming back to Key Largo tomorrow," she said.

"Um, great." Jessie sounded distracted. In the background, the baby cried. "You're a few days early."

"True, but I did say I'd be back the end of February. And you were going to find another place to live by March first, remember? Is that still workable?"

"Sure, no problem. Drive safely." The call went dead.

Maybe it was the reception.

Karen stuck her phone in the cup holder. She felt anxious about the prospect of sharing such a small space with a woman and child she'd never met. On the other hand, it was only a few days. How bad could that be?

At the Savannah turnoff, Karen programmed her GPS app and meandered through the streets, familiarizing herself with the city's layout. In a gentrified neighborhood shaded by live oak canopies, she parked in front of a two-story brownstone. Inside, the agent, an older woman in an expensive suit, greeted Karen with a warm smile. "There are four commercial units in this building, as well as two apartments on the second floor. Let's look at the vacant office suite first."

The agent opened the door and let Karen go in ahead of her. Her first reaction was to feel her shoulders relax—she loved it at first sight. The white walls rose to a high ceiling adorned by a chandelier. An arched bay window looked out toward the park across the street, lush with ancient oaks and lawns. An old fireplace, fronted by a brass grate, was topped with a marble mantel. The office smelled of lemon polish and old wood. Even without furnishings, it felt dignified and solid, a firm foundation for her new life in the city.

"This used to be the library. Many features in the building are refurbished and historically accurate to the late eighteen hundreds."

Karen wandered around, imagining clients visiting the office of Grace and Associates. The front of the room would make a perfect reception area where they could relax with a view of the park across the street. A cupboard was built into the wall, from which she could serve her guests coffee and cookies before they got down to work.

"And this could be your office."

The long room had been divided in half by the tasteful construction of a wall, creating a private space for her. Spacious windows, laced by crape myrtle trees, afforded a veiled view of the backyard. Karen imagined a desk and file cabinets and a small conference table filling the room. This would be the heart of her business—of her future.

Alone.

She closed her eyes and exhaled.

Just put your head down and keep moving, she told herself.

When the agent unlocked the second-story apartment, Karen nodded in approval. The ambience welcomed her, reassuring her with abundant light from many windows, high ceilings with decorative moldings, and hardwood floors throughout. A cozy dining room looked out toward the park, while on the opposite wall, the kitchen had a view of a neatly maintained garden at the back of the house.

"The other renter maintains the garden," said the agent. "She says you're welcome to whatever veggies and flowers you like." She continued down the hall. "The master bedroom has a walk-in closet."

Karen followed. "The apartment is beautiful, but I didn't realize it would be furnished."

"It won't be after the current resident moves out. Her lease is up April first. Is that a concern?"

"I'd hoped to move in sooner." Karen stuck her head into the other bedroom, which was smaller but perfect for guests and storage. "But no, it's not a problem. In fact, it'll give me time to prepare."

The office and apartment exceeded her expectations, the lease was within her anticipated budget, and the city was lovely. She could imagine greeting clients in her office downstairs, someday with the help of a receptionist. She would attend local events, make friends and contacts, and put down roots. If she had to wait an extra month, it would be worth it. "Where do I sign?"

The agent whipped out a pen. "I sent your deposit receipt by e-mail. Do you need anything else?"

Karen smiled. "No. I'm excited about the place. It's gorgeous."

"Great. Call me in four weeks, and I'll meet you here with the keys." They shook hands, and Karen walked out to her truck, but before getting in, she looked back at the brownstone. In its stately gentility, it seemed to offer comfort, safety, and a gracious start for the second half of her life. If she had to choose between love and business—and apparently, she did—this new home would ease the pain. Savannah would make a wonderful foundation for her future. Curt would have loved it here.

She swallowed hard and climbed into the truck.

Returning to Jekyll Island, she cruised slowly past the golf course and the ruins of Horton House and parked at Driftwood Beach, where she sat on a log and stared at the Atlantic. In a few weeks, Curt would be living on the other side of the ocean. No doubt he'd take up with that woman, Isabel. And once there, why bother coming back? Would she ever see him again?

It wouldn't matter. He'd made his terms clear.

She took a deep breath and straightened her back. Any man who'd make such a rigid ultimatum wasn't for her, anyway.

He was just being passionate. He didn't want to lose you, so he doubled down. You're a fool for letting him go.

If he didn't want to lose me, Karen argued back, he'd have been more flexible. He'd wait for me.

No, he's doing what he needs to do. You should do the same. After all, you're both adults. And you're both control freaks.

Karen made a face. Yes, we're perfect for each other, she thought.

Sliding her feet into her sandals, she trudged back to the truck. That afternoon, she visited Ida and confirmed her plans. The older woman nodded sadly, wished her well, and told her to hide the key under the mat. By nightfall, Karen had packed, cleaned, and removed every indication that she and Curt had been there at all.

Chapter Thirty-Six

*O*n the way home from Jekyll Island, Karen tried to rehearse her speech about Jessie clearing out, but Frieda kept interfering, griping about the girl and her baby thrown out on the streets.

At Paradise Shores, Karen drove to her trailer, but a primer-gray sedan was parked in the short driveway, and there was no room for her truck. The neighbor, sipping a cocktail on his patio, scowled as if angry at all the cars crowding his property, so she parked in the visitor lot and hiked home. A tall, thin blonde with her hair in a towel answered the door.

"Jessie? I'm Karen."

Jessie held the door open. "I'm sorry about the mess." The living room was filled with diaper boxes, baby clothes, a toy box, and a playpen, in which stood a one-year-old baby.

Karen set her suitcase on the floor. "So this is Sunshine."

Jessie leaned down and picked up the little girl, who tucked her face against her mother's neck. "She's shy with strangers."

"Most babies are."

"It's her bedtime. We were waiting on you."

Karen glanced toward the bedroom.

"It's all yours," said Jessie. "I'll sleep on the sofa. She's fine here." Jessie laid the baby in the playpen and dimmed the lights. Sunshine popped up and began wailing.

Karen pulled the flimsy divider closed. The bed looked freshly made, and the room was empty and clean. What now? It was too early to sleep, but she sensed the baby needed to forget about the stranger who'd just arrived. Karen flopped on the bed, feeling awkward. She busied herself on her phone, checking email and the news. Eventually silence fell.

Karen slid the divider open and tiptoed into the bathroom. There she found childproof locks securing every door and cabinet.

"I'm sorry for the hassle," said Jessie. "When I realized we'd be staying a while, I put them on."

"It's not a problem. They'll come off." Karen felt like a jerk, but she had to ask. "How's the house-hunting going? Have you found a place?"

"We're waiting for a couple of callbacks, tomorrow or the next day. I don't have that much stuff, so when we get the call, I can be out of here pretty quickly."

"Okay, well…goodnight."

"Goodnight."

Karen escaped to her bedroom. She put on her pajamas, laid the Sandford novel on the nightstand, and slipped into bed. She reached for the phone to text Curt good night but then remembered and leaned back against the headboard. She looked up at the ceiling. Her eyes stung.

Well, what'd you expect? You let a man like that get away like he don't matter at all. If it was me, I'd be chasing after him with everything I had. Maybe there's no hope for you.

Karen turned out the light. *Good night, Frieda.*

***

Baby laughter woke Karen. She smiled at the sound and then remembered and pulled the pillow over her head. No way around it, this was going to be awkward. Hopefully, the apartment prospects would pan out today and Jessie would begin packing. Soon, Karen would have the place to herself.

Sunshine began fussing.

"No, you can't." Jessie spoke in a loud whisper.

Fuss, whine, fuss.

"Shhh."

The trailer jiggled.

"Stay here. Sunshine, no." With the single-mindedness of babies everywhere, Sunshine grasped and pulled at the flimsy divider, trying to get into Karen's room. When Jessie pulled her away, the baby began to cry.

"You can open it," said Karen. "I'm awake." *As if I could sleep.*

"Are you sure? I can take her for a walk."

"It's barely light out."

The divider slid back, and Sunshine crawled over to the foot of the bed and pulled herself into a standing position. Karen, propped on her elbow, smiled at the baby, who simply stared.

Jessie stood in the doorway. "She's a very curious little girl."

"She's okay. I'll keep an eye on her."

"I'll make coffee."

Sunshine eased closer to the nightstand, eyeing Karen's red phone. Karen grabbed it and stuck it under her pillow. The baby saw where it went and lifted one foot, expecting to find a toehold in order to climb onto the bed. Her little hands grasped at the bedding, trying to haul herself up.

"Where do you think you're going?"

Jessie called from the kitchen. "She's used to crawling in bed with me in the morning."

"Want to come up?" Karen lifted the baby onto the bed. Sunshine scrabbled to the pillow and lifted it, but the phone was gone. In its place was a silly-looking back scratcher with jiggly eyes glued onto the handle. The baby reached for the tool.

"Coffee's ready," said Jessie. "Looks like you two are going to be friends."

"She's adorable," Karen said, "but would you mind getting her? She can have the scratcher to play with."

"She has her own toys." Jessie picked up the baby and left the room.

Karen shrugged and stuck the back scratcher up in the closet. Then she closed herself in the bathroom with its profusion of baby locks. After dressing, she poured a cup of coffee and sat on a barstool to drink it. The baby's antics served as distraction in what would otherwise have been an uncomfortable silence. Karen finished her coffee. "I'm going to say hi to Fern and Belle." Outside, she felt free, sprung from the stifling closeness of the overcrowded RV.

"Figured we'd see you one of these days." Fern held the screen open.

"Welcome home," Belle said. "I made cinnamon rolls. Did you eat?"

Karen asked about Eleanor, who was still hanging on. She got updates on everybody, and then the conversation turned to Jessie. "She says you found her a couple of rental options."

"I was hoping." Fern set her coffee cup down. "But there's nothing."

"Rents are sky-high, and there are no vacancies anywhere," said Belle.

"What about Homestead or the towns around there? I'd think the housing there would be a lot cheaper."

"It's an hour away," said Belle. "She wouldn't have anybody to help her."

234

"Bigger problem is that Jessie has no money," said Fern. "Flat broke and no child support."

"What's she planning to do? Does she have any ideas?"

"Other than going back to Atlanta?" asked Fern. "Nope. So I guess you're stuck with her for a while, until something turns up."

"*I'm* stuck?"

"Not you alone," said Fern. "We'll keep looking. Something will turn up."

Belle said, "The Andersons might let her rent their RV for a couple weeks. They're flying home to Texas for a wedding."

"Forget that," said Fern. "Renee'll never let anybody stay in her trailer. It's too tricked out. She's too prissy."

"We need to think of something." Karen stood. "Thanks for the coffee."

"Leaving so soon?"

"I want to see Eleanor. Also, I need to think, and it's hard to do in the trailer."

"It's just short term," said Fern. "She's a good kid. Don't be a grouch about it."

Belle pulled on a sweater. "I'll walk with you."

As they headed for Eleanor's, Karen said, "She had a month to resolve this, and now I'm the bad guy."

"I feel terrible. We tried to find her a place, but everything is so expensive. Short of driving to the mainland, there is nothing," said Belle. "On the plus side, we lent her our laptop, and she's doing her college classes while we watch the baby. Everybody in camp loves the two of them."

"I'm glad for all of you, but the trailer isn't that big," said Karen. "It's uncomfortable having all three of us in there."

"It's always harder at first, but you'll adapt. I have faith in you."

"Faith or not, Jessie needs to find another place to stay. I'm leaving at the end of February."

"Why? I thought you were a part of our group now."

"Belle." Karen stopped walking and looked at her friend. "I can't live in an RV forever."

"I know it's small but I thought you'd trade up."

"It's not that. I rented a place in Savannah."

Belle's shoulders slumped. "What will happen to Jessie?"

"I did what I could. What else do you want from me?" A gust of wind came out of nowhere, whipping up dust and sand from the campground and lashing the two women so hard that they raised their arms to shield their faces.

At Eleanor's driveway, Belle said good-bye. "I need to speak with Fern."

Karen knew the two of them would be back, working her over, trying to effect some compromise that suited Jessie.

Doc let her in. "She just woke up."

Karen stood at the foot of Eleanor's bed. The old woman opened her eyes, blinked, and then smiled. "I knew I'd see you again."

"I'm glad you're still hanging in."

"Yes." The word came out a croak. "I'm too tough to kill."

"I knew that."

"But this isn't much of a life." Eleanor gestured for her water bottle, and Karen handed it to her. "On the plus side, the child is delightful."

"And her mother is a good person, everybody keeps telling me." Karen sighed. "I'm so stuck."

"I knew that the first day." Eleanor closed her eyes.

"I can't boot them out on the street."

"No, that would be cruel."

Chapter Thirty-Seven

*L*oud music and laughter blasted out of her RV as Karen approached. She stood in the doorway, her mouth a straight line. She'd hoped to get some work done, but inside, it was like a reunion of the Golden Girls television show, if they were hosting a baby shower. Doc, Patti, Fern, and the rest of them crowded into every inch of seating. In the middle of the room, Sunshine held on to a chair and danced—or tried to—to a Beyoncé number. Knowing she was the center of attention, the baby laughed as she wiggled and jerked, up and down on her fat little legs, occasionally plopping down on her well-padded rear. The ladies wiped their eyes and howled, the trailer jiggled, and the baby danced on.

Not exactly a place to get any serious work done. Karen remembered seeing a public library by the grocery store, so she threaded her way through the crowded living room into her bedroom, gathered up her laptop and files, and left.

The girl behind the desk pointed her over to a bank of carrels, and Karen got busy developing new job descriptions for Ben's employees. The library wasn't very busy midweek during the school year, with all the retirees outside enjoying the tropical sunshine. It was easy to be productive, here in the quiet with no dancing babies or hysterically-laughing grandmothers. Karen was able to focus, and she raced through her work.

After an hour, she stood and stretched. The library was a tomb. She sat back down, ready to start on Ursula's work, but since the free Wi-Fi was so fast here, she decided to play around with Google Earth instead. She found her destination and zoomed in. The University of Barcelona looked to be within walking distance of the ocean, with beaches and attractive boardwalk areas. The university sprawled across the city with multiple campuses; a cosmopolitan environment, offering every kind of cultural opportunity. She was proud of Curt for landing such a gig—a year in Barcelona, beginning in August. As she tumbled deeper into the rabbit hole of blogs, websites, and YouTube videos, Karen began to understand what she was missing. He had offered her all of that—romance, art, beauty, culture, dining, nature, and history in a Mediterranean setting— and all she had to do was give up her thriving young business.

She'd seriously considered whether it was possible to work in Europe while maintaining her business here in America, but the answer was no. So instead of working at a desk overlooking the beaches of Barcelona, she was hunched in a small cubicle while people took over her trailer. Tomorrow was supposed to be the day Jessie moved out, but clearly, that wasn't going to happen.

Karen had bristled at the way Fern and Belle acted like it was no big deal for Jessie to move in indefinitely. The crowding was bad enough, but the feeling of being a doormat was worse. She knew they meant well, but she felt taken advantage of. Not that she didn't want to help Jessie, especially given that she was Frieda's family.

Thank you.

You're welcome.

But how were they supposed to manage for the next month? And whether Jessie believed it or not, in thirty days the RV would be sold. Then what?

Not like it was Karen's problem.

Karen packed up and drove a few miles down the highway to Lorelei's, a bayside waterfront café whose dock served as a hot spot for the fishing guides in the area. She munched on fish tacos watched boatloads of tourists arrive and depart. Tarpon splashed madly in the shallow water of the bay, fighting each other for the occasional dropped French fry. While she watched, inspiration struck.

On the way home, she stopped in at Fern's and told her what it would take for Jessie to be able to stay another month in Karen's RV. Fern stood listening, hands on hips, nodding.

Back at the trailer, the ladies had cleared out. Jessie looked up from hand-stitching a hem. "The baby was late going down for her nap, and it's my shift with Eleanor. Would it be okay if I left her in your care?"

"You're helping with Eleanor?" Karen set her briefcase on the counter.

"We all take turns. I don't think Sunshine will wake up for a while. The ladies wore her out this morning." Jessie folded up her sewing and stuck it in a bag. "So is it okay?"

"I guess I could. Since she's sleeping."

"Thanks! Her diapers and everything are right here. I use these wipes because she has a little rash. She might be hungry, so you could give her some chopped-up bits of cheese and blueberries. Her apple juice is in her sippy cup, in the fridge. Her toys are in this box over here, and I'll have my phone close by if anything happens."

She slipped out the door. Karen was tired already.

After Jessie left, Karen tiptoed over to the playpen, which was covered with a lightweight blanket. She lifted one corner. Sunshine lay on her tummy, knees drawn up underneath her, her bottom in the air. Karen fought the urge to reach down and touch the cherubic curls around the nape of the baby's neck. Better she sleep.

Karen got comfortable in the recliner and began reading a novel. Outside, the campground was quiet. Peace settled over her, and she was able to imagine what it would be like to be a grandmother. She was reconciled with her own childlessness, the pain receding years ago in the normal course of life. At times, it reoccurred, but at the moment she was content.

The baby rolled over and mumbled in her sleep. Karen froze. Sunshine coughed, whimpered a little, and struggled to her feet, trying to look around in spite of the blanket. She whimpered, and Karen jumped up. "It's okay, honey." She pulled back the sheet and reached for the child, who hesitated and then went into Karen's arms.

Karen circled the trailer, jiggling the baby, rubbing her back and cooing. Then Sunshine got restless.

Now what?

She opened the fridge and handed the sippy cup to Sunshine, who took it in both hands, raising the cup and tilting her head backward to drink. Karen sat in the recliner and let the baby stretch out in her lap. The child studied Karen while she drank, even reaching up with one hand, her little fingers exploring Karen's face. As any human would naturally do, Karen smiled and tried some baby talk.

Sunshine emptied the cup and threw it across the room. Then she smiled, shimmied off Karen's lap to the floor, and crawled to get the cup, her soggy diaper sagging on her backside. She picked up the cup and threw it again. This time, it flew behind her, whacking the window.

"Come on, let's change you." Karen knelt on the floor, laid the baby on a blanket, and took care of business, pleased that she was able to manage without any special training. When she finished, Sunshine didn't jump up right away, so Karen leaned over and blew a raspberry on her bare belly. Sunshine giggled, so Karen did it again. They played that game until the baby rolled over and went into the bedroom to explore.

Karen followed her, removing breakable or unsafe objects just in time or, if too late, convincing Sunshine to relinquish her hold. They played peekaboo, rolled a ball, and tossed stuffed animals around the room. When the baby giggled, it struck Karen as funny, so she laughed, making the baby giggle more. By the time Jessie returned in late afternoon, the trailer was a mess and Karen was exhausted.

But she'd had fun.

While Jessie distracted Sunshine, Karen dragged herself into her bedroom and pulled the divider closed. She hoped the baby wouldn't come looking for her. Feeling grateful for this small amount of privacy, Karen closed her eyes, hoping Fern delivered on her promise, and soon.

Chapter Thirty-Eight

The next morning, Karen washed down a piece of toast with coffee as the big Chevy dually backed into the driveway, a large roll of canvas in the truck bed along with Doc and Patti.

Jessie looked up from the floor where she was playing with the baby. "What's happening?"

"Moving day." Karen hurried outside. A man rode in the cab with Fern and Belle. When everybody piled out, Fern said, "This is Mack. He says we're good until he and his wife leave in April."

The short, well-fed man reached out to shake Karen's hand.

"I appreciate the loan," Karen said. "We won't need it that long, though."

"Karen, you and Patti get one side," said Fern. "Mack and I'll get the other. Belle, you get the poles. Doc, you're on glue, Velcro, and side skirting."

"I brought an air mattress and pump," said Candace, walking up with Margo.

"Good thinking." The women hefted the canvas out of the truck and onto the ground. With Mack directing, they began unrolling the canvas and laying out the hardware.

"What is it?" Jessie came outside, holding Sunshine on one hip.

"It's a screen porch," said Karen. "This way, you and the baby can have the bedroom."

"Awesome!"

"But I'm not going to bunk outside forever."

"I'm doing the best I can."

"There must be apartments all over the place."

"I was hoping for something with a yard." Jessie blew a strand of hair off her face and went back in the trailer.

Whatever Jessie's best was, she was still here. Karen dashed over to steady an upright as Doc pounded the stabilizing stakes into the ground. Soon the canvas walls were in place and the ceiling panel secured. Velcro strips were affixed to the side of the RV, to which skirting was attached. The screen porch took shape quickly. In less than two hours, the trailer had expanded with what amounted to a small bedroom.

After she had thanked everyone and promised to return it in a month, Karen moved in. She inflated the mattress, tested it, and propped it out of the way against the back wall. A stack of boxes served as a dresser, and a lamp was connected via a heavy-duty cord snaking under the RV to the electrical outlet. All the while, Jessie remained inside with the baby.

It was lunchtime, and Karen was hungry, but she didn't want to go inside and hassle with the closeness of the RV. Instead, she stuck her head inside the door. "I'm off to run errands."

Jessie nodded, a flash of understanding in her eyes. "See you later."

Karen hopped on her scooter and headed for the local deli for a sandwich. She had them double wrap it with a bag of ice and went to Pennekamp to rent a kayak. Out in the mangroves, she stashed the paddle and unwrapped her lunch, chicken salad with nuts and dried cranberries. She closed her eyes, tilted her face to the sky, and filled her lungs with the clean salt air. What a relief to be able to escape for a while into such beauty. With a bottle of iced tea propped between her knees, she ate in the silence. Karen wasn't a hermit, but after all that had happened in the past few days, she needed this—needed time alone and quiet. By the time she'd finished her dessert, a white chocolate–chip cookie with macadamia nuts, she felt more settled, but still weighed down with the sense of loss.

She tried to put it into context. In spite of her hopes and aspirations, one of the cruelest lessons of her life was it wasn't possible to have it all—that a person sometimes had to choose—and the choosing sometimes required sacrifice. Losing Curt felt like the biggest sacrifice she would ever make, and she had to reassure herself constantly that it was the right decision.

That night, in the screen porch with the lights off, Karen changed into her nightie and slipped into bed. It was weird sleeping outside, but she thought she would like it. The enclosure kept the bugs out but let in enough air that she didn't feel closed in. The campground was quiet tonight. In the distance, she heard a bullfrog sing. She drifted off, feeling more settled than before.

The next morning, Karen went into the trailer to use the restroom and make breakfast.

"There's coffee." Jessie was trying to cut up a pancake while keeping Sunshine from climbing on a shelf.

Karen grabbed the baby and steadied her. "Go ahead. Finish up. I'll watch her."

Jessie ate while Karen played with Sunshine, and then they switched. Or tried to. Sunshine wanted to be in Karen's lap constantly, fussing when she put her down.

Jessie rinsed her dish. "I know it's not really fair to you that we're here, crowding into your trailer." She prepared Sunshine's breakfast, chopping up mangoes and little squares of cheese along with Cheerios.

"It's not a question of fairness. We don't have any other choice."

"Still, I have a suggestion." Jessie lifted the baby into her high chair, but Sunshine balked, screaming. Karen offered to hold her in her lap and feed her.

"I'm not sure that's a good habit to start," said Jessie.

"Who cares?" Karen took the baby and chuckled at Sunshine's joyful reaction to being held. "It's only temporary."

"I'm sorry, but no." Jessie shook her head and stuck the baby into the chair anyway. In spite of the screaming, she explained, "According to my textbooks, babies have to start feeling independent, and mealtime is a perfect setting for them to explore."

"It's not going to kill her this one time."

Jessie finally got the baby to quiet down and start eating. "One time leads to two times, and then where are you? You completely lose control of the situation."

"You're a psych student?"

"I'm halfway through my degree in social work."

"Good for you. What did you want to ask me?"

"If you'd accept rent. I'd like to give you a hundred dollars for the month."

"Your grandmother would kill me, so no."

"I want to pay my way. I've been working."

"Doing what?"

Jessie's phone beeped, and she glanced at it. In that annoying way kids have, she read it in front of Karen. When she looked up, her face was pale. She set the phone aside and went back to feeding the baby.

"Doing what?" Karen repeated.

246

"Huh? Oh, um, I do alterations for the ladies. Gina got me started."

"She tried that on me," Karen said. "I kept telling her no. You have to be careful. She can take advantage."

"I'm aware of that," Jessie said. "I charge all of them ten dollars for simple hemming and mending, but anything more complicated is twenty-five dollars an hour. And I'm as busy as I can stand."

Karen admired Jessie for that. "You're handling them better than I ever did."

"So can we agree on rent?"

"No." It was time for Karen's second idea. "But you can agree to go apartment hunting with me."

Jessie shrugged. "If you think you can find something, let's look. But I still wish you'd let me contribute."

Karen shook her head. If she let Jessie pay, the girl would feel more entitled to stay.

The psychology student had probably already figured that out.

"I'm going to the library," Karen said.

Jessie bowed her head toward Sunshine. She didn't answer.

Chapter Thirty-Nine

*T*he next morning, Jessie was resigned, but Karen was determined. They would find an apartment, and Jessie could begin making plans to move.

After leaving Sunshine with Belle, Karen and Jessie headed north to the mainland. They exchanged a few pleasantries and then fell silent. Karen drove, while Jessie bent to her phone, nimble thumbs flying. The tide was out, leaving mud flats baking on both sides of the roadway. The sky was hazy, a southerly wind blowing the crud from Miami toward the Keys. To break up the silence, Karen rolled the window partway down, letting in road noise. Jessie spoke only to give her directions from GPS.

At the first address, a guard waved them through gates. Karen parked in front of the office. "Looks expensive."

"That's because it has a yard. I hope it's big. I might have to find a roommate." Jessie hopped out of the cab. The manager, a thin woman with a strong jaw, said, "You're lucky. We have one apartment available." They hurried after her as she marched toward the back end of the property. "We don't get many vacancies, so you caught us on a good day." She unlocked the entry door, located under the stairs to the upper residence. The porch-light fixture lacked a bulb and was covered in spider webs.

The unit, shaped like a shoe box, consisted of a bathroom and a combination kitchen-living room with a Murphy bed. A slider opened to a slab of cement that ended in a wooden fence.

"That's the yard?" Jessie asked.

"Perfect for relaxing outside," the manager said.

The fence was broken in places, and on the other side, a back-yard skateboard ramp rose above the fence line. Several young men sat smoking at the top of the ramp. They stared at the women. One of them scratched his crotch, and another laughed.

"You've got to be kidding me," Karen muttered.

Jessie swallowed. "How much?"

The manager told them.

"That's outrageous," Karen said.

"It's the going rate. This one won't last."

"Thanks anyway." They returned to the truck. Jessie consulted her phone. "The next one is an apartment on the ground floor and has a little yard." She grimaced. "I hope it's better than this one."

"What's the area like?"

"Affordable."

The Richelieu Apartments were painted bright pumpkin. The windows of the rental office were painted over, and the air stank of fried fish. When a cockroach ran across the manager's desk, Jessie stifled a shriek.

The man laughed, exposing three missing teeth.

"Let's get out of here," Karen said.

The third apartment complex looked clean enough on the out-side, but as the manager led them through the courtyard and past the pool, Karen saw that it was drained, the bloated carcass of a rabbit half in the puddle of muddy rainwater in the deep end. She grabbed Jessie's arm and headed back to the truck.

They kept looking until it was dark, but everything affordable ranged from disgusting to frightening. Dejected, they headed back to Key Largo.

"Something will turn up," Karen said, but she couldn't imagine Sunshine toddling around in such places.

"I'll keep looking," said Jessie.

That evening, Karen went to get a bite at Lorelei's. Out on the patio, she finished her drink and sat, her thoughts morose in spite of the peaches and pinks of sunset over the sound. When she got back to the trailer, Jessie had just finished bathing Sunshine in a little rubber wash-tub on the shower floor. She put the baby to bed and came to the door of the screen porch. Karen sat in darkness, lit only by a distant streetlight.

"Can I come out?"

"Sure." Karen unfolded a second camp chair.

"Today was such a bust. I never saw so much filth."

"Horrible," said Karen. "Hard to believe some people live that way."

"Even when I was living in a single-wide in backcountry Georgia, it wasn't dirty. Those people were horrible."

Karen was still trying to get her brain around the idea of Sunshine living on the other side of the fence from the skateboarding ramp. Jessie would be a prime target. They'd both seen the way the young men raked her over with hungry eyes. Still, she had to help Jessie find a place, or she would never be able to sell the RV. "Have you looked at the flyers at the grocery store?"

"I don't even know why they print new ones. There's nothing."

"Things can change." Karen hoped.

A car went by, and the women fell silent as it traveled slowly past.

"You want a beer?" asked Jessie.

"Sure."

Jessie came back out with two bottles and handed one to Karen. "It's actually kind of nice out here."

"It is. I feel like I'm camping," said Karen. "Your grandmother got me started. If it hadn't been for her, I'd never be here."

"What would you be doing?"

Karen took a swig of beer. "I might have gone back to California eventually and tried to start over there, working for some big corporation again."

"Might have been a little more secure."

"That's always the gamble, isn't it?" There were no answers in life, Karen thought. You were constantly making them up for yourself and might never know whether or not you were right. "I'm pretty happy, all in all. But nothing's perfect."

"Um. Along those lines." Jessie took a sip of beer and then put the bottle down on her knees, playing with the condensation and studying the cold beads.

Karen waited.

"So I talked to Lenny a little while ago."

"Today?"

"A few minutes ago."

"I didn't know the two of you were in contact."

"We have been, a little." Jessie sighed. "He sounds sorry."

Karen clamped her mouth shut. It wasn't her business, she repeated in her head. Not her business. Not her business. "Just be careful, okay?"

"Of course." Jessie finished her beer and went back inside.

Karen sat in the dark for a long time after that. No sense trying to sleep yet. Her mind was a jumble of anger and fear. The night fell quiet, and the campground grew dark. After a while, she went to bed, but she didn't sleep for a long time.

Chapter Forty

*T*he roar of a boat motor woke Karen. She tried to go back to sleep, but Jessie's revelation made it impossible. In the darkness, Karen turned on her reader, but she was too sleepy, and the words were wasted. She set it aside and lay in the dark, waiting for dawn.

Instead, flashing lights lit up the night, and an ambulance appeared, rolling quietly down the road through the campground. As it passed Karen, she sat up.

Eleanor.

Karen slipped into her clothes and flip-flops and quietly unzipped her door flap. In the damp cold, she walked quickly down the roadway toward the back edge of the campground, following the vehicle. Fern and Belle came out of the darkness and joined her. Their anxious whispers increased Karen's concern.

Doc and Patti were already at the campsite. Margo and Candace appeared. They stood and waited, but then Fern couldn't stand it anymore and elbowed her way inside. When she returned, her face was grim. "She's not breathing. They're trying to revive her."

***

In the late morning, they trailed down to the gazebo on the beach. More women joined them, and the story unfolded. Candace had been with Eleanor, watching a movie, when the old woman slumped sideways. Candace called 911, but the paramedics couldn't do anything.

Margo and Candace had looked through Eleanor's address book and found a nephew. He contacted the office, and the campground manager shooed them away and locked the place up. When Candace objected, the manager said the nephew had directed her to secure the property.

Karen sat atop the picnic table, her feet on the bench, head hunched between her shoulders. It had been only six months since something similar had happened with Frieda.

"We should have a memorial, at least." Belle's voice was barely more than a whisper.

"Goddamn it." Fern stormed around the table, hands jammed in her front pockets. "We're her family, but they act like we're a bunch of vagrants wanting to loot the place."

The sun rose, and Jessie showed up holding Sunshine, oatmeal crusted on the baby's mouth. Belle reached for the child and hugged her close. Jessie climbed up next to Karen. "What's going on?"

"Eleanor died."

"Oh, no." Tears welled in her eyes.

The kid's new at this, Karen thought. She patted Jessie on the back.

"I loved that old lady. I'm going to really miss her."

"We all will, honey," said Belle.

"What fries my bacon is they just hauled her body away, and we'll never even get to be part of a service or anything." Fern dropped onto the beach.

"We could have one ourselves," said Patti.

"We're all here now," said Doc. Karen looked around. More of the CRS ladies had gathered silently.

When Margo stepped forward, even Gina bowed her head. "Oh Lord, we thank you for this day…" Karen and Jessie slipped off the table and stood together, heads bowed. The rest of the women followed suit. As they prayed, Sunshine began to fuss, and Belle handed her to Fern. The baby laid her head against Fern's shoulder and fell silent. A light breeze rocked the sailboat masts, and their riggings rang like church bells.

***

Afterward, Karen folded up her bed and straightened the screen porch. She showered, ate breakfast, and went to the library. Ben was expecting an update this morning, and she wanted to check in with Peggy in California. She opened a file and turned on her laptop. The computer hadn't been shut down the last time she used it, and a web page about Barcelona reloaded onto the screen.

She didn't want to think about Curt right now. She didn't want to miss him or wonder if he was already in Spain and if so, who he was with. It would be early evening there. Soon he'd have dinner— alone? Doubtful.

She tried to return to work, but Eleanor's death had knocked her off-balance. Thoughts of illness and mortality interrupted her concentration. In a couple weeks, she'd be in Savannah starting a new life, at fifty. Knowing only a handful of people, loving no one. If she had a stroke in her apartment, who would come to her aid besides a couple of hired EMTs? Karen had admired Eleanor's self-sufficiency, but now she wondered if it was enough.

After another half-hour of dithering, she couldn't fight it anymore and dialed Curt's work number. His autoresponder said he'd be gone for two weeks and if the caller needed help before that, to please contact the main office. Karen hung up, packed her briefcase, and climbed on her scooter, raising the kickstand with a vicious kick. She drove all the way down to Duck Key and Marathon, and then she turned around and came back.

That evening, Eleanor's death cast a pall over the trailer. Karen and Jessie were both morose. Over a dinner of fried chicken, biscuits, and gravy, Jessie told Karen more about contacting Lenny. He'd been so happy to hear from her, and he'd begged and pleaded with her to come home. Swore he'd stopped drinking, picked up the trailer, and watered her flowers a lot. Jessie was wary but felt it had been a good conversation, and that fact both reassured and confused her.

"Well, you're twenty-two." Karen helped herself to another drumstick.

"That's condescending," said Jessie.

"You're right. Sorry."

They ate in awkward silence.

"What about you?" asked Jessie. "You and that professor."

"What about him?"

"Belle says you're in love, but Fern says you'll never let a man stand in the way of your ambition."

"I guess that about sums it up. They think I'm a fool," said Karen.

"Are you?" Jessie refilled Karen's wineglass.

"I don't know."

"The ladies talk about you."

"I'm sure they do."

"They admire you. They just don't understand you."

Karen was in the middle of a sip of wine, and she started laughing and choking all at once. Her eyes teared, and her nose ran as she coughed. When she calmed down, she said, "Me, neither."

Jessie folded her arms on the table. "I'm not going anywhere."

So Karen told her about Curt and their long crush and her dreams and his visit to Georgia and her new office and his offer for her to come to Spain.

And Jessie told Karen about Lenny and how she didn't know how to decide what to do, but even if he wasn't exactly right for her, she would tough it out for a couple more years with him because she had no other choice, and by the way, he wasn't the father. She elaborated in full detail, while Karen tried to keep her eyes from bugging out. When Jessie finished, they both sat there for a minute, not knowing what to say.

Karen sighed. "Kind of a relief, though, right?"

"I guess. But it's so sad. What am I going to tell her when she gets older?" Jessie held out her glass, and Karen refilled it.

"You're the psychology major. You'll figure it out."

"I almost wish I were older," Jessie said. "I hate all the uncertainty about my future."

"Get used to it."

"But you—"

Karen looked up at the ceiling, shaking her head. "I'm more than twice your age, Jessie, and I still don't know what the hell I'm doing. All you can do is decide what your values are, what's most important to you, and then try to stick to them. Nothing really changes with age. I still have as many dreams now as I did when I was twenty-two."

Jessie said, "I didn't realize you could be going through the same thing…"

"At my age?"

"I didn't want to say it, but yeah. When does a person ever get old enough to have everything figured out?"

"Never, I hope." Karen wiped her eyes. "Because then where's the magic?"

Chapter Forty-One

*T*he cab let Curt out in front of a complex of buildings with Moorish arches and tiled hallways. He stood for a minute, trying to get his bearings.

That morning, after only a couple hours of sleep, he had shuffled downstairs to see what the Barcelona Hilton offered for breakfast. At the café, the voices were a mixture of Spanish, Catalan, English, and German. His waiter had zipped around refilling coffee and conversing in all four, but Curt felt so jet lagged, he had a hard time communicating in his native language.

At the geology building, Curt pulled open the front door and stepped inside. From her perch behind a pristine white desk, the receptionist directed him down a series of long hallways to the office of the department head. There, a woman in a tight skirt and low-cut blouse looked up, delight flashing in her eyes. "Yes?"

"I'm Curtis Hoffman, visiting adjunct from the United States." He held out his hand.

She came around the desk and took his hand in both of hers. "Ah, yes, Dr. Hoffman. We were expecting you." She looked up at him. "Would you like me to introduce you to the department chair?"

"Thanks." Curt held back a smile. It was nice to be welcomed so warmly.

Dr. Lorenzo Fernandez, skeletally thin but with a ready smile, greeted Curt warmly and introduced his associates. The woman was Monica. The other colleague, Sergio, was a jocular beach ball with a too-short tie. The three of them showed him around, starting with faculty offices to classrooms to labs to the amphitheater where visiting notables addressed crowds of hundreds. They spoke formal English with an accent.

"We have taught geologic studies since 1910," said Fernandez. "Our school sets the European benchmark for scientific research."

"And we're the biggest," said Monica with a little smile.

Sergio opened a door. "These are the geochemical-research offices, where you'll be working."

"What about this?" Curt reached for an adjacent door.

"Don't go in there," said Lorenzo. "That's the back of the amphitheater, and there's a program in process."

"At the north end of the building, you'll find a cafeteria, which has a dining room for staff. It's very private," said Monica.

"We also have a gym," said Sergio, who looked as if he didn't use it.

Curt wasn't interested in the gym. Instead, he planned to swim in the ocean, jog along the beach, or borrow a bike and explore the area.

"Have you decided where you'll be staying?" asked Monica.

Curt stuck his hands in his pockets. "I was hoping to get some suggestions."

"We can talk about that at the orientation lunch." She smiled, her eyes narrowing like a cat eyeing prey. "Sit with me. I'll tell you everything you need to know to be happy here."

"Thanks," Curt said.

"It would be my pleasure."

After the tour, Curt ducked out for time alone. Lunch wasn't until two. He would have to get used to the later mealtimes.

After another hour of looking over the grounds and meeting other staff, he felt worn out. He found a quiet nook in the library and checked his phone for messages, but the one he hoped for wasn't there. He ran through his e-mail, but time dragged.

A couple of young women sashayed past in short shorts and tank tops. Their laughter provided a stark contrast to his bleak mood. Finally, it was time to join the others in the faculty dining room where he was introduced to the expat community, a friendly, talkative group. Along with lunch, they listened to speech after speech. By the time the program ended and he was back at his hotel, Curt was stumbling from fatigue. He pulled the curtains closed and fell into a deep, dreamless sleep.

When he awoke, it was dark, and he felt ravenous. He showered and dressed and hailed a cab to Las Ramblas, the world-famous promenade. There, he located a café recommended by one of his new colleagues and sat outside in the balmy night, dining on tapas and watching the crowd flow past. He'd wanted to enjoy himself, but felt a dark mood descend.

When he left the United States, Curt had been excited, with a list of plans for the year abroad. He would make friends at the university and learn to live like a local in this historic city. He would explore the parks and museums, enjoy the beach at the city's edge, and learn the languages, both Spanish and Catalan.

He would forget the fact that Karen chose to put her work ahead of their relationship.

Couples strolled past, holding hands, laughing, kissing. He pushed his plate away and signaled for another bottle of wine.

It was her choice, and he accepted that, but he wasn't built for being alone. He was past the age when it would have shamed him to admit it. Her decision stung, but he had to adapt. With a million and a half people in the city, surely he could make a few friends. Someone to share dinner with, tour a museum, or explore a romantic garden. Curt was in Barcelona for the experience. Life as a monk wasn't in the cards.

He strolled Las Ramblas, watching the street performers, artists, and living statues. Barcelona was a cornucopia, spilling out her riches to tempt him. At the foot of a soaring tiled fountain, a classical guitarist played flamenco, his partner twirling and stamping in a blur of red silk. The notes evoked deep emotion as Curt's thoughts ranged from loss of Karen to his daughter growing up and leaving the nest to the sunset years of his own career. As the guitarist finished with an enthusiastic flourish, the crowd clapped and shouted its appreciation. Curt handed the guitarist a generous tip, but his mood remained bleak as he returned to his hotel room for the long night ahead.

Chapter Forty-Two

*K*aren and Jessie formed a routine, falling naturally into a process of helping each other. While one did housekeeping or took a shower, the other played with the baby. In things related to childcare, Karen was less rigid than Jessie, although it never became an issue. But Jessie had her ways.

"You don't have to hold her." Jessie stood in the bathroom doorway. "Usually I just leave her in the Pack 'n Play."

"But she wants to get out."

"You'll spoil her."

"She's just such a cuddle bug," Karen said. After a while, she couldn't help it. She was getting attached. She felt like a grandmother.

While Jessie showered, Karen held Sunshine, enjoying the solidness and warmth of the baby. She was growing more attached every day. The two of them played games, like make-a-face and talking-teddy-bear. Sunshine's four teeth gleamed like adorable corn kernels in her pink gums.

Karen found she could speak Sunshine's language, baby talking right along with her. She showered Sunshine with kisses on her nose and cheeks while the baby grabbed her hair and pulled it. At times Karen wondered what it would have been like to have a daughter, a baby girl like Sunshine. She held the baby close.

In the shower, Jessie was singing.

When she was dressed, Jessie took the baby back. "I'm making slow-cooker stew tonight, if you want to eat with us." She began changing Sunshine. "It's a family recipe."

Karen hesitated on her way out. "What time?"

"Six?"

"Okay."

When Karen came home from her day at the library, the aroma of sage and garlic wafted out of the trailer. She poured a glass of wine and read while Jessie put the baby to bed. Then they feasted on Russian chicken on rice, with a salad on the side.

"You're a good cook," Karen said.

"It's a hobby. Trying out new recipes, gathering them in one place—" Jessie took a swig of wine. "Which unfortunately is a shoe box in Atlanta."

"Is he still texting you?"

"Twenty times a day."

"He wants you back."

"Yeah." Jessie heaved a big sigh, and Karen found it contagious.

"What do you think you'll do?" she asked.

Jessie shrugged. "I don't know. He's pathetic. But then I kind of understand, too, you know?" She explained about his concussions and the football history. "So maybe he's sick and needs help. And maybe I'm bailing when he needs me most."

"But you have to think of your future."

Jessie rolled the stem of her wineglass between her fingers. "I grew up watching my mother, and I never wanted to be like her. It's why I love psychology so much—trying to figure out why people are the way they are. But here I am, in the same frickin' situation as her."

"Your dad was violent?"

"No, he's a quiet drunk. But it's the same thing, you know?"

The baby cried out in her sleep, and the women lapsed into silence. Night fell, and the neighbor's Christmas lights blinked on, flashing diffuse red and green through the kitchen curtains.

"I don't want to be codependent," said Jessie. "I don't know what to do."

"So going home is a nonstarter."

"Yeah, but it's worse than that." Jessie sucked down another glass of wine and refilled it. "Lenny doesn't acknowledge Sunshine."

"What do you mean?"

"He doesn't touch her or hug her or talk to her or anything. It's like he doesn't see her."

"You know that's bad, right?"

Jessie picked at her meal. "But it could be for a lot of reasons. I read about this. Sometimes men don't bond right away. Or he feels unsure of himself. Or a lot of things. I can't condemn him for that. She's barely a year old. It might take more time."

"Jessie?"

Jessie put her face in one hand. "I'm rationalizing, aren't I?"

"You might be." Karen got up and pulled the curtains shut. "Hard to say. The most important thing is safety, for you and the baby."

"He promised to go to counseling."

They all did that. Karen had seen it over the span of her career. Sometimes it helped. "Has he gone yet?"

"I don't think so. I think he's waiting for me."

Karen sighed. "What are you going to do?"

Jessie drew a line through the condensation on her wine glass. "I told him he could come here."

Chapter Forty-Three

"*O*h, man." Karen drained the rest of her glass. "Really?"

"Yep. I did it."

"What were you thinking?"

"First of all, I don't know if he's totally bad. All I know is he got drunk and did it this one time. There are a lot of reasons it could have happened, but it's out of character for him. If I give him up now, I could be making a big mistake."

"That's what you're telling yourself, right? You asked me about rationalization. Do you hear yourself?"

"I have to try."

"Why?"

"What else am I going to do? I don't have any place to live. I don't have a job—"

"You have your clothing business."

"It's not enough. I can't afford rent and childcare and food if I'm living alone. At least with Lenny, we can live cheaply in the trailer."

"Another thing, he wants you back, but he doesn't seem to care about the baby. How can you live like that? And what are you going to do if he goes nuts again?"

"He won't."

"You don't know that."

Jessie pulled on her jacket. "I'm going for a walk."

Fine, Karen thought, sinking into the sofa. What a mess.

You're tellin' me.

Karen closed her eyes and leaned her head back. *You could fix this, Frieda.*

How?

I don't know. Make him get in a car wreck or something.

Don't be saying things like that.

I didn't mean it, Karen thought. *But what am I going to do?*

There was no answer.

Karen wanted to throw something or run away, neither of which would protect any of them. And since Jessie wasn't thinking straight, protection would fall to Karen, at least for the duration of Lenny's visit. After that, she wasn't responsible.

Except what if he sweet-talked Jessie into coming home with him, and then they'd be out in the countryside, helpless. He'd probably take her phone and car keys. She'd be trapped.

Karen felt like throwing up.

***

A week later, a beat-up work truck rumbled into the driveway. Karen opened the door. Lenny was a little taller than her, and he wore prison pants, a white tank and a plaid overshirt, unbuttoned. His flat stomach and broad shoulders spoke of physical labor.

"I'm looking for Jessie?" He took off his sunglasses and smiled, and Karen saw why a young woman might make the mistake of forgiving him.

"I'll take you to her." Jessie and the baby were down at the clubhouse, sewing with the ladies, so Karen locked up and walked him over there. When they came through the door, the women fell silent.

"This is Lenny." Karen stepped away from him.

"Hello, ladies." Lenny stood erect, flashing that thousand-watt grin, and Jessie put her sewing aside.

Fern reached him first. "I heard about you."

"Whoa, how about 'Nice to meet you'?"

"It isn't nice. You're not nice, from what I heard." Fern stuck her barrel chest out at him, as if daring him to make a move.

Lenny glanced away. "Whatever you heard, I take full responsibility."

"How, exactly?"

He tilted his head as if he didn't understand.

Fern tapped him on the chest with one finger. "How did you take responsibility? Did you turn yourself in for domestic assault and serve time yet?"

The young man shifted his stance, his feet apart, chest thrust forward.

Jessie, not smiling, stood and placed her sewing on her chair. She straightened her blouse and walked slowly toward him.

Fern held out her arm, barring Jessie from coming any closer. "He wants you to run off with him, and that little child as well. We're your family now, and I don't think it's asking too much to expect him to answer our questions."

"He agreed to go to counseling when we get back."

The ladies gasped, and Belle clutched Sunshine.

"*When* you get back? You're actually going?" Fern's face turned purple.

"I haven't made up my mind," Jessie said. "He has to agree to certain conditions first."

Lenny raised his chin. "Which I said I would do. Case closed."
He looked down at Jessie. "You hungry?"

"I could eat."

"Why don't you show me where it's good, and we'll get a bite,
and then I'll bring you back here so your friends won't have to
worry about me being unresponsible with you."

"Irresponsible," said Doc.

Jessie turned to Belle. "Can you watch her for a few hours?"

Belle hugged the baby and nodded.

"After you." Lenny held the door and followed Jessie through it.
Then he turned and gave them a sloppy salute. "Ladies."

The door closed, and chairs scraped backward as they all ran
to the windows to look. Lenny was swaggering away, his arm en-
circling Jessie's shoulders. Watching, the women were apoplectic.

"Did he just flip us off?"

"What a bastard."

"If he hurts her, I'll kill him."

"You and me, both."

"How can she risk this?"

"It doesn't look good."

Karen held her breath for the next few hours, but Lenny
dropped Jessie off at nine. Jessie went right to bed, but her light
was on for a long time, and Karen could hear her laughing and talking on her phone, late into the night.

The next day, Karen agreed to babysit while Jessie and Lenny
hung out. He dropped her off around ten that night, and when Jessie
came in the door, she was flushed and happy. Lenny had bought her
a cute bikini, and they swam with the dolphins at the wildlife park
down the highway. As Karen watched Jessie float around the room,
she wondered if the girl could possibly be objective about the man.
Had he really changed, or was this an act to get her back to the
trailer near Atlanta?

Chapter Forty-Four

*O*n the third day, Jessie asked if Karen would babysit so she could spend the night with Lenny at his motel room.

When Karen hesitated, Jessie sat down on the sofa, one leg folded under her. "I do think he's learned his lesson," she said, winding a strand of hair around one finger. "He's being really kind and thoughtful."

"Have you actually talked about what happened?"

"He blamed the fact that he was drunk and promised to drink less in the future. So far, that's what I've seen. He orders sodas a lot when we go out."

Karen agreed to babysit, but she had a bad feeling about the evening. As she watched Jessie pack an overnight bag, she ran through her observations. In all the time Lenny had been visiting, he'd avoided her and the rest of the ladies—not a good sign. She didn't see any repentance coming from him in the small amount of time she was able to observe him. Plus, he hadn't shown the least bit of interest in Sunshine, and the baby acted like she didn't know who he was. But Jessie was a grown woman, however young, and it wasn't Karen's place to mother her. Jessie would have to explore her world and make her own decisions.

Young people were hard to judge. Sometimes they made mistakes but then straightened out as they matured. Karen didn't want to condemn Lenny without knowing more about him. Maybe it was just one time, a mistake, a terrible alcohol-fueled lapse of control— but the thought of Jessie sticking with him, living in an isolated single-wide out in the country, raised too many worries to name.

That evening, Karen watched them drive away, trying to ignore the cold feeling in the pit of her stomach. Her phone was charged and the ringer set to high. She checked on Sunshine, who was sleeping soundly. Then she opened one of the romance novels from Jekyll Island. The last time she looked at the clock, it was almost one. She fell asleep in the recliner.

At two, she awoke to the sound of the door being unlocked, and Jessie walked in, her face red and her makeup streaked. One sleeve was torn. Her eyes blazed.

"What happened?" Karen jumped up and went to her. "Are you hurt?"

"Not as bad as him." Jessie let her purse and shoes drop to the floor and sank onto the sofa.

"Where's Lenny?"

"Writhing around on the floor of his hotel room, most likely." Jessie allowed herself a little smile. "I fought back."

Karen wanted to drag Lenny behind a fast-moving vehicle, but she kept her voice even. "I'll make tea," she said, opening a box of chamomile. "I'm glad you're safe."

"I can't believe I was that stupid." As she said it, Jessie's voice broke. Karen sat next to her, gave her a hug, and handed her a box of tissues. When the tea was ready, she brought two cups over.

"How did you get back here?"

"I walked." Jessie picked up a steaming cup.

"In heels? It's two miles."

"How did you know that?"

Karen looked guilty. "Fern and I drove by the place."

"I'm sorry for scaring you. And except for a couple of little cuts on my feet, I'm fine," she said. "Which is more than I can say for Lenny."

Karen wanted the story, but she heard a noise and looked out the window. "Do you think he'll come here?"

"No. He can't drive." The night had begun with a romantic dinner and many tropical cocktails, followed by a visit to his hotel room. When Lenny told Jessie she'd be returning to Georgia with him, she balked, and they argued. When it escalated to yelling, she yelled back. When she decided to leave, he grabbed her. She shook him off, and the fight became physical. Now her left arm was red and beginning to bruise.

"I was so mad, Karen. I cussed him out and pushed him off me, and he backed up a few steps. Then he stood there like a gorilla with his arms out to his sides. He was all red in the face, and he said, 'Do I have to beat you?' Can you believe it?" Jessie shook her head. "I ran into the bathroom, thinking I could lock myself in, but I wasn't fast enough. He came in after me, and then I was trapped." Jessie rubbed one eye with the heel of her hand, smudging her mascara further. "He had his arm back like this, in a fist. I thought for sure he was going to break my jaw. I was going to start screaming my head off, hoping somebody would come save me, but then I grabbed my hair spray and let him have it right in the eyes. Then I ran."

Karen hugged her. "Good for you."

"Yeah, good for me." Jessie started crying in earnest now. Karen rubbed her back, offered tissues, and kept one ear cocked toward the highway. She didn't know what hair spray would do to a guy, but if he came after Jessie, all they could do was lock the doors and call the police. The muscles in Karen's jaw twitched. She did not like being a victim.

Minutes later, they both heard it. A vehicle coming too fast into the campground. It screeched to a stop in the driveway. "Stay here," Karen said. "Call nine one one."

"What about you?"

"Lock the door." Karen pulled it shut behind her. She slipped through the zippered entrance to the sleep porch and secured it behind her.

Lenny jumped out. His hair dripped onto his shirt, wet from trying to rinse the painful spray out of his eyes, which were bulging and red. "Where is she?"

"Get back in your truck and leave," Karen said. She stood in front of the canvas porch, her arms folded and feet planted, trying to look as formidable as possible. In one hand was a tiny canister of Mace, so old it was probably inert.

"Make her come out here."

Karen spoke calmly. "Get back in your truck, and leave now."

"Jessie!" Lenny bellowed. Lights came on next door.

"She called the police. They'll arrest you."

Lenny glared at Karen. "Maybe, but I'll still beat the shit out of you first."

Karen looked into his ravaged eyes and knew he meant it. She glared back at him, gripping the little canister.

The porch light came on at the trailer next door. The neighbor came out of his trailer, holding up a phone. "I'm filming you."

"Stupid fuck." Lenny ran to the man, wrestled the phone from him, and hurled it down the street. It pinged against a metal object and then shattered in the darkness. He shoved the old man up against the side of his trailer, lifting him off his feet. When Lenny let him go, the man folded to the ground and lay still.

Lenny ran back to the screen porch and tried to unzip the opening.

"Jessie, lock the door!" Karen yelled. She picked up a lawn chair and swung it at the back of Lenny's head as he was bent down, fumbling with the zipper. It was featherlight and useless, but it distracted him. With a roar, he grabbed the broken chair and swung it at Karen. She stepped back out of range but was now trapped against the wall of the RV. Lenny wound up again. Karen flattened herself against the trailer.

Just as Lenny swung again, the big black-and-tan Chevy Silverado roared up, bounced over the curbing and skidded to a stop with Lenny in the headlights.

Fern jumped out and planted both feet. She held up a Maglite like a billy club, slapping it into the palm of one hand. "Off the property. Now."

Lenny raised a fist. The truck shifted gear. Behind the wheel, Belle raced the engine, twice. Candace and Margo appeared out of the darkness to stand beside Fern. Both of them held up bear-spray canisters.

"Come on, mister," said Margo. "Let me feed you some of this."

Lenny clenched his fists. His head jerked at the crunch of taillights shattering. He cursed and tried to get around the truck, but Belle inched forward and cut off his pathway. Glass exploded again.

"Ima fuckin' kill you!" Lenny screamed.

Sirens pierced the night. Belle shifted into reverse.

Lenny ran to his truck. Patti stood brandishing her fire ax, a wicked smile on her face. Behind her, Doc raised a shovel and brought it down hard on the windshield. The glass spiderwebbed into a million little pieces.

Cursing and wailing, Lenny jumped in, and the truck fishtailed out to the highway, broken glass raining from its cab. Belle reversed the Chevy and parked it in the lane. The women huddled to debrief, shaking with adrenaline and pride. When the neighbor hobbled over, they shook his hand and hugged him. Jessie came out of the trailer.

Belle hurried to her. "Is the baby okay?"

"She's still sleeping," said Jessie.

"Thank God."

The police arrived and took a report but weren't optimistic.

"We can't sit outside your door and watch for the guy," said one officer. "You should think about what you're going to do. Get a big dog, at least."

"Or move to a someplace he can't find you," said the second officer.

Karen was dismayed, and Fern muttered under her breath, but unless they hired private security, the women would have to protect themselves. When the police left, the women went back to their trailers.

Jessie and Karen sat at the kitchen table, too keyed up to sleep.

Jessie wasn't crying anymore. Her face was pale but determined. "Now I really do need to find a place to live. I wanted to stay around here, but that's out."

"What about Denver? Sandy's got that big house, and your dad makes a good living. I'm sure they'd love to help."

Jessie made a face. "She'd love to have me back to keep her company, but she made it clear a baby would be a competitor."

"Surely she didn't say that."

"Not in so many words. Sandy's crazy. I can't be around her."

Karen wondered if this was youthful drama.

"When I got pregnant, Mom—I mean Sandy—went nuts. She tried to get me to abort Sunshine. We argued, and when I told her I was keeping my child, she tried to push me down the stairs. My dad saw it all, and he had her committed. She was hospitalized for several months. Dad tried to get me to stay." Jessie's eyes narrowed. "He said Sandy would need me when she was released."

Karen ached for the girl. "So you felt like they both deserted you."

"I told Lenny, and he came and got me. I moved out that weekend." She looked toward the bedroom where Sunshine was sleeping.

"You're in a rough place right now, but it will get better."

"Can't get any worse." Jessie smiled, and then her face crumbled, and she began to weep.

Karen scooted over and hugged her. "You'll be fine," she said. "You'll get a good job and fall in love again, and Sunshine will thrive. It might take a while, though, so you have to stay strong."

"I'll try." But Jessie didn't sound like she believed it.

"You will be fine. I promise."

"Sorry, but that sounds crazy."

"Listen to me," Karen said. "I had four miscarriages. Four pregnancies—four children, buried. Do you know what I would have done to have a child? You have a child."

Jessie heaved a big sigh, and Karen continued.

"When I went to my hometown for my mother's funeral, I was served divorce papers, and then I lost my job."

"God."

"My point is we go on. Most people suffer. It's just a fact of life."

"And yet, you seem so normal."

"I wouldn't go that far," Karen said.

Jessie wiped her eyes with her shirt sleeve. "I need to start making plans. I'll get an apartment in a city, maybe find a roommate. I'll find childcare and a job and do classes online at night."

"You've got your business for extra income."

"That will help." Jessie sighed. "Someday, it'll be easier, but right now, it's overwhelming."

"I understand," said Karen. "I wish there was something I could do to help."

"You gave me refuge when I was on the run and a chance to see how I was living and break free. Now it's up to me." Jessie stood.

"It's almost morning. I'm going to try to grab a few hours of sleep before Sunshine wakes up."

The two of them hugged, and Karen went to her sleeping porch, but she wasn't the least bit tired. She locked the RV's door, zipped her enclosure shut, and walked down to the water's edge to sit and think.

In spite of all the drama and heartache of the night, Karen felt optimistic. Jessie would have a rough time of it, but she would gain understanding and self-sufficiency. In another year, she'd have her degree. The economy was improving. Jessie would find a job and settle in to a new city. In time, she would make friends, fall in love, and build a life.

The parallels weren't lost on Karen, who would soon be settling into a new home herself. The app was off and running; she had money coming in and a growing roster of clients. In time, she'd settle in to life in Savannah.

The sky lightened to charcoal and then pink. A light breeze rippled across the water, rocking the boats in the marina.

As to love? There was only one man she wanted. Karen closed her eyes. It was true, what she'd told Jessie. She did feel stronger, but it still hurt like hell. She'd experienced loss before, and she knew she'd get through it, but just for the moment, grief took her breath away.

A motor started up in the marina, and a few moments later, a small aluminum fishing boat putted past. The fisherman saw Karen and waved, and she waved back. Silence returned to the water, and the sun lit the clouds to peach and then gold. She regretted having to leave this place, but like Jessie, she would start over again, no stranger to the process, having moved away twice from North Dakota and once from California.

The pain of leaving battled with the excitement of a new beginning. She would miss Jessie and Sunshine and the CRS ladies, but maybe when work slowed down, she could join them somewhere at their various camps. Like Rita did, for a month every year. She could maintain their connection, knowing they were her family for life.

Jessie had the harder road in front of her, being only twenty-two and a single mother. The CRS ladies had been such a big help, with meals and childcare and companionship. If it took a village to raise a child, Jessie had lucked into one. Sunshine would miss the ladies. They would miss her, too. Especially Belle, who seemed to have a special bond with the child.

The thought of Jessie moving on alone made Karen unutterably sad, but Jessie had to grow up and make her own way, like everybody else in the world. She wasn't Karen's responsibility.

A couple of grackles landed nearby and fought over a bit of bread they'd found in the camp. Somehow the smaller one won and flew off to a nearby tree, where a nest was wedged into the branches.

No, Jessie wasn't Karen's responsibility, but she was Frieda's granddaughter, and Karen owed that woman a debt of gratitude. While traveling with Frieda on her last road trip, Karen had finally become an individual in her own right. After a lifetime of following the rules and being a good girl, Karen had learned to stake out her own territory and follow her dreams and passions.

And in so doing, she'd learned she could choose whether and when to sacrifice herself. No longer an obligation based in faith and family, the decision was a choice now, an opportunity born of middle-aged clarity. Karen had a choice. That was a privilege. She watched the bird feeding its young and had an idea.

She smiled at its brilliance. Nodding at the sky, she thought, *Are you happy now?*

The palm fans fluttered, as they always did, in the gentle breeze.

Feeling lighter than she had in ages, Karen slid off the picnic table and walked back to the trailer. In the early morning light, she unlocked the RV, and while the girl and her baby slumbered on, Karen located the pink slips for the truck and trailer. She dug a pen out of her office supplies and, with a smile and a flourish, signed her rig over to Jessica Larson.

Chapter Forty-Five

FIVE MONTHS LATER—AUGUST

"*G*et in there. Go on." Curt slapped the horse's flank, and the big gelding clopped into the trailer to join the mare, already secured at the front.

Patrick stood waiting with the colt, who rubbed his head against Patrick's arm. "You'd think he was a pet."

Curt said, "To us, they are."

"How will Erin feel about this?" Patrick led the colt up the ramp and snapped the lead into the D ring on the wall.

Curt wiped the sweat out of his eyes and slammed the tailgate shut. "She's not happy about it." Erin had a harder time saying good-bye, but now that summer break was over, she was heading back to California to finish her veterinary program. In fact, his daughter was a grown woman now. She would probably never be back. "I ned I had a chance to try something new before I got too old. e backed off and told me to have fun."

Patrick pushed up the front of his Stetson with a thumb. "I didn't think you'd go through with it."

Curt leaned against the trailer, arms folded. Gazing across his land, he saw the old farmhouse in which he'd grown up, the barns his father had built, and the rolling acres tilled now by a neighbor. Red roses twined around the white picket fence that outlined the front yard. He would miss this place, and he wasn't sure he'd be back. The couple who'd agreed to lease it were expecting their third child, and he liked the feeling they'd be warming up the house with their noise and messes.

"I almost changed my mind." Curt had stuck out the two weeks in Spain, getting to know his future colleagues and making other friends. Lorenzo and Sergio were solid dudes, but he'd have to watch out for Monica. Whenever other women came into the office to meet the American professor, she got all snarly. Well, that was amusing, nothing more.

He'd placed a deposit on a two-room apartment not far from the university, where expats tended to gather. He'd met some of his students, and for all their rolling *R*s and rapid speech, they were the same as the kids in North Dakota. Together, they would explore the geologic mysteries of the Iberian Peninsula for the next year. After that, who knew? His future was open-ended, a prospect he found both thrilling and daunting. He preferred certainty, but life wasn't certain, and he had learned to live with that if he couldn't make it otherwise. So on the flight home from Barcelona, he found a measure of peace with his decision.

At least, in every other matter besides love. Regret over Karen flooded his heart, and he shrugged and walked around the horse trailer, pretending to check the electrical connections but, in fact, trying to shake it off. She had made her decision, and so had he.

Although he would always love her, he wouldn't stand in the way of her goals. She had to find happiness on her own terms. As would he. They were both hardened in life's fires. They'd survive.

"Safe travels." The men shook hands, and the rig rolled down the driveway. Curt watched it go and then crossed the yard to lock up the barn. Inside, pigeons fluttered up to the rafters, but the stalls were empty and quiet. He'd miss Duke and Missy, the way they'd stomp and nicker in greeting in the morning when he arrived to feed them, or petting them with a fair amount of baby talk before locking up for the night. Even that nosy colt, whom Erin had named Argo at the last minute. Hell of a handle for a little horse.

He stopped by Aunt Marie's new place, checking to make sure the drip system was working right in her container garden on the porch. The old woman gave him a hug and a sad kiss on the cheek, and then she hugged him again. He sat in his truck a minute, watching her go back inside. The humidity was up, and over to the east, the sky filled with monsoon clouds. He'd miss the way clouds turned the sky purple against the golden fields in late summer and the crisp dryness of winter.

Heidi, Jim's elderly German shorthair, padded across the yard and flopped on Aunt Marie's porch. Curt put the truck in gear. North Dakota had never seemed so sweet to him, and the combined grief of leaving it and losing Karen felt like a knife in his gut, but he knew that nothing good came of wallowing, so he turned onto the highway and tried to find a reason to be happy about Spain.

Chapter Forty-Six

SEPTEMBER

"So ah was gettin' coffee, and guess who ah ran into?"

Karen looked up from her desk, smiling at the mellifluous drawl of her new assistant. Della, a willowy six feet with her hair cropped in a short natural, set the tray on Karen's desk.

"Ah got you a peach-raisin muffin and a mocha. That all right?"

"Fantastic." Karen pushed her work aside, unfolded a paper napkin, and broke the muffin in two. "So who'd you see?"

Della sat at the round conference table at the window overlooking the garden. Outside, the neighbor was harvesting tomatoes and peppers and clearing out old vegetation for fall planting. Della took a bite of her pecan Danish before answering. "Remember that guy you pitched last December, Trevor somethin' or other, one of Ted Natchez's group?"

"He almost looks like Elon Musk, right?"

"Um hm. That guy. Anyway, his business is takin' off—he's in the energy sector—and he gave me his card. Said he wanted to talk to you about doin' some hiring." Della grinned.

"Your coffee shop–trolling strategy is a success," said Karen. "All this good food and new clients, too."

"Yeah, don't forget that at my six-month review." Della had elbowed her way into the job at a chamber of commerce mixer last April. With her background in publicity, she had introduced Karen to the business community of Savannah almost faster than she could handle it, and the app enabled Karen to increase her office's efficiency tenfold. At the rate they were going, she'd need to hire an HR technician, and she'd already alerted the property manager she'd be expanding.

Della finished her pastry and went back to her desk in the front office. Karen turned back to her work, but she couldn't concentrate. So much had happened since leaving Key Largo in March.

When she'd handed Jessie the signed pink slips for the RV and truck, the girl first hugged Karen. Then she cried. While Karen shielded Sunshine from her mother's tears, Jessie said, "I was so scared, thinking of trying to find someplace to live in some strange city and not knowing anybody. Doing it all on my own. Worrying about Sunshine being babysat by strangers while I worked all day. And I had no idea how I'd manage classes on top of all that." The speech brought on a fresh deluge.

"I was worried about that, too," said Karen. "Now I don't have to be. You can stick with the ladies until something better turns up."

"It's more than me," Jessie cried. "It's Belle. It would kill her if we left. She had a little girl. I don't know what happened, but she passed away when she was three. That's why she's so attached to Sunshine."

"I didn't know."

"She doesn't tell people." Jessie wiped her eyes and then looked at Karen with alarm. "But what about you? I thought you needed the money."

Karen reassured Jessie that she'd be fine, and the girl accepted this as true.

"And guess what?" Jessie said. "Fern owns a duplex in Palm Springs. She said if she and Belle ever get tired of driving, they'd move there."

"Maybe you could move with them."

Jessie smiled, her face tear-streaked. "Do you think it's too early to go tell them the good news?"

They piled into Fern and Belle's trailer, and a fresh round of tears ensued. Fern asked Karen to look at something outside, and Karen followed her down the steps.

"You going to be okay?" asked Fern.

"Yeah, but could you give me a ride into Miami tomorrow? I need to find a pawnshop."

***

Karen used the earrings to make a down payment on a car, and a few days later, with help from Fern and Jessie, she emptied the RV of her things and moved to Savannah. Soon after, the CRS ladies broke camp and headed to New England for the summer. According to her latest e-mail, Jessie was making a pretty good income by rehabbing classy old garments. She was also closing in on her degree. Sunshine was cutting teeth, but the ladies still clamored to babysit, so Jessie had plenty of help. When the truck needed brake work, Fern found a reliable garage while they were driving through Connecticut, and the ladies passed the hat to offset the cost.

So Karen didn't have to worry about Jessie anymore. It wasn't worry that had her dragging around her apartment and work lately. Maybe it was the change of seasons in a new place. Fall was coming, the light was turning to amber, and the trees were beginning to drop their leaves. In the morning, instead of flying out of bed, enthused about her day, she hit the snooze button repeatedly. Her lethargy was inexplicable for a woman who normally functioned as a laser-focused fireball. She should be happy, having acquired the trappings of a good life—the office, the business, and new friends.

Maybe it was the fact of turning fifty-one. She'd had a couple of hot flashes, but nothing horrible, except this crazy lack of energy. She scheduled a physical, but her doctor told her she was in perfect condition.

Logically, she assumed there was some low-level grieving going on. But even though she felt deep sadness about losing Curt, she knew that if she kept putting one foot in front of the other, in time, life would return to normal, and she would recapture her zest for life. A person could only wallow so long. Nothing in life was perfect. You did the best you could and moved on.

So Karen threw herself into her work. It had been a busy six months. Her bank account was growing, as was her list of clients.

And yet.

At times, while at her desk, in the quiet of an afternoon, she'd find herself staring out the window, seeing nothing. She occasionally called Peggy to ask what was going on in Newport, or Aunt Marie, who was thriving in her new house. Karen had a large network of friends and acquaintances that she kept in touch with through e-mail and social media.

Savannah helped, yet for all the company of her colleagues and coworkers, the new friends she was making and the male attention she was attracting—even going on a few dinner dates, nothing more—she couldn't shake this growing feeling of lethargy.

Della tapped on the door. "Your ten o'clock is here." She stuck her head in. "You okay?"

"Sure. Why? Do I look all right?" Karen reapplied lipstick from a tube in her desk drawer.

"Just kind of pale. I'll send her in."

Karen greeted her new client. The hour flew by in the excitement of business, but when the woman left, the gray blanket settled again.

"I need some air," she said to Della. "Be back in a few hours."

Karen got her purse and went to her favorite restaurant, a seafood place with a patio. While she waited for her food to arrive, she watched boat traffic on the river and hoped her spirits would lift. Sailboats flitted by, darting around larger vessels. A massive tanker crawled upstream, her entourage of tugboats fretting alongside, but Karen only stared without thinking.

When the server brought her lunch, she took a bite, then another. She put her fork down and stared at the colorful plate, mystified at its lack of flavor. Was her sense of taste disappearing, too?

She gazed out at the brown water of the Savannah River, rolling along on its way to the Atlantic. Her interest in work was flagging. Her clients were beginning to bore her. After a big start, her business now failed to capture her attention.

It was ironic. After clearing the decks of her life so she was free to focus on work, work no longer compelled her. She was drifting, and she knew why, but there was no answer for it. She needed to snap out of this malaise. She told herself it would pass if she applied herself.

Over the next few weeks, she went to the gym every day and worked out under the direction of a trainer. She got blond highlights and went shopping for a new wardrobe. She began meditating in the evening and listening to motivational lectures on YouTube.

And then her hair began falling out. She stood in the shower one morning, watching strands slip down the drain and thinking, *I am an idiot.*

You're not a total idiot, she heard back. *Just very, very slow.*

When Della arrived at the office the next morning, Karen was waiting. She told Della to hold down the fort; she'd be back in a few days. And then she rolled her suitcase to the taxicab waiting on the curb.

***

Fifteen hours later, Karen arrived in Barcelona. She'd slept on the plane as well as anyone could, which meant she was tired and bleary-eyed when she trudged up the Jetway. She retrieved her suitcase from baggage claim, found a restroom, and changed into fresh clothes. In the nasty fluorescent light, she washed her face, brushed her teeth, and applied a little makeup. Outside, the late-morning sun seared her tired eyeballs.

Even though she was exhausted and nervous, she felt a rising sense of excitement as the cab pulled away from the curb. Three-lane roundabouts circled triumphant statues in the city. Iconic Gaudian loops and swirls awakened her imagination. Lush parks and verdant gardens soothed her eyes every few blocks. By the time she arrived at the University of Barcelona, she felt revived.

At the geology department, Karen tucked her suitcase behind the front desk and followed the receptionist to the long hallway leading to faculty offices.

"Professor Hoffman is in two thirteen," the receptionist said. Her heels clicked in the silence as she walked away, leaving Karen to wander on alone.

His door was open, and a woman was leaning over a desk, rifling through files. Her ample breasts nearly spilled out of a low-cut blouse.

"Hello?" Karen said.

The woman straightened. She looked Karen up and down. "May I help you." It wasn't a question.

"I'm looking for Curt Hoffman."

"And you are?" She lifted her chin and stuck her chest out.

Whoever this woman was—Karen guessed a secretary—she was certainly protective. "I'm a friend."

"Do you have an appointment?"

Karen shrugged disarmingly. "I thought I would surprise him." In fact, as soon as she'd landed, she'd tried to call his cell, but his number was out of service.

"I believe he is at lunch with his fiancée. I do not expect them to return for several hours, if at all." The woman smiled.

Karen stood like a lump of clay, trying to process the statement. She looked down at the floor, hiding her shock and thinking of what she should say next. What she should do. Did the woman mean Curt? Had she confused him with someone else?

"I'm sorry," said Karen, "did you mean Curt Hoffman?"

"*Jes*, Dr. Hoffman, the professor of geophysics. The tall, handsome man from America? He is out with his fiancé." The woman all but purred, a sickly smile on her face.

Karen's purse strap began to slide off her shoulder. She grabbed it and straightened, and when she looked up, the woman's smile was gone.

"If there is nothing else."

"No," Karen said. She walked down the hall, her ears roaring. She found a bench and sat, trying to organize her thoughts. A fiancée? So he was serious when he said he was tired of waiting for her. He wouldn't put his life on hold anymore, even for a year.

A door flew open, and students poured out, yammering and jostling each other on the way to their next class. All that energy, all that future in front of them. Somewhere in this building, Curt spent every day with that youthful energy, thriving and happy while she trudged around Savannah with her hair falling out. How completely depressing.

What a fool she had been to make this trip. Her face burned. She should have told him ahead of time but thought he'd be surprised and happy. What a mistake. What a gigantic waste of time and money.

Well, she'd learned her lesson. She should have taken him at his word. He'd said he would get on with his life, and he had.

So would she. She would get a hotel for the night and fly home tomorrow. Now that she knew the truth, she would be able to make progress again in her own life, no longer weighed down by thoughts of what could have been. She would return to Savannah and start over, this time for real. She would shape a life without him. In time, she would heal. Again.

The click of high heels roused her out of her nightmare.

"You didn't find the professor?" It was the receptionist.

Karen cleared her throat. "His assistant told me he was away from the building for a few hours."

The receptionist glanced at her watch and shook her head. "No, he's here. If he's not in his office, he is in lecture hall C. Just follow the noise." She gestured toward the far end of the building and clicked away.

Karen held her purse on her lap. So what if he was here? His fiancée would probably be in the audience, hanging on his every word. She was probably a student, like Madison Hesse. Now that she knew the truth, there was no point. Karen would never see him again, and that was as it should be.

She stood, intent on collecting her suitcase and hailing a cab, but part of her brain wanted her to go in another direction, because she couldn't leave without seeing him one more time, and if he didn't like it, and his fiancé was pissed at her for breaking into their cozy little world, who gave a flying—she got madder by the minute.

Karen followed the noise. She heard the sounds of applause and pulled open a door, but the room was empty. She hurried farther down the hallway and yanked open another door. Nothing.

Where *was* he?

Anger battled with dismay. If he would so quickly dismiss her, how much could he really have loved her? What was she to him, a toaster? A modern convenience, to make his life easier? She would not leave until she told him exactly what she thought of him and had closure. Then she would reclaim her life. She would be brilliant— the most successful businesswoman the South had ever seen.

She yanked open another door and heard the sound of a lecture. She followed the sound, turning right and left. Then she yanked another door open stepped into the lecture hall—and onto the auditorium stage, behind the speaker, in front of hundreds of students and faculty.

Karen froze, horrified.

The speaker, a burly man with a walrus mustache and round glasses, stopped talking and turned to her. "Can we help you?"

She stared at him and then the crowd, momentarily unable to grasp that she'd made her way to the stage door of a lecture hall. "No, sorry." As she escaped, the sound of laughter burned her ears. She found her way back through the warren to the main hallway and ducked into an alcove to gather herself.

It was all too much. What a disaster. She felt like a fool.

How much time, money, and energy do you have to sacrifice to get this lesson into your head? You called the shots. All he did was give you what you said you wanted. You need to own that. Now go home.

She headed for the front desk and her suitcase, anxious to get the hell off campus. As she rounded the corner toward the exit, her phone rang.

"Were you looking for me?"

Karen stopped walking. Her mouth went dry. "I was," she croaked.

"Turn around."

Curt stood in the middle of the hallway, arms open, waiting for her. Her shoulders sagged, her purse dropped unnoticed to the floor, and then she was in his arms, kissing him with every ounce of passion she had, right there in the middle of geological science, in the middle of a growing flood of students leaving the lecture hall. She didn't care who saw them or if he was engaged to some woman or not.

They broke apart, arms around each other's waists, staring into each other's eyes. A throat cleared, and the receptionist said, "Excuse me." She stood nearby, holding Karen's purse and phone. "Professor, is this your fiancée?"

Curt looked at Karen, one eyebrow raised in a question.

Karen laid her head against his shoulder.

"Estella, could you please let my assistant know I'll be gone for the afternoon with my fiancée?"

Karen laughed. "I think she already knows."

***

Later, in his bed, Karen awoke from the coma brought on by sexual gratification and jet lag. She sat up, looking around his bedroom. A small suitcase stood by the door, zipped closed. She fell back asleep. When hunger drove them from bed, Curt fixed a plate of prosciutto and melon slices, and they sat on his balcony and watched the lights of Barcelona wink on.

"I was in the audience," he said, telling the story of seeing her on stage in the lecture hall. "At first, I thought I was hallucinating or something. But I knew it was you because of the way you stand when you're processing information."

"You know that?"

"Yeah. You do this little thing with your left shoulder, and you stand like—" He posed himself, and it was ridiculous, and they both laughed.

"I can't believe you've studied me to that extent."

"But I have," he said. "You're my life's work."

She cut a bite of prosciutto, laid it atop a melon slice, and placed it on his tongue. "Your assistant told me you were engaged."

"She's possessive." His eyes lasered into hers, and she felt her breath leave her. Again.

"So she just made it up?"

"Karen, don't you know me by now?"

"If I didn't, I wouldn't be here. And I have something to say to you." She refilled their glasses with a crisp, cold white. She held both glasses and studied him before handing one to him. "You need to wait for me."

"I could as easily say you need to move here." His eyes narrowed.

"We're both used to doing things our own way. We've lived a long time, and we have our routines. But we have decades ahead of us, another whole lifetime. For you to say you can't wait for me is crazy. I flew here to tell you that. And if you want to call me selfish, so be it."

"You are selfish. So am I." He pushed back his chair and went inside.

Karen stared across the cityscape of Barcelona. Her speech wasn't going that well. How else could she say it? She didn't think she could function without him. They could live on separate continents for a few more months, and then he could come back to Savannah—she dropped her head onto her hands, imagining another fight looming.

"Karen."

He leaned down, cupped her chin in his hand, and kissed her deeply. Then he knelt at her side and handed her a small velvet box. "I told Monica I had a fiancée because she got a call from the jeweler I was working with. She was very angry at me."

"I'm sure she was." Karen eyed the box. "What were you going to do with that?"

"Fly to Savannah and convince you to marry me. My flight left two hours ago."

Her eyes widened. "We would have missed each other."

"But we were thinking the same thing, and you moved first. Karen, look, I don't care how long I have to wait. I just need to know you're in my future for sure. And the only way I'll feel sure is if you agree to marry me."

She opened the box. It held two blinding carats on a white gold setting.

Then she looked up at him.

"I agree."

"You do?"

She laughed out loud, leaning away from him, holding both his hands. "Is that what you're supposed to say?"

They kissed, standing on the balcony, overlooking the city, the sounds of Barcelona the backdrop for their new life together.

He asked, "What changed your mind?"

"I tried living without you," she said. "And I couldn't."

Chapter Forty-Seven

TWO YEARS LATER

"**C**ome on. We're going to be late." Curt held open the front door of the brownstone.

Karen dashed down the stairs, fastening her earring. "Did you get the present?"

"It's in the car. Do you have the address of the place?"

"Down by the river just outside town. Jessie told me what spaces they're camping in."

Karen got in the passenger side of the Mercedes coupe and shut the door. The CRS ladies were making a loop through the South, and she couldn't wait to see them again. Since she'd left Key Largo, she'd stayed in touch with Jessie via Skype and other electronic means, but this would be the first time Karen would have a chance to see them again in person—and to hold the new baby.

With Curt behind the wheel, Karen kept glancing at the speedometer, wishing he'd go faster, but he liked to see things along the route, as opposed to her tendency to race around getting things done. In the two years since they'd married, they found that they balanced each other.

Karen told herself to calm down. She gazed out the window, appreciating the oak trees and azalea bushes dazzling every flower bed. The city was so rich in history and culture that they never went more than a few days without attending a gallery opening or a famous author's book signing or a lecture by a visiting notable.

After their passionate reunion in Barcelona, she had returned to the States to continue building Grace and Associates, and the business had expanded into three of the four office suites in the brownstone. When Curt's year in Spain ended, he had resigned from the University of North Dakota and leased the fourth office for his consulting business.

"You look happy." Curt rested his hand on her leg. She felt the heat and, if it weren't for the reunion ahead of them, would have told him to pull over. She placed her hand on his and met his eyes.

"I am happy." Of all the surprises in this second half of her life, the best was the discovery that lovemaking wasn't just good; it was even better than when she was younger.

They left the city limits and rolled through the rural countryside, heading for the camp. Eleven months out of the year, Jessie lived in a real house with her husband and two children. They'd built a successful business sourcing and updating vintage clothing, and then selling it at the price of new. Jessie wished they could camp more, but they were too busy. When she said that, Karen would remind her about the importance of balance. She hoped Jessie wouldn't wait until she was fifty to learn that lesson.

"I've been thinking," Karen said.

"Hmm?" Curt signaled to exit the highway. They were almost at the campground.

"You know we're getting older."

"Speak for yourself."

She slapped him playfully. "In three years, I'll be fifty-six. I never intended to work forever. We're doing well."

"Yes." He turned down a country road alongside the river.

"And we've still got the farmhouse."

"True. The Eastmans are very good tenants." He turned to look at her. "What are you thinking?"

Karen leaned her head back. The deep greens of a lush southern countryside rolled past, and she felt lucky to have experienced it—to have experienced all the places she'd lived. Yet, for all her affection for her new home in Savannah, for all the beauty of Jekyll Island and Key Largo, and for all the golden sunsets of Newport Beach, her heart would always reside in the northern plains. That was where she'd met Curt, that was where she'd matured, and that was where she wanted to spend the rest of her life.

"I'm thinking we need a three-year plan. And then we go home."

"Home where?"

"Home, as in back to North Dakota." She reached over and touched his face. "Could I talk you into it?"

He parked in front of the campground office, turned off the car, and took her in his arms. His kiss was so tender it brought tears to her eyes. "You don't have to talk me into anything. I want to go home, too."

She touched his lips, and he kissed her fingertips. It was the right decision. She'd savored every minute of her time away, from California to the Keys to the southeast edge of the country. But now she wanted to grow old in the land of her ancestors, to see the storms rolling in off the prairie and to be near her parents' graves. To make a life with this man she'd loved since high school, this man who shared her prairie roots.

"What about the winters?" he asked. "You said you never wanted to deal with the cold again."

"We'll meet the ladies in Florida. We'll buy an RV. A big one. With a dishwasher, and slide outs——"

"And a TV compartment on the outside, and a barbecue——"

They were interrupted by a pounding on the window. Karen opened the door and fell into the arms of Jessie and the CRS ladies.

Acknowledgements

Gratitude and love to my family. You mean everything to me, and I am proud of all of you.

To my critique group who made me feel smart when it was warranted and the rest of the time told me when my writing stunk. To my Hemet and Palm Desert friends who've cheered me on without hesitation, and to the members of the Diamond Valley Writers' Guild, who have given me a virtual campfire around which to warm my writer's heart.

Thank you.

About the Author

This isn't the usual bio-info you'll find in the back of most novels. Because, having spent time with you, in Dakota Blues and Key Largo Blues, I'd like to chat. No, we can't do that on this page, but you can go to my website, **http://www.AnyShinyThing.com**, and say hello.

Many novels and movies feature the coming-of-age story, in which young people figure out who they are and what they want to be. That's compelling, but so is this: what happens afterwards, twenty or thirty years later, to these interesting people?

At about age fifty, people have a second coming-of-age to go through, but now the stakes and rewards are even greater. This is the time of life to make it happen, reexamine choices, and forge new paths. We know the clock is ticking, so we're on fire to make our time count. Plus, we face unique obstacles, whether illness or death, or life-threatening heartache, or the low expectations of the culture.

As we age, our characters deepen. We might decide to stop being doormats and take a stand, or make the greatest sacrifice of our lives. We have dreams. We lay out goals and objectives. We start businesses. We cook up schemes. We fall in love.

We throw the Hail Mary pass, risking everything, just like young people.

That's the Older Adult coming-of-age story. As fascinating as the kids are, I think older peeps are just as fascinating. We may not be as pretty, but we're more devious and complicated. And so are our stories. These are the stories I'm passionate to write about, God willing, for the rest of my life. Which, if I'm as lucky as my mother, will be at least another thirty years.

For more information about my books, blog, or present state of mind, please visit **http://www.AnyShinyThing.com**.